In Trouble

In Trouble

To: Val

Thanks for the support

Dianne

Dianne Palovcik

IN TROUBLE

Published by Dianne Palovcik, Edmonton, Canada

Author photo by Carlyle Art

ISBN: 0-978-1-77354-169-3 Paperback
      0-978-1-77354-185-3 eBook

Disclaimer
This is a work of fiction based on historical facts. Names, characters, businesses, events and incidents are either the products of the author's imagination or used in a ficticious manner. Any resemblance to actual persons, living or dead, or actual events is purely coincidental.

Publication assistance and digital printing in Canada by

PUBLISHING
PageMaster.ca

Chapter One

January 6, 1961
Northumberland Strait, Canada

Sarah Gardner leaned against the ship's rail. She'd lost all hope and decided to jump. The future she longed for was gone forever, destroyed by those she trusted. *I'll jump and make them all feel guilty. Show all those perfect people with 'holier than thou' attitudes.*

The north wind howled across the ship's deck and slapped Sarah's scarf across her mouth. Stinging spray from the frigid Atlantic gale peppered her face. She took off her glove, eased her hand into her pocket and stroked the leather cover of her diary. It was the only part of Myles she could hold on to. She closed her eyes against the chilling dampness and summoned his face. Her index finger moved over the zipper, its tiny teeth rippling along the tip of her nail. The moment of pleasure was swept aside in an instant. With her back braced against the deck rail, she pounded the deck floor with her heel, pleading for pain to chase away summer memories. Even now, he owned her heart.

While Sarah fought the blustery weather and her demons, other ferry passengers enjoyed a warm journey and food inside the passenger lounge. Large windows offered watery views without the bitter cold.

Sarah's parents sat side by side in silence, removed from the other passengers. There was nothing left to say. They simply needed to complete their commitment, take Sarah to Rose Hill Home and leave her there. Neither one was convinced family and friends bought the idea their only child would be spending time in Halifax taking an art course. It was true, Sarah was exceptionally talented, but leaving school part way through the year was a dead giveaway. But they had no choice.

It was 1961, Sarah was seventeen, pregnant, and society expected her to be out of sight. Like many others over the years, she was going to an unwed mother's home. This one was in Halifax. There, she would wait for her baby to be born, give it up for adoption and return home. Bad girl problem solved.

For weeks Sarah pleaded with her mother not to take her away. She hated the calm, preachy phrases her mother used to defend the need for her to leave home. 'Sarah, you're 'in trouble' and you can't stay here. It's best for you. In time, it'll get easier and you'll forget.'

Sarah grasped the deck rail with both hands, took a deep breath and exhaled. She placed her left foot on the cross bracing ready to swing herself up, over and into oblivion. *Okay, on three. One, two....* The metal lounge door clanged shut. She turned. A tall, dark haired young man in a navy pea coat strolled toward the railing. As he pulled up his collar, he looked straight at her. Sarah wasn't in the mood for polite conversation. She looked away.

"Pretty snappy out here. You're experiencing the crossing at its worst, stinging salt water and fuel smell. Got a bet on with someone inside to see how long you can stay out here?"

Sarah lifted her head. "No, just avoiding them."

"Ahhh. I might have chosen a stay in the bathroom instead." He received a snort in response. "Going to Halifax for a day or two?"

"No, going for a while. Not my idea. Parents think they know better." *Okay, let's get this little chat over with.*

"Yeah, I know what you mean. My name's Andy. And yours is...?"

"Sarah."

"Live on the Island?"

"Yeah." *Time for you to stop now.* Sarah returned her gaze to the water.

"My office is in Halifax but I travel all around the Maritimes. Just visited my mother on the Island. It's great, except on cold days like this one. Been to Halifax before?"

"Once. Art show with my parents."

"Cool. Visiting friends?"

"No. My parents think I need to grow up." Sarah wrapped her arms around the slight bulge in her midsection and met Andy's eyes head-on.

"Ahh." He nodded, stepped forward and saw puffy, red eyelids. Dried tears marked her cheeks. Wisps of curly light brown hair escaped the hood of her jacket and clung to her face. She was taller than he expected, probably five feet, seven inches. He guessed her age to be sixteen, maybe seventeen.

Sarah maintained eye contact as he drew closer. "They found a place for me to stay. Told me it's for my own good. Well, that's what my mother says, anyway. As if she knows what's good for me. What I want doesn't matter. They just want me away from home for a few months. It's all about them."

Andy heard the edgy tone in her voice but saw growing ease on her face. "Earlier you mentioned an art show. Do you draw, paint?"

"Yes, mostly watercolours. I was in an art program with Miss Mayne in the city this summer. She's from Halifax. Maybe you've heard of her?"

"No, I haven't but I have friends in Halifax connected with the College of Art. I could send info. Do you know where you'll be staying in Halifax?"

Sarah hesitated. "Not exactly."

"So, are you thinking about studying art? Maybe becoming an artist or teaching art down the road?"

"I love to draw and paint, so yeah. Maybe."

"Well, if it's something you love, don't give up....."

Andy was interrupted by the presence of a woman who intentionally avoided his glance and moved toward Sarah. She lowered her voice but there was no mistaking the angry quality of the words.

"Sarah, why are you still out here in this freezing cold? We can't be late for your appointment. Now stop being stubborn and get inside, right now. What is the matter with you?"

Sarah stared, stone faced at her mother then headed toward the door. *The matter is, I'm being shipped off to Halifax like a piece of furniture. Nobody believes your stupid story about an art course and staying with a cousin in Halifax for months. What a crock! I hate you! You ruined my life!*

As the port come into view, Andy left the deck and headed toward the stairway leading down to the car deck. Unexpectedly, he was near enough to overhear Sarah's mother speak.

"Sarah, speed up. Dad's already at the car. The Matron at Rose Hill Home is expecting us no later than four thirty. Why were you talking to that young man on the deck? Who was he? You know this trip is to be kept quiet. Oh, never mind answering. You've lost all common sense."

Sarah's father was standing beside the car. "Not long now. Did you get something in the cafeteria?"

"No, wasn't hungry."

"We'll stop in Amherst, about an hour from now. How's that sound?"

"Good. That sounds good, Dad."

Andy turned his head, rushed past Sarah and her parents toward his car. *Rose Hill. My gawd, that's where my sister stayed. Next stop, Amherst for gas. I better beat them there and be gone before they arrive. That mother sounds like mine! Stick to what society expects of your moral behaviour or you'll be shamed and shunned.*

Sarah scarcely noticed the blue, green and yellow clapboard siding on homes scattered along Route 16 leading away from the ferry terminal. She slouched in the back seat of the family car and stared out the side window. Her mind was focused on the white leather suitcase with red stitching on the seat beside her. It had been tedious to stitch the red lining back in place but it looked almost as good as new when she'd finished. She patted it, tilted her head back, closed her eyes and recalled the happy times of summer.

***

Myles Alexander eclipsed every other person and event in Sarah's life when he arrived in town during the summer of 1960. He filled her mind and body with fiery longing that only his physical presence could release. Hiding in the sand dunes was their favourite pastime. One blanket to lie on and another to snuggle under. She melted when he wrapped his arms around her and caressed her body. She memorized everything about him. Blue eyes, English Leather cologne, a brown birthmark on the inner thigh of his right leg, his laugh and gentle hands moving and exploring her body.

"I love this tiny cove. Warm sand under a hot summer sun and nobody can see us. It's the best place ever. How did you find it?"

"A friend at the bank told me about it and I could hardly wait to share it with you. You're right, nobody can see us. Let's enjoy ourselves. I brought along your favourite drink."

"My mother would kill me if she knew I liked wine. It makes me feel relaxed and happy so it can't be bad, right?"

"Well, your mother isn't here and I'm sure she wants you to be happy. Besides, you're making your parents proud with your art. You should celebrate."

"You're the best. I feel giggly already." Sarah wiggled her toes into the sand then looked up to see Myles striding to the water without his swim trunks. "What are you doing? Are you crazy?"

"I'm waiting for you. Ditch the swimsuit. Let's have some fun. Then you can tell me your great art story. Come on, beautiful girl."

After the swim and more wine, Sarah stretched out on the plaid blanket and began her story.

"Well, you know I'm in the summer art program. Miss Mayne has classes in her studio in the old brick factory downtown. Every day we walk in a part of the city to get ideas. Last week we toured the basilica down the street. After the painting session, she took me aside and said I had promising talent with watercolours. She said I should focus on my flower pieces as they were exceptional. That's the exact word she used. Exceptional. Can you believe it? She wants to feature two or three in her gallery. Then she asked me how I would like to sign them. I told her I didn't want to be Sarah. I want a mysterious, exotic name. So guess what I decided? Eva, for my Grandma Eva. I think I might add a little Lady's Slipper or Tiger Lily in the corner under my signature. So what do you think about that? Pretty great, eh?" Hearing no response, she glanced over. Myles had rolled onto his side away from her and was sound asleep.

***

"Sarah, are you listening?"

"What? Sorry, Dad. I was day dreaming about summer."

"That's not a good idea, kiddo. It makes you sad. We'll soon be in Amherst. Food?"

"Food?"

"You know.... things you eat like sandwiches, banana splits, butterscotch pie."

"Sure." Sarah closed her eyes, huddled under a blanket and pulled the diary from her pocket. She ran her fingers over the embossed '1960' on the top right corner then opened the black tab for May twenty-fourth.

Tuesday, May 24, 1960

I had the most wonderful day of my life today because I met the best looking guy, ever. He started work at the bank today. Myles Alexander is from Halifax and will be here for twelve weeks. He is gorgeous. He wore a dark suit, white shirt and tie that matched his dreamy blue eyes. Wow. I think I'll find an excuse to go to the bank every day. Ha ha.

Sarah's early memories of Myles gushed forward and pulled her back in time to June. The sun streamed through the bank's windows as she made her way to the teller's station.

"Hey, Sarah. Good to see you again. How can I help you today?"

"Hi, Myles. Mom asked me to deposit this cheque in her account. My English class starts in twenty minutes so I'm kinda in a rush."

"No problem. You're lucky the school is so close to the bank."

"Yeah. That's how small villages are. Schools, churches, stores, library, everything close together. Bet you think it's strange for the manager, Mr. Baker and his family to live above the bank!"

"Yeah but the best part is the staff can use the picnic table in their backyard."

"Neat."

"Wanna join me there for lunch tomorrow?"

"Sure." Sarah could hardly imagine her good fortune.

The next day Sarah walked quickly down the street from school, past the doctor's home and office then slowed her pace as she turned the corner. She didn't want to appear too anxious but was dying to see Myles again. Her heart was going a mile a minute. She found him at the picnic table beside the stream that wandered through the village. A large weeping willow cast a cooling shadow over the table.

"There you are, gorgeous. Sit beside me. You look great in that yellow sweater."

"Thanks." Sarah couldn't pull her eyes away from his smile and dimple in his chin.

"Mrs. Baker sure knows how to grow flowers. Which one's your favourite?"

Sarah was floating away on the scent of Myle's after shave. The butterflies in her stomach weren't helping either. She focused on the first flower she noticed. "Tiger Lily. The orange one."

Sarah was totally infatuated and barely recalled anything else except he'd asked her to the beach for the following day.

Now, seven months later, the sensation of warm sand under her feet remained strong. She was powerless to control her urge for more Myles. She opened the diary again.

Saturday, June 4, 1960

Myles was very polite with my parents today. I'm sure they think he is grand, just like I do. We drove to the beach and walked in the dunes. He smells positively divine. It's English Leather. He took my hand and I tingled all over.

He's soooo dreamy and sophisticated – even opens the car door for me. I love his stories and jokes. We had a great time and he asked me out next Saturday. He really, really likes me!

Saturday, June 11, 1960

We drove to the city for a movie today. 'Pillow Talk' was on the screen. We ate popcorn and cuddled in the back row. I love the way he wears his polo shirt collar up and sunglasses on top of his head. He looks like Ricky Nelson. He's so cool. I didn't want the day to end. I dream about him every night.

I invited him to my school dance next Friday night. Everyone will be so jealous.

The memory of that Friday evening was so special, Sarah was unable to resist reliving it.

"Good evening, Mr. and Mrs. Gardner. Sarah, you look beautiful. I brought you a wrist corsage. Hope you like red roses. May I put it on for you?"

Sarah could see her parents out of the corner of her eye. Neither looked happy but muttered a few words of welcome.

"Do we have a curfew, Mrs. Gardner?"

"Midnight is the usual." Sarah's mother replied quickly and firmly.

"Sarah will be home before the clock strikes twelve. Neither of us wants to be a pumpkin! Hope you like to dance, Sarah. Let's go."

Sarah wrapped her arms around her upper body and brought back that Friday night. At her door, Myles encircled her in his arms, then brushed his lips across hers. She felt light-headed and clung to him to keep upright. Suddenly, she was spinning around in mid air, flying in body and soul. A moan escaped her lips into his ear.

"Shhhh. See you tomorrow at six for a movie."

Sarah knew the end of this story but could not stop reading, She blinked back tears.

Saturday, June 18, 1960

It rained all day so being at a movie was perfect. I don't remember much of the story! We sat in the back row and cuddled through most of it. He smells so good.

Had our pictures taken at the photo booth in the theater lobby. One is really mushy! Glad this diary has a key.

Thursday, June 24, 1960

Lunch today was fun. Myles has a younger brother. He told me stories about the jokes he plays on him. Sounds like they live in a very big house.

Grade Eleven is over for me so I want to visit his family in Halifax one weekend soon. What will I wear?

Saturday, June 25, 1960

I'm so bored and lonely this weekend. My Myles is in Halifax visiting his family. He said he'd rather be with me but his parents expect to see him once a month.

Mom and Dad don't really like Myles. It's a good idea we're apart for awhile and I'm too young to be so serious. Baaaa

Dad said Myles is having a good time for the summer and I need to look after myself. Mom was quiet about whatever that meant.

Yeah well, what do they know and who cares what they think anyway? Not me! I'll show them.

Sunday, June 26, 1960

Myles came back this afternoon. He hardly spoke to Mom and Dad when he picked me up for supper. I asked him what was wrong. He told he had a big argument with someone in Halifax. It must have been a whopper. He didn't tell jokes and I was home early.

Thursday, June 30, 1960

Yeah. Found out today I'm going to a 6 week summer art program in the city. Mom promised to drive me back and forth. It starts July, 4th. Can't wait to tell Myles.

Saturday, July 2, 1960

Went for a drive today and parked on an old back road. He told me I am his best girl. I know we will be together for a long time.

He's getting really, really serious. I feel nervous about what comes next. What should I do? I'm sure I can trust him to make everything safe.

Sunday, July 10, 1960

We went to the lobster supper in the church hall last night and took a drive to the beach.

That's where 'it' happened. We will be inseparable now. It feels so great to think about our future together. I'm so happy to be a part of Myles' future.

He told me he really misses me when he visits his family.

I'm sure his family knows about me. I bet he'll take me to see them in a few weeks. I'm going to start hinting about that. I'm the one for him.

"Sarah, did you pack those new slippers?"

"What?"

"What are you doing back there?" Sarah's mother turned to the back seat. But Sarah was quick and dropped the Chatelaine magazine over the diary. "New slippers. Did you pack them?"

Andy knew all the passing zones from the ferry terminal to Amherst. He managed to pass Sarah's family car in less than half an hour. The exit sign for Amherst appeared as his rumbling stomach became impossible to ignore. He'd passed several cars so Della's Diner probably wouldn't be too busy. He could hardly wait for the homemade rhubarb pie and coffee. Seeing Della again would be good too. He dashed into the diner and plopped down on a red vinyl stool at the counter.

"Coming from or going to, Andy?"

"Hey, Della. Coming from the Island. Been busy today?"

"Steady."

Della Logan could read people. She sensed when to talk and when to let people keep their own company. She moved away after taking Andy's order and greeted a family coming in the door.

"Hi, folks. Sit anywhere you like. I'll be right with you."

Sarah made a beeline for a booth in the corner and slid in the side with her back to the door. She was unnerved to see Andy. If he acknowledged her, mother would have something new to berate her about. She kept her head down.

Della approached their booth. "What will you folks have? The grilled cheese sandwich, rhubarb pie and coffee is on special."

"Sounds good." Sarah wanted to eat and get out, quick.

"Make it three, miss." Sarah's dad spoke calmly, like they had all the time in the world.

"Coming right up."

Della headed to the kitchen and returned with Andy's order. "Head's up, Andy. I added ice cream, no charge. Looks like you need it."

"You're the best, Della."

"Careful, now. I might think you mean it."

"Hey, Andy. Phil from the record store. Good to see you again. You're a real regular here. What's the attraction, Della or the food?"

Andy spun around and shook Phil's hand. "Hey, Phil. Bit of both. What's new?"

"Couple of new LPs you might like. Drop in, if you've time."

"Thanks. Maybe next time." Out of the corner of his eye, he saw Sarah. The look on her mother's face was so frosty he decided to let them leave first. No point in riling her up. Sarah reminded him of his sister Liz. His stomach began to knot. *Breathe, breathe.*

Two coffee refills later, Andy couldn't wait any longer. He dashed to the washroom, paid the bill, called 'see ya' to Della and walked straight to the front door. Sitting in the Bug, he took a deep breath and turned the key in the ignition. He pushed Liz from his mind by thinking about Della. Despite her brief, modest comments today and on previous visits, Andy knew she and the diner were success stories. Savouring the pie today had rekindled the memory of his overnight in Amherst last winter. He hadn't planned to stay but Mother Nature gave him no choice but the local hotel. Despite their different backgrounds, their conversation that evening had been easygoing and natural, like friends. He wanted to know her better.

Back on the highway to Halifax, Sarah sat quietly in the backseat. Joyful and sad memories mingled in a relentless assault. This would be her life for a while. No way out, yet. She'd be a victim of her memories until she could reach Myles and make new ones. He was in Halifax and soon she would be too. She slipped the diary from her pocket and placed it inside the open Chatelaine again. She began in early August when times were good.

Saturday, August 6, 1960

What a wonderful day. Miss Mayne had an Open House and Myles went with me. Happy, happy, happy.

"So, this is your artsy hang out, Miss Gardner. Or should I say, Eva?"

"Don't be a silly goose. I'm still Sarah. I'll be Eva when I'm famous." She took Myles' hand.

"Hello, Sarah. I'm glad you could make it today."

"Miss Mayne, this is my boyfriend, Myles."

"Welcome. Have you seen Sarah's work yet? She's very good."

"So she tells me." He pulled his hand away and walked to the display tables. "Wow, you are pretty good." Returning, he leaned into Sarah and whispered, "How long do we have to stay? It's cove day."

Miss Mayne interrupted her response. "Sarah, I sold a piece of your work earlier. Can you come to my table?"

"She sold one of my watercolours. Holy cow! I'll be back in a few minutes."

"We can leave then, right?"

"If you want to, sure."

Sunday, August 7, 1960

We had a romantic picnic today. Walked on the beach searching for interesting shells. I'm going to save them forever. It's so exciting to be in love. I see my happy future every time we hold hands.

My period's a few days late. Sometimes it happens.

Friday, August 12, 1960

I don't feel myself these days. Really tired. Probably a cold starting. Off to class in the city.

We're going to the drive in tonight. Hope I feel better then.

Saturday, August 13, 1960

Feel queasy this morning. Maybe it's the 'flu. At least I didn't throw up.

The sun's pouring in the window and I'm so drowsy. My life is great. It'll be better in September when Myles finishes his bank training. We'll have plans to marry and move away.

Yikes, it's almost four. Can't keep my FH (future husband) waiting. He told me he'll have a surprise soon. Bet it's a ring.

August 17, 1960

Wish I could stop feeling so queasy every morning. It must be nerves. So much is happening to me. It's exciting. Art classes and Myles. Life is perfect.

The Sears Fall and Winter Catalogue has pretty clothes this year. I looked at furniture too. First time ever. I'll sneak it out of the house Friday night. Myles and I can get ideas for our apartment.

SG loves MA

MA loves SG

Sarah knew what was coming but couldn't turn her eyes away from the page. She was pulled into the pain, written by her own hand.

Sunday, August 21, 1960

My period is really late. I told mom this morning after breakfast. We're going to the doctor tomorrow. I hope it's appendicitis. What if it's not and I'm pregnant! This isn't fair right now.

Monday, August 22, 1960

I saw the doctor today. He checked my stomach and asked if I had a boyfriend. Then he asked for a sample of my urine. It goes to a lab in the city. He asked me if I might be pregnant!

Myles and I will have to get married sooner than I thought. I want a big church wedding. This is so exciting.

Friday, August 26, 1960

Mom and I saw the doctor today. I feel so grown up but nervous too. I'm going to have a baby in April. I waited for Mom to talk to the doctor alone.

When we got home she said we would talk with dad at supper.

I'm sure the wedding plans will have to start right away. I want to wear white no matter what mom will say.

Supper was awful. I couldn't eat. They are sending me away after Christmas. It's some secret place in Halifax for girls like me to hide.

This is the most horrid day of my life. I'm really, really mad at them. I can hardly write. They don't understand anything. I'm not, not, not going.

They told me I had to tell Myles I'm pregnant. I could tell they think he'll dump me. Smug faces. He won't. I see him tomorrow and he'll help. We'll start planning ourselves. It's earlier than we thought but this is going to work out okay. I'll show them.

Myles' arrival at Sarah's home was the only normal event of their usual Saturdays together. The day unraveled the minute she sat in the car.

"You look awful. Are you sick?"

"No but our lives are going to change." Sarah smiled, holding his eyes in her gaze.

"What the heck does that mean?"

"We are expecting a baby." She placed her hand on his arm.

"What!" He pushed Sarah's arm away. "Don't you take something so that doesn't happen? This can't happen. You're ruining my life. I refuse to be trapped into a mess you've made."

"We love each other, Myles. It'll work out, just sooner than we thought." Sarah struggled to keep her voice calm.

"We had a great summer. That's all it was. You're in high school. How does that work out? It doesn't. You need to get rid of this baby."

"But it's our baby." She touched his hand.

"The bank offered me a job in Halifax. I can't have a wife and kid to look after. Get your mother to talk to the doctor. They'll think of something. I'm going back to Halifax next Friday."

"That's my surprise? You've got a job and leaving!"

"What did you think it was...something about you? I was coming back to visit in a couple of weeks but not now." Myles continued to stare out the car windshield.

"Myles, please. You're in shock. We love each other. You have a job offer. We can work this out. I'll move with you. I'll go to school in Halifax." Sarah could hear desperation in her words, feel her eyes tear up, her chest tighten.

"You're not listening, Sarah. I want the job not an instant family. I think you should go back inside. Talk to your parents. It's better this way. Good-bye."

Saturday, August 27, 1960

My world's a mess. I'm a mess. There's no way out. I can't go back. What am I going to do? I feel stupid.

Is this all my fault? Was I supposed to know all about getting pregnant?

Why is this pregnancy stuff a secret?

Mom never talked to me. She ordered a booklet about menstruation and told me to read it. It's so confusing. Is it only my fault? I'm the only guilty one?

I need to see Myles again.

Sunday, August 28, 1960

I couldn't sleep last night but I feel better this morning. If I can't see Myles, I can write to him. That's exactly what I'm going to do.

He was in shock yesterday so he's scared. I'm sure he loves me. I'll go to the bank tomorrow and ask someone to give him my letter. I'm not giving up.

"We're here, Sarah. Rose Hill Home looks like a nice house. Bring your suitcase."

Chapter Two

January 6, 1961
Halifax, Nova Scotia

Rose Hill Home stood hidden from the street by towering spruce trees standing shoulder to shoulder inside a fenced front yard. The semi circular driveway permitted cars to park unnoticed and people to enter unseen through a sturdy oak door. Black wrought iron fencing and several spruce trees created a shield on the remaining sides of the three story red brick structure. The message was clear. The uninvited were unwelcome.

Sarah didn't care what the place looked like. She reached over the front seat, hugged her dad and left the car, cradling her suitcase. Her mother was already facing the front door, eager to get them inside. She pushed the door bell before Sarah managed to reach the top step.

A middle-aged woman with short, dark wavy hair opened the door. "Welcome to Rose Hill Home. You must be Sarah. Hello, Mrs. Gardner. Come in. My name is Mrs. Andrews and I'm the matron." She smoothed the jacket of her navy suit and led them into her office where she stepped behind the large wood desk and sat on a brocade fabric chair. "Please have a seat. Thank you for choosing us."

Sarah flushed. The idea that she had any say in this choice was ridiculous. Her snide snort of anger followed. She glanced sideways at her mother, who frowned. Sarah quickly recognized her opinions would not be welcome in this room.

Matron cleared her throat, straightened her back and continued to speak. "As I mentioned, welcome Sarah. First, your room. You have been assigned a room on the third floor, overlooking the front yard. You currently do not have a roommate but I believe that will change in a few days. You are expected to make your bed and tidy your room daily. These and other chores will keep you busy and help you forget your problem. Any questions so far, Sarah? Mrs. Gardner?"

Sarah shook her head. Her mother, perched on the edge of her chair smiled feebly and replied, "Not at the moment." She unbuttoned her tweed coat then continued to twist her leather gloves around the handle of her purse.

Matron placed her horn rim glasses on the desk. "Although we live in a quiet neighbourhood, you are not permitted to walk alone. We encourage only small groups of two or three walking together."

Sarah blurted, "Why is that? Do you think I'm planning to run away?" She thought it sounded like a good idea already.

Matron ignored the cheeky attitude and answered calmly. "Well, large groups attract unnecessary attention and of course, we want to protect your privacy. We do not want strangers staring and making you feel ashamed, especially as your pregnancy becomes more obvious." She smiled at Sarah.

"That sounds reassuring, doesn't it?" Sarah's mother cast a quick smile in Sarah's direction.

Matron continued. "There is a school on the next block and teenagers can be very unkind. But a large park and a small shop for candy and ice cream are in the neighbourhood. Any other questions about walks?"

"No." Sarah exhaled long and loud.

"We have a daily work roster which includes the dining room, sitting room, kitchen and bathrooms. This work is an excellent way to learn skills, self-discipline and acquire training for future employment or marriage. Many girls from Rose Hill obtain work in restaurants, hotels and private homes after leaving us. You and your parents may want to consider one of these work options after you leave Rose Hill. Questions?"

"I'm sure you're right. Those skills are certainly worthwhile, aren't they, Sarah?"

Sarah turned toward her mother. Her piercing glare was pure anger.

Matron noted the animosity then quickly carried on. "I see you brought a suitcase, Sarah. We provide most of your indoor clothing. You are allowed to wear your own coat, shoes, boots, hats, gloves and slippers. In the meantime, we keep your other clothing. Your Rose Hill clothes are in your room."

Sarah added panic to her not so subtle attitude. She needed to keep the suitcase and get into the lining. Matron was droning on about something but she wasn't listening.

"Sarah? I just asked about relatives in the Halifax area."

"Hmm?"

"I understand you have relatives around here. Is that correct?" Matron did her upmost to maintain a pleasant tone.

"Yes." Sarah replied firmly with the full expectation that some good news was finally on its' way.

"Rose Hill Home does not allow visitors with the exception of your parents. Your time here will pass quickly when you focus on acquiring new skills and how your behaviour brought you to Rose Hill. However, you can call or receive a call from your parents once a week. We monitor all mail sent and received. Any questions?

"No." She really wanted to ask this matron person who died and left her queen?

"Mrs. Gardner, I need you to inform your relatives about these visitation rules. However, they may send mail so I would like their names to add to Sarah's contact list. We will deal with that in a few minutes."

"Finally Sarah, about your name. Our girls use only first names they chose for their time with us. What name do you want to have while you are here?"

"Why can't I use my own name?" *I have a name. How's this help anything?*

"Well, you and your family are putting this unfortunate event in the past. A new name helps the past disappear. You can become someone else for a while."

"Can't I tell you later?"

"I'm afraid not. We must begin your first day here with a clean slate. No past to interfere with the new life you are beginning. So what will it be?"

A fond memory of her grandmother Gardner popped into Sarah's head and she blurted, "Eva. Eva's what I want."

"Good. Now, you must not tell anyone your real name, first or last. It is expected you will not talk to anyone about your family, where you are from or any personal details of your life. Understood?"

Sarah stared at Matron and answered with forced certainty, "Sure."

"Do you have questions, Eva?"

"Yes, who answers my questions about pregnancy? Do I see a doctor? Will my baby be born here? What do we do here besides chores?"

"Sarah, don't be so snippy. Apologize to Mrs. Andrews." She reached out to pat Sarah's arm.

Sarah winced and clenched her fists.

Matron answered quickly. "You will be able to talk about your pregnancy with the caseworker. We have reading material and arts and crafts supplies in the sitting room. A local minister leads a weekly discussion group on Sunday afternoon."

Craft supplies and the minister be damned. "When can I see the caseworker?"

"In a few days. I will let you know before she arrives. Unless you have other questions, this would be a good time to say good-bye to your mother. The two of us have a few topics to discuss after you've gone to see your room. You can remove your clothing here and put the empty suitcase under your bed. I will get a worker to take you to your room. She will tell you about supper and the evening routine. I'll be back in a few minutes."

Left alone in the room with her mother, Sarah hoped the few minutes would be a few seconds. She turned her back, crossed her arms, marched to the office window and stared toward the street.

"Sarah, I hope you use this time away wisely. Think about your future after this is over. You can begin a new life." She paused. "Also, you better knock that anger out of yourself or life is going to be very hard. Turn around, right now!"

Sarah spun around. "Knock it out of myself! I didn't put it there in the first place. Why do you think I'm angry? Could it be I can't trust anybody? Could it be nobody will help me? Could it be everybody knows what is best for me but me? Could it be I have no idea what will happen in this prison? Now I can't use my own name, wear my own clothes or use my brain? I don't have a life. How do I start a new one? Tell me that!"

"Shhhhhh. Here comes Matron. Don't make a spectacle of yourself. I'll call you in a few days. You'll feel better then. Give me a kiss."

Sarah leaned toward her mother and tolerated a kiss on her forehead as Matron entered the room.

"Eva, this is Bernice. She's here to help while you stay with us. She has several years experience in our home. Don't hesitate to ask her questions."

Sarah looked into Bernice's eyes and was met with a cold stare. Her thin lips moved but the result was more sneer than smile. Sarah saw no indication of helpfulness let alone kindness. This was a job. Her hands were rough and red, old beyond their years. Her dull hair was gathered into a scraggly ponytail. A once bright housedress, faded from drying too many times on an outdoor clothesline hung on her bony frame. Its yellow roses were now muted, a match for her sallow face. So far, life had not treated her kindly. Sarah had a strong sense Bernice passed her unkindness to others. She decided to keep her distance.

"Come on, Eva. Tomorrow I'll add your name to the duty list. We might as well start in the kitchen. Can ya cook? Doesn't matter. We'll start ya cleanin' the floor. You can start at the bottom and work your way up. Never hurts to have a little joke at work, eh?"

Sarah stood at the kitchen door gawking at all the pregnant young women in one room. The noisy cross-conversations were overwhelming. As an only child, she had no experience in a kitchen full of busy people. She gripped the door knob and took it all in.

Several young women stacked cutlery, plates, glasses and paper napkins on the counter. One carried jugs of milk toward the dining room. Beef stew bubbled in two huge pots on the stove. The steam rose to the ceiling and drifted toward the window. Bowls of butter and multiple loaves of homemade brown bread covered the laminate counter top. Pans of apple crisp sat on cooling racks beside the bread. Two large serving spoons were immersed in a thick filling topped with a mixture of oatmeal, brown sugar and butter. Wind rattled the back door trying to get past the deadbolt. It held but a draft seeped through the hinged side. A light frost covered the lower half of the window despite heat from the stove. Heat and chatter.

Reality hit Sarah hard. She was now one of them. To control the urge to escape, she stared at the biggest pan of apple crisp she'd seen in her life. The aroma was sensational. She imagined it topped with vanilla ice cream.

Bernice's voice snapped her back to real life. "Seen enough? Let's get outta this oven. I'll take ya to your room." She headed for the stairs, glanced over her shoulder and pointed to the left. "That's the dinin' room there and the sittin' area is opposite. Its got a window on the front yard and some books, magazines and craft stuff. No questions, right? Let's see your room." They began the silent climb to the third floor.

"Well, here's your home away from home, Eva. There's two beds so pick one and shove your suitcase under it. Ya got two drawers in the dresser so don't get grabby. Your donated clothes are in the closet. Bring the ones you're in down at supper. And don't expect to have this room all to yourself, missy. Girls are always comin' and goin' here. The bathroom's down the hall. Any questions now?"

Sarah shook her head, sat on a chair and stared at the floral bedspread and tired blue carpet.

"Don't say ya didn't get the grand tour, eh? You'll hear a bell for supper. Get right down or one of us'll come lookin' for ya. Oh, don't keep yer door closed. We make sure yer all okay, day and night. The night lady does bed checks. Lights out at ten."

Sarah lifted her head. Cabbage rose wallpaper covered all four walls. Big pink flowers everywhere. Her room was scarcely big enough for two single beds let alone the four-drawer dresser and two cane bottom chairs. She smelled faint odours of laundry soap and stew wafting up the stairwell. Fearing a nasty shout from Bernice, she went to the closet. Five faded, flowered maternity tops and five pair of maternity pants hung listlessly on wooden hangers. Three pants were black, one brown and the fifth green, her least favourite colour. In the top dresser drawer, she found seven new white maternity underpants, five large white bras, an assortment of coloured socks and a new navy wool cardigan. Four extra large white nightgowns and a yellow housecoat filled the second drawer.

With her Eva clothes on, Sarah gently moved her hands across her abdomen then stepped into the hall. She was now a stranger to herself and everyone else. Eva no name.

"Hello. Anybody here? Hello. I'm the new girl. Anybody else on the third floor?"

"Me." A soft, hesitant reply drifted across the hallway.

"Hello, Me. I'm Sa....Eva. Can we talk?"

"Okay."

Sarah found 'Me' sitting on her bed in the dim light clutching a small photo and a handful of tissues. Her trash can was full of used ones. A blue mouse-shaped lamp with a red nose sat on the dresser. The lamp belonged in a child's room, certainly not in the room of someone soon to be a mother. She was afraid to speak for fear of shattering the frail form in front of her. She leaned forward and spoke in a soft voice. "What's your name?"

"They call me Ellen." The voice was tiny, just like her.

"Cute lamp. Was it here when you arrived?"

"Oh, no. It's my night light. I brought it from home."

"You're all alone in the dark. Bad day?"

"Yes. "

"I'm sorry to hear that. What kind of place is this? Phony names, secondhand clothes. I'm ticked, already."

"There's no point getting angry. You can't leave." Ellen began a gentle rocking motion while chewing her thumbnail.

"But what's this place really like?"

"It doesn't matter what I think about it. I'm here and some day, I'll leave. In between, I eat a little, sleep a lot and wait."

"But why are you in your room right now? Don't you have chores? They sound serious about chores around here."

"Mine are always the same. I tidy the sitting room after breakfast, lunch and supper. Matron says that's all I am able to do."

"What do you do the rest of the time? Do you go out?"

"I usually sit in my room and look at magazines."

"How long have you been here? Have a roommate?"

"I arrived at the end of September. I had a roommate. She moved into another room because she said I was sad all the time. She's gone now."

"Do your parents visit or call?"

"My mother came two weeks ago for a couple of hours. She always says I'll be well after I leave and forget this place. She calls every week and sends magazines."

"Maybe you should talk to the caseworker."

"I did. She said my mother was right."

"Hey, there's the bell for supper. Let's go down and sit together." *This girl needs help. What's the matter with this place?*

"I'm not hungry."

Sarah tried again. "You can introduce me to everybody. I'd like that."

"Oh, I don't know. I might come down later."

"I really need someone for my first meal here. You're the perfect choice. Please."

"Well, I'll try."

Sarah was astounded when Ellen stood up. Her hand went to her mouth in shock. Ellen looked no older than fourteen. She was about five feet tall and Sarah estimated she weighed less than ninety pounds. A large pink flower barrette adorned her dark, shoulder length hair. She wore black patent Mary Jane shoes with pink ankle socks.

Ellen gripped the handrail tightly and started down the steps. They descended one flight of stairs in silence. Ellen made a sudden stop and grabbed the newel post with both hands.

Sarah whispered. "You okay?"

"I'm not hungry. I'm going back to my room."

"You're leaving me alone for my first meal? How will I know what's good to eat? You're the expert. What's your favourite food here?"

"The stew's pretty good."

"We're in luck. It's on the menu tonight. Let's go." Sarah held her breath.

Ellen muttered a hesitant "Okay" and released her grip on the post.

Sarah and Ellen served themselves in the kitchen. Ellen skipped the bread and took a tiny portion of beef stew. She picked up the smallest portion of apple crisp and waited in the hall for Sarah. Everyone was seated by the time they arrived. All conversation ceased and without exception, everyone stared at the latecomers in silence. It was an awkward moment as Sarah stood in the doorway waiting for Ellen.

Lunch at Rose Hill was casual with soup and sandwiches. Supper was a different event. Matron always joined the girls for the evening meal. She fancied herself as the mistress in a boarding school and took her role seriously. She reasoned a meal in a well appointed room would train young women for marriage or future employment in better homes and hotels. It exposed them to the trappings of a world outside their usual experience. Supper was her time to create the appropriate setting. A three leaf walnut dining table with white tablecloth easily accommodated twelve girls. It dominated the room. The matching buffet and china cabinet stood against the wall opposite the window to the backyard. The wallpaper was multicolour roses on a cream background and the drapes were yellow. In the corner, a glazed green Majolica pottery jardinière with pedestal held trailing ivy.

Matron's idea was true for some residents of Rose Hill. Society, however, played no favourites with unwed mothers. Homes for unwed mothers sheltered girls and women "in trouble" from all backgrounds and walks of life. Single, working women, young girls, married women, wealthy, poor and everyone in-between sat at Mrs. Andrew's table.

Despite Matron's desire and the genteel surroundings, conversation was stilted. Girls and women with made up names and no past could not settle around the table for conversation about school, work, friends, family, parties or even themselves. They shared meals with others they did not know and very likely never would. Sadness, fear and loneliness were all present at the 'family' table. For some, anger was not far away.

Matron broke the ice. "Everyone, this is Eva. Please introduce yourselves. Nice to see you join us for supper, Ellen."

Sarah glanced around the table and nodded in the general direction of the Matron. Phony people were sure to create lively, honest conversation. She didn't care anyway. She didn't need anything from any of these people. She'd be out of here soon.

"Eva, I'm Joan. My room is right below yours. I think you are alone in your room right now... just like me."

"Hi, Eva. I'm Marjorie. I've been here since August. Anytime you need help, let me know. We're all friends here."

"Hello. I'm Betty."

"Welcome, Eva. I'm Alice. I'm almost ready to leave. Guess you can tell though!"

"Hello, Eva. Welcome. I'm Emma."

"Eva, I'm Karen. Marjorie is my roommate." She smirked and rolled her eyes toward Marjorie.

"Welcome to Shangri-la, a quiet oasis in a world of turmoil! I'm Mary, your comic relief in a storm of emotions."

Sarah snorted. Then for the first time in too many days, she laughed out loud. "Thanks for that, I think!"

"Mary, don't be so silly. Sometimes I just don't know what to make of you." Matron stared hard at her.

"Well, Matron. I'm trying to make a little fun so we can laugh once in a while. Life can be serious and you don't get out alive."

"Oh, good grief. Let's get back to supper."

The meal dragged on with meaningless conversation. Sarah encouraged Ellen to eat. Gratefully, it was over in less than an hour and she escaped to her room and sat in the dark. She puzzled over why everyone appeared to have accepted their fate. Two of them actually looked happy. How bad was home if this place looked good. Anyway, she had no intention of conforming to this herd mentality, talking about due dates, trips to the bathroom and swollen feet. She had much better things to do with her time. Number one was a plan to see Myles. The sooner the caseworker showed up, the better.

"Lights out, girls. It's ten o'clock." Bernice smiled with satisfaction as she ascended the staircase. *Get to bed, princesses. Tomorrow is another workday.*

Sarah changed for bed by moonlight. It wasn't easy but better than seeing the room she had to live in. Lying in bed, she gave herself permission to cry for the loss of her old life. Then she vowed to spend her time planning for her future. It would not be the future her mother saw nor the one Matron predicted.

But first, she needed comfort. She removed her suitcase from under the bed, broke the lining thread and took out her art case. Between the pages of her sketch book, Myles smiled at her. She kissed his photo and whispered, "I'll find you, my love. Soon the three of us will be together."

Chapter Three

January 7, 1961
Halifax, Nova Scotia

"Rise and shine, ladies. It's Saturday. This is Nancy, your morning sunshine. Breakfast is in thirty minutes. Chores begin at nine."

Sarah had a quick bath, wrapped the towel around herself as best she could and pulled her hair into a ponytail. Back in her room, she scanned her closet. Baggy maternity pants with an out of shape stretch panel and a hand-me-down maternity top were the options. She closed her eyes and let her fingers make the decision.

Breakfast was a quiet meal. Girls drifted in and out with little conversation. Porridge and toast were in the kitchen. Brown sugar, milk and homemade strawberry rhubarb jam were on the table. Alice, Emma and Karen were eating when Sarah arrived.

"Good morning, Eva. The first night can be difficult. Sleep okay?"

"I did. It's Emma, right?"

"Yes. Alice and I are next door to you."

"Alice, you look really uncomfortable. When are you due?" *Damn, now I'm talking like them!*

"Any day now. My back is killing me and it is hard to sleep. Poor Emma has put up with me for three months. She'll be happy to see me go."

"It's okay, Alice. I understand. I'll actually miss you, bunky."

Karen jumped in. "I don't sleep well any night but nobody believes me. I've been here since the end of August and it doesn't get better."

"Well Karen, Marjorie has a different story. She says you saw logs every night. She's your roommate so I think she might be right."

Emma's hard edge of sarcasm wasn't missed by Sarah. She rushed to change the subject. "You've been here since August? Wow."

"I'm due around the end of next month. My family travels a lot so I came early. They want me to have good care near a hospital."

Emma glanced at Sarah and rolled her eyes. "Alice, if you're finished, I can help you upstairs."

"I'm staying downstairs this morning. I can't wait to get this over." She sighed heavily.

Sarah leaned forward over her coffee, hands wrapped around the cup. She couldn't imagine looking or feeling like Alice. Even the idea frightened her. When delivery time came, she planned to ask for serious painkillers.

"Good morning, girls. Hello, Eva. I'm Eleanor. Welcome. Matron sorted yesterday's mail last evening. It's in the kitchen for pick-up. The Saturday newspaper is also here. Chores start soon. Eva, did you check the list?"

Sarah started toward the kitchen but quickly darted up the stairs. At Ellen's door she paused and knocked. "Are you awake?"

"Come in, Eva. What's in your hand?"

"I couldn't sneak out jam but here's toast. Eleanor almost caught me but this top has big pockets."

"She's nice. Probably wouldn't say anything. Nancy also works in the morning. She's okay, too. Bernice is the nasty one. She's cranky and snoops in our rooms when she thinks nobody's around. I don't know if she takes anything. Thank you for the toast."

Back in her room after kitchen duty, Sarah stared past the huge spruce branches toward the brick church across the street. The stained glass window twinkled in the morning sun. It reminded her of rock candy in her Christmas stocking. She got on her knees and reached under the bed. Suddenly Marjorie was standing over her.

"What you doing under there? Got secrets?"

Before Sarah could say anything, Marjorie was at the window. "You've got quite the view. I'm stuck at the back. Nothing happens there." She wandered to the closet, opened the door and rummaged through the clothes "You smoke? I'm looking for someone to smoke with."

"Smoke!" Sarah was dumbstruck by the rude behaviour and that Marjorie could smoke at Rose Hill.

"It relaxes me and boy do I need that here." She sat on Sarah's bed and continued. "How do you like it so far? What do you think of Mrs. Andrews? She's too bossy for me. Did you meet Nancy this morning? She's better than Bernice but Bernice smokes so that's good. You should see the nice ring Betty has. I'd like to know who gave it to her but she's tight lipped. She's snobby, ya know, thinks she's better than the rest of us 'cause she takin' some school course. Same for that Joan one. Always askin' questions and mouthin' off with ideas. Thinks she's so smart."

"I see."

"Want to be my friend? You're new so I'll take you for a walk after lunch."

"No, thanks. I'm still tired from travelling."

"You're not from here?"

"I'm going to lie down now. Bye."

"I'll be back later."

Sarah closed the door and opened her art case. She placed her sketch pad against the window. Within an hour, her sketch of the church window emerged from the paper. She felt relaxed and satisfied with "Rock Candy." It would be terrific in watercolour. Marjorie might need cigarettes but art would be her lifeline until Myles was back in her life. In the meantime, she'd keep to herself. Except for little Ellen.

In mid-afternoon Sarah put on her coat and went to Ellen's room. "Let's ditch this joint. Come to the backyard with me. I need some fresh air and a change of scenery. The sun's out but put on your coat and gloves."

"I don't know. It's too cold to be outside."

"Come on. Just for a few minutes. It'll be a change for both of us."

"Okay, just for a little while."

Eleanor watched the two girls come into the kitchen and exit the back door. She absentmindedly made hot chocolate for their return. Her brain was preoccupied by Ellen's gaunt appearance.

Outside, Sarah noticed Betty sitting on a wooden bench with a blanket over her knees. A very large book rested on her lap.

"Hi, Betty. Can we sit with you? What are you reading?"

She responded without enthusiasm, "Sure. It's an art textbook from university."

Sarah settled on the bench. "So, what's the art book about? I like to draw and paint but I've never seen a book like that one."

Without lifting her head she replied, "It's for an art course I'm taking about the history of art and artists."

"Sarah, I'm cold. I'm going back to my room."

"But, we just got here. It's warmer on the bench with us. Want to sit down?"

"No. You can stay. I have to go."

"Okay, I'll see you later."

Sarah turned to Betty. "So, could I take a course like that?"

"Are you in university?"

"Not yet."

"There are high school correspondence courses from the Nova Scotia Department of Education. It's education you take without a classroom. I don't know if art is offered. You better ask the caseworker or Matron."

"Thanks. Your book looks interesting. Could I look at it sometime?"

"I have to study to write a paper but you can borrow it for a couple of days when I go to the hospital."

"Thanks. See ya. I'm going to check on Ellen and make sure she eats tonight."

During supper, Sarah could hardly wait for the meal to end and chores to be finished. The picture in Betty's book had given her a new idea. After lights out, she took her flashlight and art supplies into bed. Myles rested on the pillow.

Sunday morning was overcast, cold and a day of rest, sort of. Breakfast and lunch were extended by thirty minutes and chores kept to a minimum. No dusting, no vacuuming, no furniture polishing but attendance at Reverend Miller's afternoon discussion group was mandatory.

Sarah stretched out on her bed appreciating the quiet and thinking about correspondence courses and the art book. She pretended to be asleep, afraid of another unwelcome visit and onslaught of gossip from Marjorie.

"Eva. It's Emma. It's almost time for the discussion group. I thought you might want to be prepared for it."

"Prepared for what? Is it some sort of bad girl sermon?"

"Sort of. It's preachy for sure. How are you doing?"

"Okay, still getting used to a very strange routine and new people."

"Well, you could have said a new routine and very strange people, so that's good!"

"That would have worked, too!"

"Time to go down to the sitting room. Can we sit together at supper?"

"Sure but I want to make sure Ellen eats something."

"I'm up for helping with that."

Reverend Miller sat before ten pairs of eyes with obvious discomfort. He adjusted his polka dot tie, tugged at his jacket sleeves and pushed up his glasses, twice.

"Good afternoon, girls. Let's begin with a prayer."

Sarah tuned out after the prayer when Reverend Miller announced the topic of the day as 'Guilt'. She tuned back in when she realized the room was deathly still and Reverend Miller's face was scarlet. His mouth hung half open. For a few moments, everyone was frozen in place.

"That's a good question, Marjorie. Would anyone like to venture a guess about guilty feelings?"

Joan waved her hand and countered, "Does it actually matter about Marjorie's question or the answer? No. It does not. Nobody, including our parents thinks for one minute about who's guilty. For them, it's us. The fathers walk away. We're the ones who carry blame for the rest of our lives. I think that's wrong and it has to change." She jumped up. "What do the rest of you think about that? What do you think about yourself? For me, that's more important than what other people think." She looked at everybody individually, then left the room.

Nobody moved or spoke. The discussion period ended abruptly with Reverend Miller reminding the group he looked forward to seeing them next week. He rushed toward the front door leaving Matron staring at his fleeing back. He clutched his overcoat to his chest as he raced to the car.

Joan was hot about the guilt topic for the remainder of the afternoon and started it up at supper when Matron stepped out of the room for a few minutes. The room went silent when Matron returned.

Sarah made no comments but thought Joan was on to something about guilt. She was impressed by Joan's ability to make her points so convincingly even if she did go a bit overboard with Reverend Miller.

After supper, her agitation about being locked away in Rose Hill returned. Soon she was as upset as she had been on the ferry before Andy spoke with her. She thought about Joan's words too. They made sense but didn't stop Joan's parents from bringing her here and they wouldn't get her out either. She took several deep breaths to calm down and let her brain work. She needed a solution to being trapped inside Rose Hill, not ongoing rants. She knew Myles was in Halifax so she decided to turn her energy into making a plan to get out. The decision didn't take away the panicky sensation in her chest.

After supper chores, Emma lingered outside Sarah's door, lifted her hand and knocked gently. "Eva, it's Emma. You were very quiet at supper. Is something wrong? May I come in?"

"I'd rather you didn't, Emma. I have some things to sort out in my mind. I can't really talk about it right now, maybe tomorrow. Good night."

Emma returned to her room and found Marjorie sitting beside Alice on the bed. Joan paced between the door and window.

"How dare that little jerk sit there spouting off about guilt. Did he really expect us to smile and nod?"

"That's right. You're right." Marjorie sensed this was her big chance to secure Joan's friendship. "She's totally right, isn't she, Alice?"

"I just want to lie down. Maybe tomorrow I'll have an opinion."

"Emma?"

"Well, I don't believe any of us will change Reverend Miller's mind. I'm sorry you're upset Joan but it's time for me to read and make sure Alice can rest in a quiet room."

Marjorie jumped up and grabbed Joan's arm. "Let's go to your room."

When they left, Emma turned to see Alice holding the box of tissues.

"Sit beside me, Emma. I am tired but I want to say a few things before I try to sleep. Sorry for being so crabby. My back is making me crazy. I can't see my feet but they must be size twenty! I know I'll never do this again."

"When do you see the doctor?"

"Wednesday afternoon. I hate that lonely taxi ride. Sitting in the waiting room is horrible too. Everyone's with someone. They are happy and excited. Sometimes the nurse calls me 'Miss' so that makes it worse. They all stare at me. Anyway, my days at Rose Hill are numbered. By next Sunday, I will be with my family and my baby in the arms of strangers. You'll be alone in this room."

Emma reached for Alice's hand and opened her mouth to speak. Alice spoke first.

"Shush. If I stop, I won't be able to start again. For as long as I live, I'll never forget this place. It kept me safe from neighbours and relatives who would have shunned me or worse. But it changed the real me. Maybe I'll never be me again. One thing

I do know is you have been my anchor, Emma. I want to thank you for that. You've been a kind friend."

Emma embraced Alice. "You're so welcome, my friend. I will miss you. You'll not be forgotten. Let's get ready for bed and try to sleep."

Alice rested with her back to Emma and quietly wiped her eyes. "Emma, my grandmother's name was Emma. It's my real name, too. Goodnight."

"Goodnight."

After turning Emma away, Sarah put on her nightgown, took her pillow to the window and looked into the darkness. The frightened reflection of someone drifting alone in open water without rudder or compass looked back. She punched the pillow with both fists, put it over her face and let out a long, low moan of despair.

Chapter Four

January 7–8, 1961
Halifax, Nova Scotia

Andy MacNeil's usual Saturday routine began with a walk to Fosters Grocery after breakfast. The local grocery welcomed a wide audience of neighbourhood customers. Fosters was the place to be on Saturday. An array of vegetables, meat, fish, dairy and bakery items satisfied every shopper's needs. Equally important were the social connections that took place in the store or on the sidewalk out front. It was a time to meet face to face and discuss the well-being of others, politics and tell a yarn or two.

Old man Foster, fondly referred to as Gimpy because of a war injury in 1917, looked after things from a stool behind the cash register. When things got too quiet he would drop a bomb into the middle of an ongoing discussion. Half of the time he didn't agree with what he said himself but that didn't matter. He just liked to hear the fireworks go off.

His sons, Alex and Ben, were kept busy serving customers. Ben's wife, May looked after the bakery and ice cream with Phoebe, aged nine. Gimpy was proud of Phoebe. He felt certain she had the makings of a third generation grocer. She was good with numbers and had charm to spare.

As Andy rounded the corner, a block from Fosters, he met his neighbour, Mrs. P and Barney, her blue merle collie.

"Rushing to Fosters, Andy? Ever wish we had Sunday shopping? It makes Saturday so busy for working people."

"Not really. I like the excitement at Fosters on Saturday and I can relax on Sunday. Hey, Barney. How ya doing? How's my favourite collie?"

"Woof."

"That's great. And you, Mrs. P?"

"Pretty good for an old girl. Barney missed seeing you the last few days. Been out of town?"

"I've been on the Island making sales calls and visiting mother."

"How is your mother and the art supply business?"

"Nothing changes about my mother. Same conversations. Same opinions. Business is good, though. It's great to travel around and meet artists and store owners. I'm adding accounts so business is going well. As you know, some of my friends are artists or art teachers or both. They help me understand what stores need to stock. Anything new in the neighbourhood?"

"A nice young woman moved in down the street at number twenty-seven. Maybe you should bake a cake and take it over."

"Me bake a cake? You must have me confused with someone who can actually cook! I like to eat though. Does that count?"

"Oh, Andy. You're such a kidder. I know you make a fine clam chowder."

"Thanks but that's as good as it gets. Here's a new topic for you. You've lived around here quite a while. Do you know anything about Rose Hill Home?"

"Yes, a little. When my husband Peter was teaching high school we knew the girls didn't receive any education during their stay. We were concerned about all the women of course, but especially about the ones under eighteen. Peter's principal approached the matron at the time but she didn't welcome any assistance. Nevertheless, we put together several donations of textbooks and general reading material. Most of it would be outdated now. Why do you ask?"

"Oh, I met a young girl on the deck of the ferry yesterday. I overheard her mother mention Rose Hill. I'd like to talk with you about the Home sometime."

"We could talk today. Do you have time for a sandwich after shopping?"

"Sure. I'll see you in an hour or so."

"Good. Barney has his routine so I'll keep moving and see you later."

"Thanks, Mrs. P. See 'ya, Barney."

After unpacking the groceries, Andy called his sister Liz, and invited himself to the Valley for a weekend in the middle of the month. A few minutes after hanging up, the phone rang. He grabbed the receiver fully expecting to hear Liz tell him not to bother coming. It was her usual routine and was wearing him down.

"Hey, Andy. It's Jane. I just came home from shopping with Norma. We are meeting Wendell at The Lighthouse for brunch tomorrow. Want to join us at eleven?"

"Sure. Are you going to the reception and art exhibit at the College tonight?"

"Yep. Norma is showing her Maple Leaf Forever piece. Will we see you there?"

"Absolutely. Wouldn't miss it. Catch you later then. I'm having lunch with Mrs. P so gotta go."

Andy and his three friends first met in a university psychology class. Three years later, Norma and Wendell had completed education degrees and were teaching. Jane finished her Bachelor's program in psychology and took a year off to travel. Now back at university, she was enrolled in a Masters program. Andy completed his business degree and accepted a sales position with a national company selling art supplies. All four had a big interest in the arts. Norma dabbled in watercolours, Wendell acting, Jane poetry and Andy photography. Their time together was always punctuated by spirited, respectful conversation. No topic was off limits and agreeing to disagree was a frequent occurrence. Norma and Wendell were the established combatants in the study group early on.

Since then, nothing had changed. Norma and Wendell rarely appeared to agree on anything, including cars, movies and food. Their jousting and antics ensured no thought was left unearthed. They were entertaining so it was easy to watch and listen. Andy evolved into the quasi-moderator of the group, out of necessity.

Mrs. P's home sat on a quiet tree-lined street within walking distance of Citadel Hill, location of the Halifax Citadel National Historic Site chosen to protect the city in 1749. Clusters of spruce, maple, fruit and ornamental trees dotted the property and framed the two-story white home. The candy apple red front door gleamed in the afternoon sun.

Andy sauntered up the walkway deep in thought about the art exhibit and Nova Scotia College of Art. Since the late 1880's, it played an essential role in the life of artists, teachers and children in the community. He tapped the knocker on the strike plate and heard Barney race to the door.

"Welcome, Andy. Come through to the kitchen."

Andy followed the petite Mrs. P. down the hall. As usual, her silver hair was in a bun. Today it was gathered at the nape of her neck. Sometimes it was high on her head. She wore tailored black wool pants with a red sweater and flowery scarf.

Scarves were her signature piece. Today it was black silk with stylized red tulips. She called them her failing.

The kitchen was an eclectic collection of history, art and convenience living together companionably. In addition to functioning as a kitchen, the room was a mini gallery with art on the walls and 1920's sideboard. Andy settled into an upholstered side chair at the rustic-finish oak table. Mrs. P brought a tray of egg salad sandwiches, homemade sweet pickles and big pot of Earl Grey tea from the counter. On the way, she dropped a few treats in Barney's bowl. Andy was certain he saw a smile appear on the young dog's face. He knew Barney was one lucky boy. Then he smelled chocolate cake and knew he was a lucky boy too.

Never one to shy away from a healthy discussion, Mrs. P launched into the topic that brought them together. "So, Andy, tell me about the young girl on the Abby."

Andy rubbed his chin, looked out the kitchen window and allowed himself a few moments to collect his thoughts. "I was on the ship deck and met a girl named Sarah near the railing. She told me she was going to Halifax for a while then said her parents thought they knew what was best for her. She was very angry. Her story sounded familiar to me. On the car deck, I overheard Rose Hill mentioned. Liz was there. She's never been the same since. So what's the story on that place?"

"Well, I've never been inside Rose Hill so I can't say anything about that part. Some of this you already know. Homes for unwed mothers have been around for ages all across the country. Many homes are operated by church organizations. The young women inside are isolated, usually far from home and live under an assumed name. They are pressured to give their baby up for adoption. Feelings of anger, guilt and mistrust flourish and are present for the rest of their lives. Why are you so concerned about this particular girl going to Rose Hill?"

"Well, it's not about this girl but meeting her got me to really thinking about Liz and her life after Rose Hill. I think I should do something about that place. Should I do something? It feels wrong to do nothing. So I guess I'm saying I want to do something. Am I blathering or making any sense?"

"You're doing both. But why are you so hepped-up to do something now?"

"Well, it's been bothering me more since dad died. I know this sounds self-important but things should be better inside Rose Hill. It's 1961, for heaven's sake! Maybe I can make it better? Do I sound crackers?"

"Possibly."

"That I am crackers?"

"We already know that! Seriously though, I'm guessing your relationship with Liz is bothering you more than even you realize. Hold your thoughts. Barney needs to go out. Come with us. We'll think outside. Also, I want to show you something in the front garden. Barney, let's go."

Mrs. P and Andy walked to a tulip bed protected for the winter by a thick coat of mulch. She explained the nurture of her favourite flower and ended with a word of advice.

"I think relationships are like these bulbs. They need nurturing but not smothering. It's not an easy balance but worth the effort. Does that make sense to you?"

"It does put things into perspective. Wendell tells me I get an idea, fire off a litany of possibilities and overwhelm everyone within earshot. That's probably not welcome by people on the receiving end of my enthusiasm."

"Probably not, particularly if you don't take action after gaining their interest. And at some point, sooner rather than later, you have to make a decision and act on it. In this case, you have to either stop thinking about Rose Hill or do something helpful. You'll feel better when you do. In addition to enthusiasm, do you have ideas about Rose Hill?"

"Well, I think art or music classes might help. After that, I'm stuck. But, how do I get any idea in there? I can't just walk up to the front door and knock. I do know I need help. You and my other friends could be part of that help."

"Okay. Let's go back inside and chase this around. Barney, come."

Settled in the living room with fresh tea, the conversation resumed.

"Let's take this slowly, piece by piece. First, how does Liz fit into this? Aren't the two of you struggling with your relationship?"

"Struggling is a kind word and yes, it's true. She doesn't see me as the brother she had years ago. She's still bucking my visits to Wolfville. She doesn't have close friends nor seem to want any. She's chippy, rarely laughs. How does she fit in? I don't know but I want her to."

"So, I still don't see how art, music and Rose Hill help your relationship with your sister."

"I figure art is a neutral topic. Liz is into art again, thanks to Aunt Helen. If I can have a conversation about art and introduce the idea of Rose Hill, she might have an idea about that. Make any sense?"

"It seems logical but is it really possible in reality? Sounds like a real long shot to me. Liz has continued to isolate herself for self-preservation. Her trust in others has been destroyed and she believes you are part of that. Seems to me, you need the trust part first before anything else gets layered on in your discussion. Just my humble opinion but you have pretty high hopes for one visit, if that's what you're thinking."

"I'm going to the Valley for the January twenty-first weekend, hoping Aunt Helen will be an ally. Liz has lived with her for four years and the relationship appears strong."

"Maybe your weekend will reveal more than you expect. I hope it works out. My best advice is take it slowly. By the way, do your friends know about this idea?"

"Not yet. I meet them tonight but will wait to talk about it tomorrow. We're getting together at The Lighthouse for brunch."

"So how do you think I fit into this 'grand plan'?"

"You're pretty creative and persuasive. I'd like to toss out my first ideas and hear your feedback."

"Toss away and I'll jump in with questions and comments. Remember, I'm not committed yet. Convince me."

"Number one, we need really good reasons for art and music classes and number two, how do we get through to the matron. She's the roadblock. I need special people to work with me on both. Where do you see yourself helping, part one or part two? Could you get into Rose Hill?"

"What? Get in there? Old girls have seen and done a lot of things but laying siege to a home for unwed mothers isn't on my resume!"

Over the following hour they created a list of reasons for the classes and every person who might be helpful in making it happen. No reason or person was discounted. A final review would come later.

"We've worked hard, Andy, so we deserve a reward. How about a piece of chocolate cake with butter icing before you leave?"

"You don't have to twist my arm!"

Andy took long strides home from Mrs. P's home and rushed into the front hall of his apartment. He glanced at the clock above the hall table and knew he had to hurry. Twenty minutes later he put on his pea coat and dashed to the car, then remembered the camera. Luck was on his side and an open parking spot was available near the Gallery. He entered the building as the 'welcome' speech began. The evening's events featured local artists and was sponsored by the hometown brewery, Alexander Keith's, a landmark in the city since 1820. Norma, Wendell and Jane waved. He skirted the room and tucked in beside them.

Following the opening remarks at the Gallery, Andy moved through the three rooms on the main floor. Each artist was present and eager to talk about his or her work and techniques. Several times he heard comments about a much-needed expansion to the old four-story hall. Artists and attendees welcomed his interest in taking pictures to record the evening. He hoped a couple of them would appear in the Saturday edition of the newspaper.

Norma's piece, Maple Leaf Forever was an eye-catcher despite the modest ten by twelve inch canvas. The maple's stunning red fall coat captured every eye. Several people recognized its' location in the city. It evoked fond memories from those who had attended school where the tree stood on guard near the playground. She was both thrilled and overwhelmed by the appreciative response.

At ten-thirty the following morning, Norma, Jane and Wendell waited for Andy to arrive at The Lighthouse. Jane savoured her coffee and twisted her antique dinner ring in thought. Wendell and Norma intently discussed kippers and the merits of waffles versus pancakes. They punctuated their opinions with arm gestures. When the back and forth became highly animated, the waiter was forced to perform a duck and dive maneuver with the coffee pot.

"What's to discuss, you two? You analyze everything to death at brunch. Kippers are just plain nasty. Waffles and pancakes are an even draw. Give it up, already. Sunday morning is all about coffee."

In the meantime, Andy was backing out of the driveway and heading for Robie Street. With businesses closed, the streets were quiet and parking easy. He opened the restaurant door, left the January chill behind and stepped into a sea of blue tablecloths and the welcoming smells, sights and sounds of The Lighthouse. Aromas of fresh brewed coffee and cinnamon buns greeted him. Lively chatter and laughter originated from the diners seated in brightly painted Captain's chairs. A few nodded or waved. Atlantic storm lanterns updated to accommodate electricity hung from the ceiling.

Photographs, watercolours and oil paintings depicting lighthouses decorated most of the wall space. Peggy's Cove and

Louisbourg caught his eye on the way to the table. To complete the mood, Celtic music flowed from the record player behind the counter.

"Morning, all. What did I miss?"

"Nothing really… just the usual agonizing brunch decisions. Or should I say, indecision for Wendell and Norma. Why do two creative people need to debate food?"

Wendell couldn't resist tossing a comeback. "We are creative and therefore, want to explore the options."

"Uh, huh and Heaven help us all if Ken ever decided to take waffles or pancakes off the menu. I analyze all week and am a happy girl to sip my coffee and order the 'special'".

Norma raised her left eyebrow and retorted. "Oh, yeah? What happens if the 'special' includes kippers?"

"Well, Miss Smarty Pants, I know you will look out for me and point that out, right? You and Wendell are hopeless about brunch but I love you anyway. And you too, Andy."

Wendell straightened his shirt collar and quipped. "Finally, some acknowledgment about how wonderful we are!"

"Cool hair do, Jane."

"Thanks, Andy. Thought I'd try a fancy scarf with a ponytail today."

Norma pointed her finger at Wendell and Andy. "You guys have no idea how lucky you are about hair. My mom was a believer in 'close your eyes and hold your nose' perms. What a way to spend Saturday afternoon, eyes watering in a stinky kitchen. Those chemicals were something else! Did you have home perms, Jane?"

"Yes, and the added fun of a cowlick in my bangs. It drove everyone crazy with perms and hair cuts."

"At least nobody called either of you 'carrot top'."

Norma didn't give up easily. "Oh, poor Wendell. I want your red hair. Straight brown is boring. Poor baby."

"Buy a box of that stuff at the drug store and try it out. We could call you 'red'."

"Right and watch my mother go off the deep end? By the way, I brought the brochure for the art sessions starting in February. All of us should sign-up for something." She bent over to her purse on the floor. "Wendell, you have Hush Puppies and argyle socks! Trying to make the front section of the fashion pages?"

"Nah. You know I can't resist window displays. They call my name."

"You folks ready to order?"

Andy looked at everyone and received nods. "Sure and keep the coffee coming."

When the waiter left, Andy turned to Norma. "I'd be the comic relief at those art classes so I don't think it's going to happen. My camera is as creative as I get. Your watercolour was a stunner last night. It captured the spirit of the old maple in the school yard. I think art must speak to you, make a connection, be meaningful in some way. Obviously, that happened last night. Good on ya."

He smiled at Jane. "How was your week?"

"Lots on my mind. I'm happy to have a weekend to regroup."

Wendell turned to Andy. "Anything new on the Island?"

"No, but on the ferry from PEI I had a new experience. I met a young girl going to an unwed mothers home in Halifax. Turns out it's Rose Hill. I'd like to talk about doing something for the home."

Andy immediately acquired a silent audience. Norma settled back into her chair and dropped her hands on her lap. Jane placed her fork on her plate then moved her hands to embrace her coffee mug.

Wendell leaned forward for a few seconds then blurted a barrage of words. "Wow, that was a mouthful! What do you mean 'do something'? Not us, right?" He paused for a second. "That girl reminded you of Liz, right? Seems to me Liz is playing a big role in your thinking these days. Is that what this is all about?"

"Whoa, whoa. Don't have a cow, man. Right now, I just want to come up with ideas, okay?"

Wendell didn't plan to give up. "I know Liz was in there but maybe you need to step back from this for a while."

"Are you really, truly thinking of doing something for Rose Hill?" Norma asked cautiously then rested her elbows on the table. "I suppose we could talk about it," came as an afterthought.

"Unwed pregnancy is taboo, even today. Maybe you should leave this alone, Andy." Jane glanced back and forth between Norma and Wendell. She began to twist her ring then continued. "What could we really do, anyway? It is what it is."

"Well, I admit I don't know how something could be done but I still believe we could come up with some ideas for activities in there."

"We?" A chorus of three responded in unison.

Jane folded her arms across her chest and leaned back in her chair. "We can't change anything in there. It feels like a lost cause but go ahead, Andy. I have a feeling you have more to say."

Andy recounted his conversation with Mrs. P. Norma and Wendell nodded mild interest. Jane listened. Her few comments were skeptical. Several mugs of coffee were consumed and by one thirty, the foursome left The Lighthouse. In two weeks Andy would test his ideas with Liz, if she allowed him to visit.

Chapter Five

January 9, 1961
Rose Hill Home

At ten thirty, Matron unlocked her office door and spotted a used envelope lying face up on the hardwood floor. 'Mrs. S. Andrews' was crossed out and underneath, awkwardly printed was 'Matron.' Inside, she found a note printed on the reverse side of an old grocery list. She read, 'I seen some girls talk after chors. They said words like misscarrige and adopshun. Bernice.'

Matron forfeited her usual morning office routine and sauntered past the sitting room, twice. Nothing appeared out of place. Karen and Marjorie were looking at a magazine and talking about Paul Anka and Elvis Presley. Sarah was reading Saturday's newspaper. Joan was leafing through one of Ellen's old Teen magazines. She looked totally bored. Alice looked up and asked if they could speak in the office.

"Matron, I have an appointment to see the doctor on Wednesday morning but I don't feel right. Can I go today?"

"What's the problem? Are you in labour?"

"No but the baby feels different. It isn't kicking as much for sure. It was very quiet last night. I'm worried."

"I don't think anything is wrong. The baby's bigger now and has less room to move. We'll talk again tomorrow morning. You're due any day now so let me know if things change."

As Alice left, Sarah passed the open office door. "Eva, can I see you?"

"I need to go to the washroom Matron, but I'll be back right away."

Marjorie met her at the bottom of the stairs. "Hi, Eva. Got time for a chat? Let's go to your room."

"Sorry, Marjorie. I see Matron in a few minutes. After that I'm sure it'll be lunch time."

"You're seeing Matron? What did you do? See me when you're done. I'll need a smoke outside before lunch."

"Maybe."

Matron's door was ajar. She motioned for Sarah to come in. "How were your first few days, Eva?"

"Okay." She responded hesitantly and approached the desk slowly.

"Sit down. I have good news for you. The caseworker had a cancellation this week and she will see you tomorrow morning. Her name is Miss Preston. She'll help you begin the adoption procedure right away. It's not complicated, just paperwork."

"Adoption? I didn't decide on that." She crossed her arms, ready for a fight.

"I'm surprised. Your mother certainly indicated otherwise."

"I don't agree with her. She knows that. She didn't tell you, did she? I'm keeping my baby and that is that. I need somebody to help me. That's the caseworker's job, isn't it?"

"I think it best you talk with the caseworker about this to-morrow."

"I know what I'm doing. I've made my choice." She stood up and glared. She received a stern look in return.

"The caseworker is the best person to talk to, Eva. She has all the information to help you make the right decision. I'm sure you will feel better after seeing her tomorrow."

"Well, that will depend on her answer, won't it."

Sarah left the office with a satisfied smile on her face. She was confident this caseworker person would see her side of the story. Anyway, what did Matron and her mother really know about what was best for her.

While Sarah was with Matron, Marjorie rushed to find Karen. She found her absentmindedly dusting in the sitting room. "Eva just told me that she's gotta see Matron right now. I bet she's in big trouble about last night. Want me to snoop for you?"

"Sure." Karen grinned toward Marjorie's back. She was thoroughly enjoying this place. It was loads of fun at everyone's expense including Marjorie, who was the perfect dupe. Eager and thick as a post.

Betty and Mary were finishing the beef and barley soup preparation with Eleanor when Marjorie paused at the kitchen door to wave. All three smiled but said nothing.

Eleanor broke the silence. "She seems to be busy today. Wonder what's up?"

Mary chuckled, "We'll find out soon enough. Telegraph, telephone or telemarjorie. Let's make biscuits for lunch. Have we got any raisins? I love raisins."

With the biscuits baking, Betty and Mary took a break in the backyard. Betty read and Mary walked among the trees. As roommates, each was respectful of the other and did not push the boundaries of their relationship toward any semblance of friendship. They were in an awkward temporary living arrangement. Betty welcomed the restrictions. Mary reluctantly accepted them.

The weak, late morning sun made little change in the temperature. Dampness was in the air and the outdoor thermometer read twenty-eight degrees Fahrenheit. Mary wished she had put on her gloves not just her coat. Her hands were already tingling. She returned to the bench.

Betty clapped her hands together. "I'm chilled to the bone. We're in for something nasty." Weather was always a safe topic. Betty often used it to fill conversation air time.

"I think you're right. Sometimes it takes a day or two to get up a head of steam but then watch out. I'm looking forward to the days when we see more sunshine. It's so damp and gloomy."

They settled back on the bench for a few minutes of silence. It was quickly squashed by Karen who arrived carrying a cup of coffee. She looked pleased with herself and wedged between Mary and Betty.

"Have you heard the news? The new one's in big trouble. What does she call herself?" She continued without waiting for an answer as she knew it anyway. "Matron thinks she started all the racket in Joan's room last night. We're not here to make trouble. Serves her right."

Mary turned to face Karen and narrowed her eyes. "Why on earth would you say that? Eva hasn't said much about anything, let alone start a ruckus. She's been here three days. Right now, you're the one causing trouble by gossiping. Cut it out. Betty, we should go. I'm sure the biscuits are ready."

Karen remained on the bench stung by the verbal slap Mary delivered. She went into retaliation mode. Her mouth twisted into a puckered knot. It relaxed when she finished the payback plan. She strolled to the house with a smug look on her face.

After lunch and chores, Sarah sat on the chair with her feet on the bed. She could hardly believe the good news about the caseworker. Tomorrow, someone was going to help. At last, someone would tell her parents she didn't want to be here and wanted to keep the baby. Now she didn't have to find Myles on her own. She was at ease and in the mood to read.

The distinctive aroma of slow-roasting beef filled the stairwell. Roast beef with mashed potatoes and gravy was one of Sarah's favourite meals. Perhaps they'd have roast parsnips too. It was a good omen for tomorrow. The book selection in the sitting room was dismal. She chose a previously read, well-worn edition of an Agatha Christie mystery and returned to her room.

At supper, Sarah was thankful she didn't have to urge Ellen to eat. It was a healthy sign. A little bit of her wanted to be around to see more of Ellen's progress but it wasn't going to be. Tomorrow her own life would take a turn for the better. She contentedly read until 'lights out'.

Late Monday evening Karen noticed Marjorie slip out the kitchen door and decided this was the time to plan revenge on Mary. She crept toward the kitchen then waited for the back door to close. She counted to ten and slowly pushed it open. A blast of cold air stung her eyes as it brushed past her face. The porch light cast a narrow beam on the back step. Taking a quiet breath, she moved into the blackness. What she needed to do would be best done in pitch black. She was about to indulge in a secret pleasure. Tonight would be the ultimate mixture of words and actions in the dark. She craved the control and respect fear gave her. Marjorie was the perfect target.

Marjorie exhaled into the cold night air and watched her cigarette smoke drift toward the spruce. Most escaped into nothingness but a wisp caught momentarily in a branch and then it too, melted away. Snowflakes nestled on the sleeve of her black coat. For the first time in her life, she felt truly safe. She had a place where she belonged and a friend, someone to trust. Karen.

Karen scanned the backyard, seeking her prey. Taking a deep breath, she stepped forward and followed the smell of smoke.

Marjorie heard rustling in the row of shrubs to her right. Jack rabbits were frequent visitors to Rose Hill. She often saw them from her bedroom window. A yard without a dog and lots of shelter was an ideal place to rest day or night. She was content to share her time with the harmless bunnies. She didn't have to try to be a friend and face rejection.

Karen took advantage of her position and pounced from behind the tree. Marjorie's heart flew to her throat and her legs turned to jelly as Karen grabbed her coat. She tried to scream but only a weak croak escaped between her lips. Karen's hand tightened over her mouth as she whispered, "Gotcha. Wanna be my partner in a secret?"

When her breathing returned to normal, Marjorie couldn't believe her good fortune. Karen needed her. She was ready and willing to do whatever was asked. "Yes, please."

"Matron talked to me this morning. She said Mary needs special attention right now. You should smile a lot at her this week. Tomorrow, I want you to put a note under her door. I'll write it and you can play postman. It's kinder if she doesn't know who's doing it so you'll have to be very careful. Do it when she's in the bathroom or gone for breakfast. It's our secret. Let's call it our Secret Friend Mission. Got it?"

"Yes. I want to help. You're really nice, Karen."

"Come on then. We'll talk in our room."

Shortly after Nancy made the Tuesday morning wake-up shout, Marjorie quietly closed her bedroom door. Karen was waiting inside for her report.

"How'd it go with Mary?"

"Easy peasy. I did it when she was in the bathroom. Where'd you get the fancy blue envelope?"

Didn't you see Matron's name on the front scratched out, dummy? "In Matron's office. Trash cans are great places to find good stuff."

Karen had been curious about the envelope's handwritten Ottawa return address on the seal flap so she'd torn it off then placed it under her mattress with her other treasures. The less Marjorie knew, the better.

At breakfast Sarah was eager with anticipation and anxious to finish breakfast but willed herself to eat slowly. She expected to be out of Rose Hill within a week. She looked at each of the girls and said a silent goodbye. Shortly before nine, she returned to her room to review everything, one more time. Her list of requests and questions was short but she knew she had to remember each of them clearly. She counted them off on her fingers. When Matron called her name, she rushed down the stairs to meet her rescuer.

From behind the desk, Laura Preston gazed around Matron's office. The dark wooden desk and chair filled the middle of the room. Two large, four drawer grey metal file cabinets stood guard on the east wall. A massive Boston fern on a wooden pedestal filled the alcove of the bay window overlooking the front yard. On the north wall, the electric fireplace produced minimal warmth but it was attractive. Pictures of Peggy's Cove and Halifax Harbour sat atop its' faux marble mantel.

Laura was bored with her visits to Rose Hill. After six years, she'd seen it all and concluded almost every case ended the same. On occasion the middle part took an interesting twist or turn but on the whole, the stories repeated themselves. Residents of the home got themselves into trouble and expected her to fix the problem. They asked or pleaded for her to find or talk to the father of the baby, get them a job, find a place to live or convince parents to take them home. She'd heard it over and over but there was one recurring outcome. When you got caught, you gave up the baby and moved on with your life.

Eva's story would be no different. She removed the gold powder compact from her purse and smiled at the mirror. The beehive hairdo gave her the perfect combination of sophistication and modern style.

Sarah knocked on Matron's door and heard 'come'. She opened the door and beamed at the person who would solve her problems.

"Hello, Eva. I'm going to use your Rose Hill name. It makes the girls feel more comfortable when discussing their situation. Please have a seat. My name is Miss Preston and I am your caseworker. I have several questions and information for you. I expect you may have a few questions but I would prefer you ask them when I've finished. So, let's begin. "What is your due date and have you been pregnant before?"

"April twenty-second and no."

"Do you have any hobbies or talents?"

"Yes, I paint. Oh, and read a lot."

"Do you have brothers? Sisters?"

"No. Why?"

"Do you live with both parents?"

Sarah began to be wary. "Of course. What's this all about?"

"We like as much personal information as possible for your file." A smug smile crossed her face. "Are your parents healthy?"

"Yes but why are you writing all this down?" Sarah had a gut feeling Miss Preston had her own plan and she wasn't in it.

"It helps me get to know you better. Do you know the father of your child?"

"Of course I do. What kind of question is that?" Sarah bristled.

"How old do you think he is?"

Sarah felt a prickle down her spine. "If it's any of your business, he'll be twenty in July. By the way, when do I get my turn here?"

"Is he tall?"

"Okay. That's enough. What's this really about?"

"Frankly, if your file has lots of information, the adoption process goes easily and quickly. I'm sure you must understand why that would be helpful for everyone."

Sarah did her best not to yell but the volume certainly went up. "Adoption! Who told you that was going to happen? I'm not doing that. Stop filling out forms so somebody else can have my baby. I need you to help me. Isn't that your job?"

"Lower your voice, Eva. There is no need to raise your voice at me. Most girls decide..."

"I'm not most girls. I'm keeping my baby whether you like it or not."

"Eva, I want to finish my sentence and tell you adoption would definitely be best for this baby. It is a positive solution to your problem. You have a great opportunity to do something good for this baby. Wouldn't you like to do that? We have many married couples who are unable to have children. The process will be easy for you and then you can forget all this and start a new life. Doesn't that sound better?"

"Better than keeping my own baby?" She locked her eyes on Miss Preston's dark eyes.

"Eva, I understand you are very upset and angry."

"You understand nothing about me. You don't even know me. Period."

"I've seen this many times so I do know something about you. You got yourself in trouble and it is my job to get you out of it."

"I want my baby and I want you to help me. What's wrong with that?"

"Sounds like you have made this about you. Let me help you understand." Miss Preston's calm tone continued. "This is for your own good and the baby's future."

"I've heard that line before. All of you have the same answers."

"Lower your voice. Do you know you will need a job and a place to live? How will you do that?"

"I'm very sure my boyfriend will help."

"Frankly, that rarely happens. They usually run or deny responsibility. Let's talk again next Monday morning. You are upset right now."

"You bet I'm upset. You have a plan for me and I don't have anything to say about it." Sarah's face was scarlet and her tone cutting.

"In the meantime, I want you to think about two questions. What did your boyfriend say when you told him you were pregnant and when did you last see him? I think those answers will give you a good idea of his help. Do you need a worker to help you back to your room?" There was no mistaking her controlling, dismissive manner.

Sarah stormed out of the office, rushed up the stairs with her head down and collided head on into Emma on the first floor landing.

"Eva, what happened? Your face is totally red. Why are you breathing so fast?"

"I'm okay. I can do this."

"Do what? I think you need to take a breather. You better lie down. I'll help you to your room."

Inside the room, Emma closed the door and sat on the edge of the chair eyeing Sarah on the bed. She wanted to understand what happened without being nosy. Her first thought was Marjorie wheedling to get personal information. Then Bernice being bossy. Perhaps it was frustration. Time was passing but still she didn't know what to do. Her heart pounded in her ears. She lowered her head and began to twist and weave her fingers together. The wind rattled the storm window and a crow cawed as it flew across the backyard. Silence continued. Alice would leave soon and she felt the loss already. She sensed a link with Eva but was frightened of being pushed away.

Sarah stared at the ceiling, breathing heavily. She ached to blurt out what happened downstairs but was too frightened to open up. She wanted to explode but couldn't launch a rant in front of someone she barely knew. In her head, Matron's stern voice played the implied threat of revealing personal information. An explosion was imminent. The pressure valve had to be released. But how? A safe, simple question might do. But first, she had to think of one. Risking everything, she blurted, "Are you happy here?"

Agonizing seconds passed. Sarah was convinced she made a mistake, ruined her only chance for companionship. Beaten, she opened her mouth to apologize when a faint 'no' crossed the hushed space between them. Their eyes met tentatively. Words were a long time coming.

"I'm lonely but it's hopeless. I can't go home." Emma exhaled and her body settled into the chair.

Sarah swung her legs over the edge of the bed. "I had a horrible meeting with that prissy caseworker. She's no help. Why do you say it's hopeless?"

"Because it is. I can't go home. My boyfriend, Mike is gone. There is no way out for me but adoption. Since I've resigned myself to it, the days are a little easier." She paused. "My name's Bonnie."

"Mine's Sarah. I told that snobby, bossy caseworker what I want to happen. I want to keep my baby. She wouldn't listen, said the baby should be adopted. What a cow."

"Anger won't change anything. I've been here since October and nobody listens. My mother said nothing so I know nothing. Here they never tell you about important things like labour and delivery. "

"How can they do that?"

"Because they can. How can you keep the baby? You have nowhere to go."

"I told her to talk to my boyfriend, Myles. Last fall, he was angry but I'm sure he'll help when he knows I'm here."

"He doesn't know you're here?"

"No. I wrote a couple of times but didn't get an answer. He works for a bank here in Halifax. I'm sure Miss Bossy can figure it out."

"Guess you should try. Mike knows I'm here but he hasn't even sent a letter."

"Maybe he did. They check your mail, you know. Probably threw it out."

"Shhhhh. I hear someone in the hallway."

Eleanor shouted from the front hall. "Bernice, are you still up there? What are you doing? We need you in the kitchen."

"Hold yer horses. I was checkin' the bathrooms."

Sarah peeked out the door. "Coast's clear."

"Is your family from around here?"

"No, I'm from the Island."

"Cape Breton?"

"No, PEI. Yours?"

"New Brunswick. I went to PEI once. I loved it. The soil is so red. How did you end up here?"

"My mom freaked out when the doctor told her I was pregnant. He told her the church minister had information about homes that would take care of me. Then she and my dad cooked up a story about an art course and staying with my cousin in Nova Scotia. What happened to you?"

"Well, Mike and I planned to get married when I finished high school. I have one more year. We've known each other since I was in grade eight and he was in grade nine. When I got pregnant, my parents said, 'No wedding. You're both too young. You go away and have the baby. After that, if you both still want to get married, okay.'

"Wow. Mike agreed to that?"

"Well, his parents agreed with mine so he went along with it."

"You're giving your baby up for adoption?"

"Mom says, this makes it all go away."

"What do you mean 'go away'?"

"That's why I'm here. It'll be adopted. My parents and the caseworker say that I'll be better off without it. I can finish grade twelve and be free to do what I choose. It's the right thing to do."

"Right for who? Do you hear what you are saying? You sure this is what you want?"

"Mom says it would be difficult for me to go to school and look after a baby. She told me Mike moved somewhere for work. Besides, when you have a baby, nobody wants to marry you. I'd be on my own."

"Sounds like your mother has all the answers. Just like mine."

Bernice shouted up the stairwell. "Anyone upstairs is late for supper. Downstairs, now."

"We better not go down together. You go. I'll wait a minute."

After Emma left, Sarah decided to set the caseworker straight, once and for all. "Round two will be mine, Miss Bossy."

Chapter Six

January 11, 1961
Halifax, Nova Scotia

Mid morning on Wednesday a wicked winter storm gripped Halifax in a white vise. Schools and businesses closed shortly after opening. Main streets were quickly reduced to one lane by drifting snow. Most side streets were completely impassable long before the invisible sun set at four fifty-five. Abandoned cars created a maze of metal.

At noon Andy crept across the bridge from Dartmouth in a long line of vehicles behind a snow plow. Two blocks later, it became impossible to make any headway. He aimed the Beetle then gunned it into a parking lot. It was twelve-thirty but blowing snow hid the street lamps. He pulled on a toque, stuffed his gloved hands into his pockets and plunged through snowdrifts up to his knees. A few blocks later, two huddled figures stumbled through the swirling snow from a side street. A male voice yelled, "Help. Help us, please."

Andy turned to his left. "What happened? Why are you two out here?"

A middle-aged man, wearing a brown taxi company parka and a red plaid cap with ear flaps, struggled to keep a young woman upright and moving. Her dark green coat was unbuttoned, exposing a very distended stomach.

My God, she's pregnant. Andy pulled her black hat completely over her ears.

"My car is stuck two streets away. This is Alice. I picked her up at the doctor's office about twenty minutes ago. Now she's really in pain. I think the baby is coming. I'm looking for any house with an outside light on. Can you help?"

"Sure. How are you doing, Alice?"

"It's really hard to breathe. The pain's bad. Something wet is running down my legs." She arched her back and screamed. Tears ran down her cheeks.

"The hospital's too far away. Alice, do you live near here? If it's closer than the doctor's office, we'll get you there and call the doctor and an ambulance."

"I'm in a home on Hill Street... with other girls."

"The three-story one across the street from the brick church?"

"Yes." Alice squeezed her fists and pounded her hands together trying to distract herself from a jabbing, grinding spasm. She sobbed, "It's bad, really bad. Please hurry."

"It's about three blocks from us. That should work. What's your name, sir?"

"Harold."

"I'm Andy, Alice. Harold and I are going to carry you to Hill Street. If you need to scream or cry, go ahead. Nobody will hear you and it doesn't matter if they do."

Alice managed a nod. Her arms encircled her swollen stomach. Then, against her will her body twisted sideways. She dropped into the snowbank.

Sarah stood at her bedroom window mesmerized by whirling snow. A car inched down the middle of the street. A large pile of snow sat on its roof. The streetlight was a snow globe. She was home again reading Christmas cards. Across the street, the church appeared briefly as the wind paused to take a breath. It changed direction and slammed snow into her window. The glass rattled. She jumped.

With a soft tap on the door, Emma's voice broke her attention. "Ready for lunch? I smell clam chowder and I'm starving."

"Sure. I'll go down but I'm not interested in food today."

"I don't want to be bossy but you should eat. The baby needs food."

"It's really bad out there. When did Alice go to the doctor's office?"

"She had an early lunch and left over an hour ago."

"She's lucky. It'll soon be over for her. Wish I was her right now, out of here."

The weatherman was on the local radio station as the girls walked into the kitchen to pick up their food.

A heavy snow fall warning has been issued for Halifax, Dartmouth and surrounding areas. Meteorologists expect a snowfall accu-

mulation of up to sixteen inches associated
with winds gusting to forty miles per hour.
Motorists are advised to avoid all unnecessary travel. Drifting snow has significantly
reduced visibility. Emergency crews are at
work but most city streets are impassable
at this hour. The storm is expected to dis-
sipate during the overnight hours. Tomorrow
we should see sunny skies and a temperature
of twenty-three degrees Fahrenheit. Stay
home folks.

"Nobody has to remind me to stay inside," Mary stared at the kitchen window and shivered.

"Me either but lots of people have to get home to stay home," pronounced Joan as she wove her way past everyone toward the dining room.

At the table, Betty turned to Matron. "Alice's chair is empty. Where is she?"

"She had an appointment. She'll be back soon."

"I hope you're right." At twenty, Betty was isolated by age and choice. She failed to see much redeeming value in casual conversation so she rarely chose to engage in it.

"Let's tell snow stories to pass the time," piped up Marjorie. She desperately wanted to be accepted. "I could slide off the roof of our house after bad storms."

"Did you have a flying saucer?" asked Karen, digging into details. Answers gratified her nosiness and opened the door for her to ask more questions. She wasn't troubled by later embellishing the answers or telling new stories she made up. But most of all, she enjoyed the thrill of creating a story from scratch. So far, nobody at Rose Hill had called her a liar.

"Yes, it was silver. It spun around going down the hill." Marjorie was thrilled with the attention, especially from her roommate Karen.

"Anyone ever get stuck on the ferry in the ice between PEI and New Brunswick?"

"Careful, Mary," interjected Matron.

"Come on, does that really happen?" Joan asked skeptically and rolled her eyes.

"I think it can because I heard a story about it. Can I tell the story, Matron?"

"As long as no personal information is used. Chores at one-thirty."

"Okay. My Uncle, let's call him Jim, tells this story every Christmas. He's a real character. I hope I can remember all the parts. Frank in the story is his friend. I'm going to use Uncle Jim's accent. Okay, here goes.

"Frank and I were on board the Abby that day. It all started about three o'clock when the Captain got on the blower and said we would be a little late gettin' in 'cause the Abby was havin' a tussle with ice. None of us paid much attention but there was one fella sittin' across from us who seemed a little bothered. He was wringin' his hands and jigglin' his left leg somethin' fierce. A few minutes later he left the passenger lounge.

Anyway, the first half-hour or so went okay. Everybody passed the time talkin' and waitin' to hear that we were close. Around this time Frank and I stepped out of the lounge onto the deck to have a smoke and look over the situation. The coast was nowhere to be seen but there was that young fella leaning over the rail starin' into the ice. We took him for a nervous sailor and went inside, leavin' him to his own troubles.

Pretty soon the Captain came on again and said we were stuck and that a call had been put in for help from the ice breaker. By now it was gettin' dark and you could tell nobody wanted to be there much longer. Kids were gettin' bored and cranky and the adults had talked about everythin' they wanted to with people they hardly knew. It was time to get ashore. I figured this was goin' to get much worse. The canteen was nearly out of food and there's only so much coffee you can handle.

All of a sudden the guy from the rail comes runnin' inside, sits down, then jumps up, starts pacin' and yells he's gotta get off now. That's when things got really interestin'. The fella next to him grabbed his coat and took him outside. We figured they were goin' down to the car deck to sit in a vehicle for a while.

They came back a while later and he still looked pretty bad. Sweat was pourin' down his face and his colour wasn't good. Frank and I figured he was afraid of drownin'. Poor bugger. Next thing, he's pacin' around mumblin' about how many people have been trapped on ships and starved to death. This got people's attention but they were also getting' pretty scared of him and started to move away. I couldn't see a good end to this.

Then things got stranger. The guy started to take his clothes off right in front of everybody. That's when I saw it. He had on some kind of rubber suit and made a beeline for the nearest door.

'Geez, he's goin' to jump', I yelled. Frank and I bolted off our seats..."

A thunderous bang on the front door was accompanied by shouts to 'open up'. Everyone except Matron sat frozen in place. She jumped from her chair.

"Who's hammering on the door? Somebody's in awful trouble!" shrieked Ellen. She began to cry.

Sarah placed her hand on a frail shoulder. "It'll be okay."

Matron spoke rapidly. "Please return to your rooms now. I'll speak to you as soon as I can."

The door was slightly ajar when Andy and Harold pushed past the matron with Alice in their arms. She was slumped over, pale, drenched in perspiration and mumbling incoherently.

"I'm Andy. This is Harold. Call a doctor. We have a baby on the way. Find us warm blankets. Now."

Matron directed them to the sitting room where they carefully lowered Alice onto the sofa. She introduced herself as Mrs. Andrews then sent them back to the front hall and called out toward the kitchen. "Bernice, bring blankets and towels from the linen closet. Quickly. I have to call Doctor Kelly." She rushed to her office, leaving Alice with Bernice.

Andy inched forward until he could see into the office and overhear the conversation.

"Doctor Kelly, it's Matron Andrews at Rose Hill. I need you here urgently. It's Alice. You saw her earlier. We will need an ambulance."

As she exited the office, she asked Andy and Harold to wait in the kitchen. Without waiting for a response, she walked into the sitting room and closed the bevelled French doors.

Everyone except Betty crowded into Joan's room at the top of the stairs. They didn't want to be alone but each was abandoned in her own world, frightened and vulnerable.

Ellen sat in a chair in the corner near the dresser sobbing and rocking with her hands over her ears.

Sarah sat on the end of the bed nearest Ellen. She surprised herself by realizing she was more concerned for Ellen than herself. She wiped her eyes with the back of her hand and turned to face the wall.

Emma sat on the side of Joan's bed and faced the closet. She stared vacantly toward the swirled design of the glass doorknob. She realized Alice was in dire straits.

Mary stood between the two beds and leaned against the window frame. The coolness of the window momentarily distracted her from the misery unfolding beneath her feet downstairs. She massaged her swollen stomach and hummed 'Silent

Night'. Christmas always brought feelings of happiness. Right now, she desperately needed Christmas.

Joan sat at the bottom of her own bed and dangled her feet over the end. She heard Alice moaning and Matron talking with men. Despite her many weeks at Rose Hill, she held fast to her detachment from the others. Her gritty anger always simmered below a calm surface. When it boiled over, the turbulence was heard far and wide.

Karen and Marjorie were barely inside the room. Karen leaned against the door frame with Marjorie close behind her. Marjorie poked Karen's arm and whispered, "Can you hear anything?"

"Not much. Two men though. Stand over there." She pointed to the other side of the open door. "You listen from that side."

Marjorie leaned towards Karen. "Glad that's not me."

"Keep quiet and listen."

Betty sat in her own room across the hall holding the textbook on art history. She read aloud to muffle the whispers from Joan's room until a quick jab of pain twisted her stomach. It was immediately followed by cramps. Her innards turned to liquid. She jumped off the bed and raced to the bathroom.

Sarah glanced at her watch and moved to position herself closer to the door. Almost thirty minutes had passed. It felt a lot longer.

Karen glared and spoke in an unfriendly tone, "Move back, Eva. We were here first."

"Don't start, Karen. I'm not in the mood to take any crap from you. I've had enough of it lately to last a lifetime. Now, move over." Her subtle tone didn't diminish the message. Karen did as she was told.

Downstairs, the sitting room was electric with uneasiness. Alice laid on towels, her body covered by a striped flannelette sheet. She clenched her teeth and whimpered as each contraction racked her body. Matron held her hands and spoke in soothing tones. Bernice wiped her face with cool cloths, removing perspiration and tears. A wicker hamper was almost full of soiled facecloths and towels.

Andy and Harold sat in the kitchen willing the front door to open. Harold asked what kind of house they were in and Andy whispered he would explain later.

Time passed in slow motion for Andy as he sat in a chair facing the doorway to the hall. Fate had offered him this opportunity to be inside Rose Hill. He intended to take it. He resolved to approach Matron and knew exactly what he wanted to say. He exhaled slowly to keep his confidence intact.

With an icy blast of air and snow, the front door flew open. Andy watched a tall man carrying a black medical bag stride over the threshold. In smooth motions he dropped the bag, removed his gloves, coat and hat then shoved fogged, wire-rim glasses to the top of his head. He stomped his feet and tiny mounds of snow puddled on the hardwood floor.

"Where is she?" he called out with an air of commanding urgency to nobody in particular.

Andy rushed from the kitchen and pointed to the sitting room. The curt nod he received inferred a salute might be in order. Still pointing he mumbled, "Sitting room" then turned back toward the kitchen.

Harold had moved to the bottom step of the stairs. His right leg bounced up and down in restless rhythm. "We're in business now, Andy."

"Yep. But I don't think she is out of the woods yet. Here comes Matron. Hopefully, she'll have good news for us."

Matron emerged from the sitting room, contrived a composed facade and greeted Andy and Harold with a hand shake. "Gentlemen, let's step into the kitchen."

Upstairs, Sarah strained to hear the hushed exchange. She inched past Karen and moved to the top of the stairs where she discreetly crouched behind the newel post.

Inside the kitchen, Matron continued in a low, controlled voice. "Thank you for the help this afternoon. You both have done yeoman's duty. What happened out there?"

"My taxi got stuck, missus. Then I saw Andy here." He motioned toward Andy with his thumb and smiled. "I was just looking for the first house with a light on. Any port in a storm, as they say. Guess Alice and I got lucky."

Matron knew luck didn't come close to describing it. It would have been a nightmare if neighbours found a pregnant teenager in labour at their front door. The newspaper headline flashed before her eyes. 'Pregnant teen from Rose Hill found on street.'

"We're all grateful that Alice was able to make it home. I imagine you are anxious to know how things are but I can't tell you anything. I am confident Doctor Kelly will do his best." She moved into the hall, a clear signal the conversation was ended and they should leave. "Do you need to call a tow truck?"

Andy replied. "No, we're okay. I live a few blocks away and Harold can make a call from there. But before I leave, I'd like a few words with you, privately."

"I can't imagine why but come to my office."

Harold shook his head, a baffled look on his face and leaned against the door frame.

Andy started across the hall. A slight movement in the stairwell caught his attention. In a split second, Sarah stood and waved at him. He froze in mid step.

Inside the office, Matron stood facing Andy with her arms crossed. She sighed heavily, impatient to get this intrusion terminated. "You look like you've seen a ghost. What's on your mind?"

Andy stood in stunned silence. Four words feebly passed his lips. "I have an idea..."

She cut him off. "I'm sure you do. Maybe you don't understand these girls are here for their own protection. It is my job to make sure that happens."

"I understand."

"You, young man understand nothing about Rose Hill. I haven't figured out what you are up to. But I will."

"I haven't asked you anything yet. Why do you think I'm up to something, as you put it?"

"For starters, I imagine you see an opportunity to expose a story. Which paper do you work for?"

"I don't work for any paper. Can we sit down for a moment?"

"No. Anything you need to say won't take much longer."

"I see."

"You don't 'see' anything. You have two minutes to make your case for taking up my time."

Andy opened his mouth to respond when Doctor Kelly knocked on the closed door and marched into the room. "Matron, follow me." He turned on his heel and left.

Without another word, Matron opened the front door and nodded toward Andy and Harold, "Thank you again, and goodnight."

Andy and Harold pulled up their hoods and began the five block slog. Each was in deep thought. Andy kept his to himself.

Harold shouted through the howling wind. "Pretty cold lady that Matron, eh? Never even offered a coffee." He paused for a deep breath. "I never knew those poor girls were in that place. I never think about that stuff."

"You're normal, Harold. People don't think about it unless it happens in their family. And then, they keep it quiet and send the girls away to a place like Rose Hill."

"You mean those girls don't have family 'round here?"

"Probably not. Could be from anywhere in the country."

"Jeez, how long do they stay?"

"Months."

"Holy Mary, Mother of God. Do you mind me askin' how you know so much?"

"No, that's okay. My sister."

"Sorry, I'll shut up now."

When Andy's home appeared through the swirling flurries, he offered Harold a hot toddy and the phone. Harold took him up on both.

Matron came to a determined stop in front of the sitting room door, steeled herself, opened it and stepped forward. Alice's screech cracked the air.

"Doctor."

He began in a subdued tone. "The baby is not doing well. Where's that ambulance? We absolutely must get her to the hospital right away. She cannot deliver here. If that happens, I'm afraid I may lose both of them. You need to contact her family before we leave. I think they should be prepared for anything."

"Oh, dear God."

"Are you able to go with the ambulance?"

"Yes, I have a worker who lives close by. I'll call her then call the parents."

Within a half hour, Alice was admitted to hospital. She was unaware of her surroundings as the medical staff swept her away from the emergency entrance.

Matron struggled with the reality of Alice's grim circumstance and her taxi ride back to Rose Hill brought no reprieve. She fled from the car through the front door and into the solitude of her office. Too distraught to remove her coat and boots, she sat at her desk and dropped her head into her hands. Her entire body shook from the inside out. For the first time in years, she was out of control, rattled, as her father would say. She felt inside the zippered pocket of her purse for the small silver key to the top drawer of her desk. Years ago, following personal troubles, she had coerced herself into rejecting self-pity and crippling grief. Family and friends were astounded by her resiliency and recovery. She held the key for a moment then opened the drawer to look at the picture.

Annie met Matron as she stepped out of the office to freshen up in the washroom. "Matron, are you doing okay?"

"Yes, thank you. We should clean the sitting room. Then I must speak with the girls."

"The room's clean. I sent Bernice home about half an hour ago. She mentioned staying in town with a friend because the roads are blocked. Here's the phone number if you need it. Eleanor left meat pies and mashed potatoes for supper. I'll put everything in the oven to reheat. In the meantime, I'll bring hot chocolate to the dining room. When you're ready, I'll bring the girls down."

"Thank you. Give me a couple of minutes."

Marjorie and Karen arrived first. They were eager to hear the news and sat on either side of Matron. They drank the hot chocolate and chattered about the weather until Matron delivered a censoring glance. Joan and Betty greeted Matron and sat beside one another on the opposite side of the table. Mary, Ellen, Emma and Sarah entered quietly without acknowledging anyone.

Matron began, "I expect none of you will sleep well but it's best I tell you what little I know. Alice is in the hospital. She and the baby are receiving good care. When I left, the baby had not arrived. Are there any questions? Keep in mind, I may not be able to answer."

"Is she coming back? Can we go visit her?" Marjorie rushed to satisfy her curiosity.

"No, we won't be visiting her."

"Is her family here?" She intended to get some gossip. Karen would like that.

"That information is private." Matron paused. "If there are no other questions, let's have supper. Annie's in the kitchen. She'll need help."

The wailing wind was the only sound during supper until Matron spoke. "I'm staying overnight. Please keep Alice, the baby and her family in your thoughts and prayers tonight. We will talk again at breakfast. Good night, everyone."

Outside the home on Hill Street street signs rattled, school flags flapped, sirens wailed and plows punched snowdrifts into submission. Inside the home on Hill Street restless bodies twisted and turned in bed or paced the floor until exhaustion forced troubled sleep upon them in the wee hours of the morning.

All but one body. Sarah thought about Andy and how he'd saved her life and her baby's life on the ferry, even though he didn't know it. She would be forever grateful. She thought about Alice. Wild and terrifying thoughts drove her beyond exhaustion. Awake at four-thirty, her mind in chaos about Myles, her caseworker meeting and Alice, she started downstairs for a glass of milk. At the top of the stairs she heard the phone ring and someone move. The phone was picked up on the first ring.

"Hello, Rose Hill Home."

"Thank you for calling, Doctor. How are Alice and the baby?"

"Both of them? Oh, no. What terrible news. The poor parents. They expect to arrive at the hospital this morning. I left your number at the nursing station for them."

"Thank you for asking. They are very upset. I doubt there has been much sleep overnight. I will speak with them at breakfast"

"You too. Goodbye, Doctor." The handset clicked into place.

Sarah crept back to her room, got under the covers, hugged her baby, then curled her shivering body around the pillow.

Chapter Seven

January 12, 1961
Halifax, Nova Scotia

Andy woke early and worn out after a haunted sleep. Snippets of the blinding blizzard and wails of a young woman in distress had dogged his rest. He threw back the covers and ambled toward the shower, hoping hot, soapy water would flush the recurring images and sounds down the drain.

After breakfast, he cleared a path to the street and walked the few blocks toward Mrs. P's home. He spotted Barney bounding through snow drifts in his front yard while Mrs. P stood knee deep in a snow bank at her front door. He waved and began shovelling. A few minutes later he pushed his sunglasses to the top of his head and squinted at her, "So how was your afternoon and evening?" His silly smirk earned a friendly swat to his shoulder.

"Don't be cheeky, young man. I spent it with a book and fireplace. I stuck my head outside when Barney needed a bathroom break. You?"

"Well, it's a long story that includes my first look inside Rose Hill. I'll have a quick coffee, fill you in then be off to unearth my car, if that's okay. At least the Beetle's not white."

Nancy enjoyed her morning walk to work no matter the weather. She greeted everyone she met and took pleasure in the changing colours of the seasons. Yesterday's storm created a brilliant glow to the new day. Trees, fences and stranded vehicles sparkled in the morning sun. She unlocked the oak door, took a deep, contented breath and placed her gloved hand on the door knob at Rose Hill. Inside, an eerie silence permeated the house. Kitchen noise was barely audible. She quietly placed her coat, boots and hat in the hall closet, cleared the steam from her glasses and ran her hand through her short brown hair. *Still no sounds from upstairs.* Puzzled, she walked into the kitchen and found Annie alone with her back hunched over the sink. Her hands gripped the counter and shoulders shook.

"Good morning, Annie."

Annie turned slowly with her eyes steadily on the linoleum floor. Her arms hung limply by her sides and her head shook side to side.

"What's the matter? Why is it so quiet?" Nancy's voice was scarcely above a whisper.

Annie lifted her eyes and mouthed, "They're dead. Alice and her baby."

Nancy moved forward to wrap her arms around Annie who sobbed, "How can you work in a place like this?"

Before Nancy could begin to comfort Annie and grasp what had happened, Matron entered the kitchen and took charge. "Good morning, Nancy. It looks like Annie told you Alice and the baby passed away overnight in the hospital. This is terrible news and the girls don't know yet. I will speak to them at breakfast. They've probably had very little sleep so I expect breakfast will be quiet. This will be a difficult day but we must keep things close to normal for everyone's sake. Nancy, you better go room to room. In the meantime, Annie and I will put food and dishes on the table and we'll skip the kitchen line up. After breakfast, we'll get the routine started."

Tired, anxious faces circled the table as Matron entered the room with her second cup of black coffee.

Sarah kept her head down. She knew what was coming.

"Good morning, everyone. This has been a most difficult night for all of us. I imagine most of you slept very little and are exhausted. Doctor Kelly called me a few hours ago. I'm saddened to tell you Alice and the baby passed away in the hospital. Reverend Miller and Miss Preston will be here at ten o'clock. All of you are expected see one of them so you can talk about how you feel..."

Ellen bolted toward the back door. Outside, she darted between trees, hysterically crying 'no'. Sarah tried unsuccessfully to catch her. In desperation, she hid behind a large spruce and grabbed Ellen's sweater as she charged past. Both fell into a mound of snow.

Breathing heavily, Sarah spoke firmly. "Ellen, we are going to stand up. You are going to hold my hand and walk to the house. Got it?"

A compliant nod was all Sarah needed to rush to the back door with Ellen in tow. Both shivered uncontrollably as a trail of melting snow followed them across the kitchen floor. Eleanor wrapped them in blankets and minutes later, each was in a warm bath. Matron stayed with Ellen. Sarah insisted on being alone.

Ellen's teeth ceased chattering soon after she was immersed in the warm water. A mass of bubbles floated over and around her tiny body. Matron sat on a footstool in the corner of the room near the door, her mind troubled about what to do for this child-mother.

Ellen's mother occasionally dropped by for brief visits but dismissed Ellen's prolonged sadness as a phase. 'Don't worry, Matron. It'll pass as soon as she's home again. My sister has these bouts every once in a while and gets over them on her own, just fine.'

Matron leaned forward and spoke quietly. "Would you like to talk? Is something troubling you?"

Ellen kept her eyes closed and replied a faint, "No. I liked Alice, that's all."

Matron opened her mouth to ask an additional question then thought better of it. She would have a word with Miss Preston. Absentmindedly, her left hand clasped her right. Her thumb moved slowly back and forth over the diamond filigree ring. Tender images flooded her memory in a gush of affection then joy followed by a rolling tide of sorrow, regret and finally, melancholy. She saw a bit of her old self in Ellen.

"Matron, I'd like to go to my room now. Your face is very sad. Are you okay?"

"Yes, Ellen. I'm fine. Sometimes memories are happy and sometimes they are not. Are you feeling better?"

"Yes. Thank you for staying with me. Maybe one day I'll feel like talking."

"I hope so."

Sarah longed to stay in the bathtub forever. At home it was her safe place. Eventually her mother gave up delivering lectures from the other side of the locked door. 'What were you thinking? Oh right, you weren't. How could you be so silly about that boy from the bank. Look at the mess we're in now. You've ruined your life. Forget about art courses and college. I'm just sick thinking about it.'

For a long time Sarah shed tears for Alice and her baby. And for herself. She thought about Ellen and felt powerless to help. She stroked her stomach and renewed her promise to find

Myles in spite of the useless caseworker. After her first shiver from the cold water, she dressed and crept to her room. She needed time alone away from the craziness. Outside her window, the neighbourhood was returning to normal. Snow slipped from car roofs and tree boughs in the warm morning sun. Two girls in parkas strolled past the home and looked up toward the window. She stepped back quickly to avoid being seen then admonished herself and moved forward. *This is my world, too. I'm not hiding from it.*

In the meantime, Emma found herself alone on the front step. Alice's death deeply frightened her. She was desperate to be alone and think of ways to get out of Rose Hill. After Matron spoke about Alice and her baby, she had shuffled to her room and found Bernice removing Alice's clothing and personal items.

"What are you doing in here? Get out, right now."

"Stop makin' a fuss. I'm doin' my job. Alice won't be comin' back and I need to clean this room. Go do your chores. You'll be better in an hour or two. Anyway, things happen to people for good reason, usually 'cause they deserve it." Her dark eyes shot a fierce glare at Emma's retreating back.

Emma stared at the street. Right now, not later she needed to think for herself and not rely on her mother's conclusions. In her heart she knew Mike loved her. Why did she willingly accept their separation? What if he didn't really have a say in this? Why did her mother tell her Rose Hill was the best decision? Why did she trust every word her parents said? Was she really here to save her family from embarrassment? Never once did her mother speak of her grandchild. She needed a problem to go away. Emma buried her head in her hands and burst into tears, mourning for Alice, herself and their babies. It was time to leave Rose Hill. Exhausted, she went to her room and fell sound asleep.

Betty had listened to Matron's words about Alice until the room began to spin. Anxiety, her frequent companion took charge. Unable to control the scene or her own innards, she ran to the bathroom. Later, lying on her bed she began rethinking the next two weeks.

Betty's parents accepted her behaviour after the family doctor brushed aside their concerns.

"She's simply a very neat child. You are lucky to have a youngster who doesn't want to get her clothes dirty and keeps all her toys in order. I have to admit that arranging her dolls alphabetically by name, is a bit excessive but she'll grow out of this phase. Don't worry."

Betty poured over every decision in her life. She demanded it of herself, uncontrollably and unconditionally. The baby was due January twenty-eighth. Her own death was not a possibility she had considered. She'd carefully orchestrated a comfortable routine at Rose Hill to her rigid standards in order of priority. First, personal time, then chores followed by limited interaction with specific people who met her criteria. She left nothing to chance and silently berated others when their issues upset her routine. Alice's event was certainly one of those.

Joan strode away from the breakfast table on fire but kept her thoughts to herself. After two months, she was totally fed up with the caseworker's attitude about adoption. She did not accept adoption as the only and right solution for her so called shameful behaviour. But the caseworker wasn't yielding on anything. It was long past time to act. She opened the bottom drawer of the dresser and retrieved the scribbler she kept underneath her socks. Her pen left a trail of frustration and accusations across three pages punctuated by question marks and exclamation points.

Karen and Marjorie left the dining room together after eating their usual hearty meal. They smiled at Matron, glanced at each other, then separated at the bottom of the stairs to attend to their chores. Their unusual arrivals at Rose Hill troubled Matron at the time. Now four months later, she was concerned about their closeness and impact on the others.

Karen was dropped off at Rose Hill on a wet August evening. Matron opened the front door and found a teenager standing silently on the top step holding a well-worn brown cardboard suitcase. A brassy, bottle blond introduced herself. 'I'm this one's sister.' She pointed to the pouting teenager then blurted, 'Her name's Adele and she's all yours. The family wants her gone. Good luck.' She turned her back, marched to the rusted, red Chevy pickup with out of province plates and drove away.

In the office, Adele stared at Matron intently and described in disturbing detail why she ran away from a nasty boyfriend. This was followed by a rendering of the heartache she endured after her family refused to take her in when she returned home. Tears occasionally ran down her face. Matron nodded as she took notes. The story sounded well rehearsed and the tears perfectly timed.

Marjorie arrived a day later from a wage home in the city where she had been caring for two young children while the parents worked. Her employer offered few details and simply declared, 'She's been with us for a month and it didn't work out. I called her family but they don't want her back until the baby's adopted. My doctor told me you take in these girls. You'll have your hands full with this one. She's got a good appetite. By the way, I did pay her the promised twelve dollars for the months' work.'

For as long as she could remember, Mary saw the positive and often humorous side of events in her life. But no levity lived in her soul this morning. She was frozen at the table searching for some flicker of light in a stone cold, black hearted morning. She remembered Alice laughing during their pitiful attempt to make a snowman in December. Everyone giggled until tears rolled down their cheeks at the disgracefully bad haircuts she, Emma and Alice gave each other as Christmas gifts. A soft tap on her shoulder brought her back to the present.

"Mary, you can go now."

Mary looked up to find herself alone at the table. Eleanor removed her uneaten oatmeal and toast.

"Perhaps you should lie down for a while."

Mary rose from the table, willed one foot in front of the other and aimed her body toward the stairs.

After breakfast Karen and Marjorie met behind the big spruce to finalize their caseworker meetings. Marjorie paced and smoked. Karen had a plan and was enjoying the control.

"Don't worry. Counselling is a snap when you're prepared. Just tell them what they want to hear."

"How do you know what they want to hear?"

"Easy. Listen and agree with everything they say. Nod a lot and look serious. They'll think you're fine and tell Matron not to worry about you. It'll be over before you know it."

"How do you know that?"

"Oh, I've seen loads of caseworkers. One came to my school. A few others visited places I stayed for a while. They were at summer camps too."

"Summer camp sounds fun. What do you do there?"

"They're really good fun, especially the ones that have a boy's camp at the same lake." She laughed and jabbed Marjorie in the ribs.

Marjorie was about to ask why when Karen spoke again. "Finish your cigarette. We'd better get back inside. Time to be counselled."

Emma woke from sleep rested and ready to share her big idea with Sarah. No laughter or shouts broke the stillness on the third floor. She found Sarah sketching with her back to the window.

"Rock Candy again?"

"Yep. Backlight from the window really helps."

"You're brave. Thought you were trying to keep the art secret."

"Today is a new day but close the door anyway. You doing okay?" She stood to hug Emma.

"I'll never see her again, never say goodbye." Emma sobbed into her hands.

"We have no choice but to get through it together, somehow."

"I know." She wiped her eyes. "Counselling is the big topic downstairs. When do you go? Who are you seeing?"

"Miss Perfect caseworker at three o'clock. I haven't been here long so she'll assume I'm fine. Works for me. You?"

"Reverend Miller in about ten minutes."

"Why are you going to see him? He's a goof and no help."

"That's what makes him perfect. He loves to talk and doesn't like to answer questions. So, he's totally perfect for me today."

"Guess so."

"I've come to a couple of conclusions. My mother is more concerned about what the neighbours think than about me and I'm going to leave."

Sarah jumped up. "What are you talking about? You have nowhere to go and the baby is due in a month. Have you lost your mind? Is this that hormone thing Joan was talking about a few days ago?"

"No. I found my mind. Now, I have to figure out the details." She spun around and opened the door then returned to hug Sarah. "I'll be fine."

"Emma, are you up there? Reverend Miller is waiting."

"Coming, Matron." She lowered her voice for Sarah. "Come to my room after lights out."

On the second floor landing Emma met Karen who grabbed her arm and pronounced, "You look terrible. You should wash your hair and change your clothes."

Emma pursed her lips, "When I want your advice, I'll ask for it."

Karen smirked. "Hey, no need to be like that."

"Actually there is. It's time someone told you to think before you speak. You open your mouth and words fall out. Nasty words. I for one have had enough of you."

Shortly before eleven, Sarah inched along the floral carpet-ed hallway. The solitary ceiling light in the stairwell guided her around the two squeaky spots. Emma's door was ajar and she slipped in quickly to find her sitting on the bed holding a fancy bottle with a sapphire blue top.

"What's in the bottle? How'd you get it in here?"

"I hid it in my suitcase. It's Shalimar. Mike gave it to me for my birthday in June."

"Aren't you the sneaky one."

Emma waved the bottle under her nose. "Like it?"

"Wow, it's beautiful. It smells like vanilla and flowers. It's kind of woody too. I like it. Too bad you can't use it. If that nosy Bernice smells it, she'll tell on you."

"Yeah. I smell it every day and hope I don't spill any!"

Sarah was quiet for a moment. "Are you really planning to leave?"

"Yes, I am. I don't know how right now but I'll figure it out. After Alice, I have to get out. Being here has been much worse than I ever imagined. I wanted to write, think about what I could do after all this but none of that happened. This place messed with my brain. First, I was told to feel guilty for getting pregnant so I wouldn't do it again. Then I was told I would be able to put everything behind me once I left. I'd forget. How can 'feel guilty' and 'forget it' both work? They're opposites. Society thinks I'm a bad person, my parents put me here and the case-worker's brain is wired for adoption. How can I trust anybody after this?"

"Don't ask me. After a week, I'm still trying to figure out what's going on. I keep thinking about Myles and how to get in touch with him. My parents didn't give him a chance. At least you have a chance with Mike. I better go. Room check might happen soon. I'm in enough trouble already. I'm sure Matron gets an earful from the caseworker."

Back in her room, Sarah took her art pencils and pad to the window. She leaned back against the ledge and released a long, deep sigh. There was no outside light to speak of. Night had vanquished day and run it out of town. Darkness ruled but Sarah felt a powerful desire to soothe her fears and sadness. She couldn't imagine how Emma was going to pull off her plan and worse, how she could live through this prison without her. She lifted her pencil and began to cry. A delicate Lady's Slipper be-gan to take shape. A tear dropped on a petal of the pink bloom. She left it in place to dry as a dew drop and reached for a tissue to wipe her eyes.

"Alice, this one is for you. Rest in peace with your baby."

Chapter Eight

January 13, 1961
Rose Hill Home

For two days, Alice's death had a firm grip on Joan's brain. Long before sunrise on Friday, she was in overdrive. She sat up in bed and imagined a dialogue with her parents. Her fingers barely kept pace with thoughts that sprung to life on paper. She read the last four sentences of the letter to her parents and declared them perfect.

It's a bloody scam here. They make us feel guilty so we do the 'right' thing, the 'unselfish' thing when all the time they are do-gooders for couples who can't have babies.

This place is a disgrace and to boot, people die here. You must take me home.

Joan was an only child doted on by her parents. Mealtimes were discussion times with no untouchable topics. With two lawyers in the room, it would have been easy for Joan to listen but that was not her nature or nurture. She had opinions and learned early on to hold her own during family conversations.

Despite her protestations, Joan was sent to a co-ed boarding school to meet people of significant social standing and make friends. There, she took revenge on her parents and majored in parties, lots of parties. As her father so pointedly told her, she paid the price. Joan arrived at Rose Hill on October 30th. She was four months pregnant. Now, her game plan was to go home, have her baby and keep it.

Betty woke at six forty-five, well before the alarm clock beeped. She needed to take control of the day after yesterday's personal disaster. Her decision to meet with the caseworker not Reverend Miller was the wrong one. Since September, her caseworker conversations had been controlled and predictable, Betty's kind of communication. Yesterday, she slipped up. She walked into the room without her usual game plan of asking the questions to keep the discussion off herself. She walked away from meeting Miss Preston with the distinct feeling that she had been found out. When Grandpa saw through her, he'd say, 'The jig's up, Missy. Spill the beans.' Miss Preston said nothing about beans but her face told the story. As a university student, Betty fell in love with homework for the control it wielded. It was the ultimate weapon to maintain control and keep people at bay. 'Sorry, I have an assignment due.' 'I have a study group tonight.' 'Maybe another time.' Social gatherings drained her battery and resulted in her total bewilderment about the value of free expression and emotional attachments. She concluded people were unpredictable and certainly less than perfect. She'd happily preferred her own company until she walked into Professor Gregory Richard's Art History class on January 5, 1960. By spring, she was pregnant and Greg was heading to Paris on a one year sabbatical. Now, less than a month from her due date, Alice's death detonated her orderly life. For the second time in an hour she sat on the toilet.

Mary woke to incessant beeping from Betty's alarm clock. She banged the 'off' button then noticed an envelope at the door with her name in block letters across the front. She retrieved it and crawled under the warm covers to open it. Her jaw dropped and her heart pounded.

Bitch,

Don't try that again or you will be sorry. I promise.

She clamped one hand over her mouth, threw the covers off with the other and swung her feet to the floor. *I'm going to throw up. Breathe slowly. Be calm. Breathe slowly. Be calm.* She lifted her legs back onto the bed and dug into her memory vault for comfort. With eyes closed, she let Christmas wash over her and hummed Silent Night.

Sarah woke feeling anxious and out of sorts. Her head throbbed. Her heart raced. She blamed it on disturbing dreams about Alice that jolted her awake twice during the night. Their shadowy fragments vaporized when she sensed she was being watched. She opened her eyes and saw Emma shifting excitedly from one foot to the other.

"What are you twitching about?"

"I'm definitely, for sure going to leave. I can't stay after what happened to Alice and thinking about my mother's self-centered ideas. Overnight, I figured out how I can do it." She smiled proudly.

"What are you babbling on about?" Sarah placed her feet on the floor. A wave of nausea rolled from her stomach to her throat. She shivered and folded her arms across her chest as pain gripped her upper body. She winced. It hurt to breathe.

"I've figured out how to get out of here."

"Okay." Sarah spoke haltingly.

"What's wrong with you? You look awful. Why are you sitting so funny?"

"Sit down. Talk while I get back to normal." Sarah took slow, deep breaths.

Emma rattled on. "I have a place to go and how to get there. By the way, I may need you to cover for me while I make my getaway."

"Right. I'll guard the front door."

"You're not paying attention to me."

"Okay, tell me." Sarah put her hand over her chest to calm the pounding.

"I stayed awake 'til I had it all worked out. It seems so simple now." She paused. "What's the matter with you? Oh God, are you going to throw up?"

"I don't think so. I felt like this after the meeting with the caseworker yesterday about Alice. It went away in a few minutes. I'll be fine." She winced.

"How'd the meeting go?"

"I didn't say much. She let me go after five minutes so okay, I guess. Keep talking. I'll get better."

Emma opened her mouth to tell the rest of her plan when Nancy shouted up the stairwell.

"Breakfast time is almost over, girls. Two of you are missing. Emma and Sarah, hustle, hustle."

Mary scanned faces as she ate breakfast. Nothing would deter her from finding out who left the nasty note under her door. But she had a couple of problems. Nobody looked guilty and nobody avoided her glances. Deep in thought, she was startled when Ellen sat beside her.

"I could really use a cheery story this morning, Mary." Her tone bordered on begging.

Torn by her own troubles, Mary couldn't pretend cheer-fulness, even for sad little Ellen. "Sorry. I just can't do it this morning."

Sarah followed Emma into the kitchen where they were greeted by Eleanor. "Good morning, girls."

Sarah kept her eyes on the floor. Her heart was thump-ing and the pressure in her chest was crushing. She was sure Eleanor could hear her heart pounding. The idea of sitting in the dining room was frightening. Once seated, she squirmed in discomfort. Fortunately, Emma's non-stop chatter distracted everyone.

"Good morning, Joan. Have any plans for the day?"

Without waiting for a response she turned to Betty. "Hi, Betty. You look tired. Did you not sleep well? It happens."

After a few mouthfuls of porridge, she started again. "Mary, you look puzzled? You working on one of those big crosswords again?"

She gulped coffee and turned to Ellen. "So, what's the latest gossip in Teen?"

Karen was next but it didn't happen. Betty jumped up and smashed her cup on the floor. Coffee splattered up the wall. Tiny rivulets of milky liquid inched over the baseboard and pooled on the hardwood floor. "Shut up. Just shut up. I can't think. I have to think." She raced from the room, narrowly avoiding Nancy who was rushing in from the hallway.

Karen banged the table, stood and yelled, "Ditto that." Grinning, she moved toward the hall with Marjorie on her heels. *Now this is what I call fun.*

Matron heard the crash, followed by shouting and raced from her office. She cornered Karen and Marjorie at the front door. "Stop where you are, ladies. We're going to the dining room for a few minutes. Nancy, bring Betty downstairs, please."

Using the distraction, Ellen leaned toward Mary and whis-pered, "Did you have a visit from Marjorie early this morning?"

"No. Why?"

"See me after breakfast."

Herded by Matron, Karen and Marjorie returned to the breakfast table. No words were spoken in the room but twelve pair of wide eyes darted about as Nancy followed Betty to her chair and moved back to stand at the wall.

Matron began,"Like you, I was saddened by what happened to Alice on Wednesday night. It was a terrible shock but it must not overwhelm us. Please understand your personal condition is making you more anxious than normal. I'm asking each of you to be calm and respectful to each other. Any questions?"

Joan saw her chance. She rose and moved to stand behind her chair, placing her hands on top of it.

"Matron, you've said we need to be calm. That won't happen by telling us to do it. I want to know what exactly you are going to do to help us." She maintained eye contact with Matron, demanding a response.

"Well, perhaps you and I should talk about this later today. Does that help you?"

"Only if we set a time to do it."

"After supper?

The reply was swift and firm."Yes."

"Anyone else?" Matron's eyes searched each face around the table.

Ellen chewed on her thumbnail and slowly shook her bowed head.

Marjorie, imitating Karen, gave a shrug and smirk.

Mary could not allow herself to reach out for help. She would not expose her weakness to others who saw her happily in control of her life. After all, she was the one who told stories to make others laugh. Appearances were important in her family. She didn't intend to fizzle out now.

Emma was confident she would be long gone from Rose Hill within the week. She saw no reason to personalize this fuss. She'd solved her own problem.

Sarah perched on the edge of her chair fully enveloped by the heaviness lingering on her chest. She could hardly breathe. She had never fainted in her life but knew this would be the moment. She buckled awkwardly and crashed to the floor, taking the chair with her.

Everyone but Nancy froze. She rushed to check Sarah as blood gathered under Sarah's head and oozed toward a leg of the overturned chair.

"Stay still, Sarah. Where do you hurt?"

"All over. What happened?"

"You fell off the chair. I can't feel any broken bones, Matron. Sarah, we'll carry you to the sitting room. Annie's going to hold a cloth to your head. Are you dizzy?"

"Little."

Emma, Mary and Ellen stayed with Sarah for half an hour. There wasn't much to talk about but they all noticed that Marjorie made many trips past the door. Eventually, they went upstairs.

Safely in Ellen's room, Mary listened to Ellen's story. "When I came out of the bathroom this morning, Marjorie was leaning against the wall opposite your room. She started down the stairs when she saw me. Something seemed odd so I peeked from my room. She came back up the stairs and bent down in front of your door. She's really different."

"Yeah, she is. Thanks for the info. Guess I better get to my chores. Let's have lunch together."

By ten, Sarah told Eleanor she felt better so Eleanor and Annie moved her to bed where she would wait for Doctor Kelly to arrive at eleven.

Sarah dreaded Doctor Kelly's visit. Thanks to her mother's secret tactics before Christmas, they drove an hour from home to see a new doctor. Doctor Willis barely looked at her during the examination. She was too intimidated to ask questions.

When the examination was over, he said, "You're fine. Go sit in the waiting room and ask your mother to come in."

A single, firm knock on Sarah's door was followed by the entrance of a tall, dark-haired doctor with wire rim glasses. He plopped his medical bag on the end of the bed and placed his hand around Sarah's right wrist while looking at his watch.

"Hello, Sarah. I'm Doctor Kelly. Matron tells me you fell off your chair at breakfast. How do you feel now?"

"Much better. But my side is really sore. What happened to me?"

"Heart rate is fine. Well, let me take your blood pressure, have a look at your eyes, head and hip. After that I'll check the baby. I hear you hit the floor pretty hard."

"Did I faint?"

"Lie still for a few minutes and then we'll talk."

"Okay."

Finished, he snapped the black bag closed. "Well everything looks good. A scalp wound bleeds a lot. It'll be fine in a few days. Don't wash off the scab. You have lots of bruises on your right hip. They'll change colour and fade. The baby's fine. What did you feel like before you fell off the chair?"

"I woke up feeling like something was sitting on my chest. I was breathing fast. I felt light headed."

"Hmm. Is there something bothering you?"

"No." She wondered if he could read the lie on her face. "What's wrong with me?"

"You had an anxiety attack. They happen sometimes when people are very anxious about something. Are you stressed right now?"

"No." She wanted to ask if anyone here wasn't stressed. As he wasn't in the habit of answering questions, he wasn't likely to answer that one either.

"Okay. If you are anxious and worried, make sure you talk to your caseworker."

Sarah knew Miss Preston was the last person to help with anything.

Eleanor peered around the door. "May I come in, Doctor?"

"Come. Looks like you are getting lunch in bed today, Sarah. Smells good. I'd like Sarah to be up for supper this evening then back to normal tomorrow. I'll speak with Matron on the way out. Enjoy your lunch."

Eleanor placed the tray and a newspaper on the dresser then offered to walk Sarah to the bathroom. Sarah reluctantly consented. She couldn't imagine someone watching her sit on the toilet but she didn't want to fall either. Eleanor got her seated and waited outside the partially closed door.

Lunch in bed was comforting. A toasted egg salad sandwich on brown bread with milk and molasses cookies for dessert was yummy. The pain was easing so Sarah carefully got out of bed for the sketch pad and pencil under the mattress. An hour later, she picked up the newspaper. The front page headline about politics looked boring although the man looked familiar. She closed her eyes and tested her memory. She opened them and smiled. *Got it. Prime Minister John Diefenbaker.* She leafed through the following few pages without interest. Her eyes got heavy. She dropped the first section on the floor. Straightening up, she reached for the second section with local, business and social events intending to toss it over the side of the bed. She stopped in mid reach. A full blown bombshell replaced thoughts of sleep. Myles smiled at her from the front page. He looked pleased with himself. No news there. His confidence was one of his appealing traits. The real news however, was the bank address where he was the new Assistant Manager. Myles was now on her agenda in bold print. She knew where he was. Soon he would know where she was. Peacefully happy, she drifted off to sleep.

"Eva." A brusque voice came from the outline of a person standing in the doorway. "Get outta bed. I'm here to get ya downstairs for supper." Bernice stepped into the room.

Sarah expected a flurry of questions at her appearance for supper. But, Emma was the only one who expressed relief at how healthy she appeared. Instead, she sat back and looked around. Everyone was savouring the shepherd's pie and cheese biscuits.

It did look tempting. In the middle of the table, a mountainous bowl of steaming rice pudding with sultana raisins wafted cinnamon into the air. On a second look around, she concluded their focus on food was purely self-interest, a distracted stare of avoidance. She followed their lead, ate in silence and hurried to her room to work on the bank plan.

After supper, Matron invited Joan to leave the table with her, intending the gesture to confirm her place in the position of authority. Prepared by writing the three page letter to her parents, Joan deemed herself an equal in the upcoming exchange. And so it began.

"How are you feeling this evening, Joan? It has been a tumultuous few days."

"Good. I feel very good."

"I'm sure you have a few ideas for us to talk about. Why don't you begin."

"First, I want to know why we don't have more information on pregnancy, labour and birth? All we do is chores."

"Well, neither I nor the workers are trained to provide that information. The doctor visits are the time for those questions."

"So why can't a doctor come here?"

"That is a good question. I will give that some thought. Anything else?"

"Why aren't we allowed to go anywhere except a few blocks from the house? We're not in prison. Do you think we're going to run away?" She raised her hands and her voice.

"Please lower your voice. We want to ensure that everyone's privacy is protected so..."

"So nobody sees us? Are you kidding! How would going to a movie take away my privacy? I don't know anybody in this part of Halifax."

"You don't have to know people in the community to have them stare and make you feel ashamed."

"I'm not ashamed. That's their problem, not mine."

"Plainly speaking, society does not want to see unwed mothers. This home and others like it exist for just that reason. After this is over, you can go home and have the opportunities you had before coming here. Your family will not be affected by your mistake. You'll forget, go back to school, marry and maybe have children."

"I can't imagine anyone forgetting all this, ever." She swung her right arm around the room.

Matron opened her mouth to respond but Joan continued on.

"Guys get off free. That's so not fair." She gripped the arms of the chair, forcing herself to stay seated. This meeting wasn't going as she planned. Her confidence slipped a big notch.

"It may not be fair but that is the way it is."

"It is what it is? That is absolutely not a good reason. It's a rotten excuse." She'd lost her usual logical, articulate momentum so stood up and hurled her final question across the desk.

"Why are you people pushing adoption? You're taking our babies. You're stealing them."

"Stealing your babies? Adoption is a wonderful choice. Your baby goes to a good home with a mother and father. Adoption allows you to put this experience behind you knowing the child will be taken care of properly. You are doing as society expects. It's the right choice."

Pausing at the door, Joan stood tall and spat a parting shot. "It's not a choice. It's also wrong when everyone but me decides I should be separated from my baby." She stomped to the stairs.

Drawing uncluttered Sarah's mind as she honed in on the bank plan. The details of the cabbage rose emerged as she pondered how to get to the bank and what she needed to say.

Emma knocked on the door and walked in. "Hey, you're looking serious. I thought you looked good at supper. Are you sick again?"

"No, but I've got to go to the bathroom. These trips down the hall are too frequent."

"Wait for another couple of months. It gets worse."

"Great." She left the room.

Emma casually picked up Sarah's sketch book. Page after page of intricate floral images came to life.

"These sketches are very good. I predict you'll be famous."

"Thanks. I try. So earlier you told me you're leaving. That's quite the crazy idea. What's going on?"

Emma began pacing in the space between the beds. She was a mix of fear and excitement. "I don't see any other way out of this mess. My mother sold me a bill of goods on hiding out here and Mike is long gone. Dying here was never a thought, ever. Now that I know it can happen, I have to get out."

"I get it. You feel trapped but honestly, I can't understand how you believe this will work. You're a month away from delivery. You think you won't be noticed on the street?"

"I saw a train schedule to Wolfville in the paper. My older cousin lives there so I plan to call her this weekend."

"And tell her what? Does she know you're pregnant, where you are?"

"No. I'll tell her I'm coming for a visit. I'll figure out what to do when I get there."

"Are you serious? Are you going to contact Mike?"

"Where? He left town."

"Says who?" Sarah tilted her head slightly and lifted her eyebrows.

"My mother." Then she caught on. "Oh my, are you thinking my mother lied abut Mike?"

"I'm thinking it's possible."

Chapter Nine

January 14–16, 1961
Rose Hill Home

The following morning, Sarah waited for Emma to pass her door, counted to ten then made her way to breakfast. As planned, they did not sit near each other. It was not safe to fuel Marjorie's nosiness and Karen's lies, especially now. Emma had far too much at risk.

Matron crossed the hall to the dining room. Standing in the door frame, she spoke in a matter of fact tone. "Good morning, girls. It's good to see everyone well and returning to normal this morning. The weather promises to be sunny so I suggest a walk in the neighbourhood after chores. Remember, not a big group, two or three together. Speaking of chores, I must remind you to be on time for work. I've been told some of you are often late getting to your duties after breakfast. You should be at work by nine o'clock. Punctuality is very important in the workplace. If you practice it here, it will help with your future employment. Eva, I want to see you after breakfast."

Sarah had a niggling hunch Karen had fed a lie to Matron. This new challenge would be number three, added to getting to the bank where Myles works and Emma's imminent departure. In the bathroom, she mulled over two options. She could deny Karen's accusation and claim innocence or ask Matron to name her accusers and face them in Matron's presence. Her mind made up, she walked to the open office door and rapped twice on the door frame.

"Come in, Eva. Please close the door and sit down." Matron rested her arms on the desk. "I hope you have settled in despite the turmoil of the past few days. Any problems so far?"

Sarah itched to recite all the problems Rose Hill had created in her life in seven days. Instead, she kept her mouth shut and shook her head.

"Good. You're probably wondering why you're in the office. Well, I have good news for you." She clasped her fingers together. "Your roommate will arrive tomorrow afternoon. You'll have someone to talk with now. Any questions?"

Sarah rose from the chair, "No, not right now." She left the office mumbling, "And this would be good news for me because...? Talk about what?"

Sarah caught sight of Emma folding napkins in the dining room as she finished her own work in the kitchen. She pointed to the backyard. Minutes later, they were exiting the back door. Marjorie was smoking on the step so they wandered toward the back fence.

"A roommate tomorrow! This is terrible for you. What if she's gossipy, bossy, snobby or all three?"

"Or Sleepy, Grumpy and Dopey."

"I'm being serious."

"I know but there's nothing I can do about it. I was hoping for a few more weeks alone. I wonder why she didn't put this new girl in with Joan? It would give her a new audience and us a rest. So, what have you decided about Mike?"

"I thought about that overnight and decided to do nothing until after I leave. I'll ask my cousin to help me find him."

"So she knows him?"

"Sort of. She met him on Easter Sunday last year when he came to pick me up for a drive in the country."

"She doesn't sound helpful. Do you have any idea at all where he might be?"

"Not really but it'll be easier to find him when I'm out of here."

"Well that part makes sense. Won't your cousin call your mother the minute you arrive?"

"Maybe, but I have to take this chance to get out. If I stay, the baby's gone forever. I signed the oath thing."

"What oath thing?"

"It says we won't try to find the baby we put up for adoption."

Sarah had no reply. Her wide eyes stared into the distance.

"Another attack?" Emma sounded worried.

"No. This place is absolutely unbelievable." Sarah shook her head in disbelief.

"That's right and I'm getting out."

Sarah opened her mouth to ask when she was leaving as Nancy called from the backdoor, "Emma, the phone's for you."

Sarah returned to her room. Tomorrow, the roommate will arrive. She had a letter for Myles to finish. She carried her writing paper set to bed and opened the flowered lid.

Emma dreaded the voice she would hear as she picked up the receiver. She murmured, "Hello."

"Hello, dear. How are you doing? Do you still have lots of snow? What's the weather like today? Hello, hello. It's your mother. Are you there?"

"I'm here. Why are you calling? Is something wrong?"

"No, we're all fine. Do you have lots of snow there? We were lucky. The storm wasn't as bad here. I do have some news for you, though. I'm coming for a visit on Tuesday. I don't imagine you have plans for that day. I should be there after lunch. Any news from Rose Hill?"

"No, nothing new. Same old routine."

"Can you tell Mrs. Andrews I'm coming Tuesday?"

"Sure."

"You still feeling well?"

"No problems so far."

"Good. I'll see you Tuesday. Bye, bye." The line went dead.

Emma slammed the receiver into the cradle. In minutes she was dressed for a walk and at Matron's door.

"Hello, Emma. You look flushed. Are you okay?"

"Yes. My mother called. She will be here for a visit Tuesday afternoon. By the way, I'm going for a long walk, alone." She glanced at her watch. "I'll be back in time for lunch."

Matron opened her mouth to object but Emma was already gone. Assuming that the phone call was a mother and daughter tiff, she returned to her work. A few minutes later, she thought better of her decision and went to find Nancy.

Emma savoured the comfort of her own company and pretended this Saturday morning walk was her usual routine. So far, she hadn't met anyone. She wasn't sure what she would do or say if she did but turning around to retrace her steps to Rose Hill seemed silly. Instead, she decided on a simple, cheery 'hello' to pass herself off as a resident of the area. She walked toward the park.

Near the park, a sharp pain seared across her lower abdomen. False labour pains were more frequent in the past month but she had learned to live with the discomfort. Today would be no different. After slowly walking a block to the park, she stretched out on a bench to change her body position. That always helped but this time she felt no better. Alarmed, she pushed herself to a sitting position and haltingly stood up. So far, so good. Placing one foot in front of the other, she walked half a block when she heard a familiar voice.

"Thank heavens, I've found you."

"Hi, Nancy. Why are you here? How did you find me so fast?"

"Matron was concerned you were alone. One day you mentioned a nearby park so I took a chance. It's actually close to my home so I knew where to look. Are you in labour?"

"I don't think so. The pains are gradually going away."

"Probably false labour. Put your arm through mine. We'll take our time. Lots of salmon sandwiches and cream of tomato soup waiting. Eleanor made a double batch of peanut butter cookies."

Sarah had no idea why Emma was late for lunch. It wasn't like her to intentionally cause problems or draw attention to herself. She concentrated on Myles' bank details. Fish was supposed to be brain food but she didn't feel any smarter after eating the salmon sandwich. No map of the city, no electric trolley coaches in the neighbourhood and no money for a cab, even if one would pick her up. Discouraged, she wandered out of the dining room, relieved to see Emma and Nancy coming in the front door.

Mary was pretty sure Marjorie and Karen were her tormentors. Divide and conquer worked in war so Mary concluded it would work for her. She became detective Mary and rushed upstairs from lunch to get a pencil and notebook. She would watch each of them then confront them individually. The plan to catch and 'out' them for their nasty behaviour seemed straightforward. She positioned herself in the reading room to watch their movements. Her crossword puzzle book was the perfect cover. Tomorrow, the stakes would get higher. She would follow them.

Saturday evening no one was interested in anything that involved another person. When Sarah's suggestion of a game of crokinole or monopoly fell on deaf ears, she returned to her room and fell asleep reading.

Sunday breakfast conversation was dominated by the weekly visit of Reverend Miller. The fiasco of the previous weekly meeting was vivid in everyone's memory.

Joan gleefully rubbed her hands together and told everyone she could hardly wait for his arrival. She posed a question, "What do you think the topic will be this week?" There were several muttered suggestions and suppressed giggles but no serious replies offered.

At lunch, Matron announced Reverend Miller was ill and would not be able to meet with them. Sunday afternoon became free time. As Sarah left the room, she heard Joan whisper, "He's got scaredycatitis." The room erupted in laughter.

The free afternoon was wholeheartedly embraced by everyone, especially Mary who had plans to carry out. She hunted for Marjorie and Karen on the second and main floors but came up empty. As she left the kitchen, Marjorie came through the back door, arms swinging freely at her sides, a yellow envelope visible in one pocket. Something was happening. The chase was on. Marjorie passed by the second floor, headed to the third. Mary's heart started to beat faster. Risking being trapped on the third, she started the climb, feeling her legs weaken as the third floor landing came into view. Would she make it in time?

A shout rose up the stairwell, "Mary, are you up there? There's a call for you."

Relieved, Mary returned to her second floor landing then slowed her pace. At the bottom of the stairs, she was passed by Marjorie. The yellow envelope was nowhere to be seen.

Emma sat on the outdoor bench silently rehearsing questions for her mother's visit. Her goal was to wheedle information about Mike without tipping her own hand.

In the meantime, Sarah buckled down to finish her plan to get to the bank. Pressure mounted as the clock ticked down on her roommate's afternoon arrival. Her letter for Myles was perfect but she still had a problem. She moved around her room talking to herself in low tones, soundly tapping her index finger on her lips. "How do I get there? Can't walk. Think, think."

"Eva, what's going on? Why are you talking to yourself?"

Sarah turned to the door and saw Ellen in the hallway, a confused look on her face. "I'm okay, just a problem with no solution yet."

"I thought you might be ill again. I'm going to check the mail. It's time for my magazine from Mom. Mail sure makes it easy to get things from home. See ya later."

Sarah rushed down the stairs behind Ellen whispering, "Thank you, thank you" as they arrived in the kitchen.

The mailbox was empty except for a magazine rolled up in 3 - 1, Ellen's mail slot. Sarah didn't look at her slot 3 – 3. She was there for the Friday newspaper. Tomorrow she would mail the letter for Myles to the bank. Tomorrow's meeting with the caseworker would be a breeze.

"Hi, Sarah, Ellen. Here for a hot chocolate?"

Sarah replied with a casual tone as her heart thumped with anticipation. "No, came to pick up the Friday paper. I didn't read the comics yesterday."

"Fraid not. It's already in the garbage at the back door. And it's not on the top either. Sorry."

Ellen's face twisted in repulsion. "Yuck. I wouldn't touch that stuff, not even for the comics. Rotten apples, stinky meat, slimy vegetables, mouldy cheese. Double yuck."

Sarah snorted. *Ellen has a sense of humour!* "I'll have a look anyway. Maybe it's not that bad."

Outside the back door she grabbed a broken tree branch and started digging. Partway down, she found Ellen's double yuck on top of a sodden mess of newsprint, curdled milk and coffee grounds. Finishing the letter wasn't going to happen today. She wandered around the snow mounds and barren trees in the backyard. An ominous slate grey cloud rolled over the sun. She shivered then scurried to the backdoor just as Bernice dropped a wet cloth into the garbage can.

That's Shalimar! She rushed into the back hallway and noticed Emma in the sitting room. "Where's the Shalimar?" she whispered.

"Upstairs. Why?"

"I just smelled it on a cloth Bernice dropped into the garbage! She's been snooping again."

"No, that can't be. Although I was in the backyard a while ago."

"I know that scent. Let's go upstairs and check the bottle. Either you have a problem or Bernice does."

They reached the third floor landing. "You stand guard. I'll go to my room. Oh, no need. I can smell it from here. Now what?"

"Well, you're leaving. You could speak with Matron about Bernice snooping in your room, right?"

"I'll think about it. I better open the window a bit and close the door."

For the remainder of the afternoon, Sarah anxiously waited downstairs for her roommate to ring the doorbell. She couldn't focus on her book and feigned interest in magazines until supper was ready. Nobody showed up. She popped into Emma's room after supper.

"Guess the roommate heard I was trouble so she changed her mind. Ha, ha."

"She'll probably show up after breakfast tomorrow. Another night on your own. Bonus."

Monday morning was a beehive of chatter and activity. Sarah guessed it was the leftover pleasure from yesterday. Another brilliant morning sun added to the upbeat mood. She was certainly ready for Miss Preston at ten thirty.

Mary brought her crossword book to breakfast. She didn't count on investigating over cereal but it happened. She noticed Ellen was unusually quiet. Her eyes darted around the table. Mary soon recognized the symptoms. It made sense. They were the same ones she displayed only days ago. Marjorie had delivered the yellow envelope to Ellen's room on the third floor. *The nasty bags. Bullying little Ellen, of all people. Well now they have me to tangle with.*

Laura Preston stood with her back to the file cabinet, arms crossed. She let her breath out slowly, confident Mrs. Bowen would shut Eva down.

At ten thirty, Sarah tapped on the office door and entered without an invitation. She received a surprise.

An older woman with wiry black hair stood behind Matron's desk. She wore a crisp white blouse with an abundance of ruffles at the neck and cuffs. Her forest green suit jacket displayed a large cameo pin on the left lapel. The black horn rim glasses went well with the stern look on her face. 'No clap trap accepted here' they said. Coral pink lipstick was a wonky match for the red rouge on her cheeks. She reminded Sarah of the goofy, frizzy haired clown at a summer fair but this one didn't look chummy.

"Good morning, Eva. Please sit. This is Mrs. Bowen. She's here to help with the meeting."

"Help? Are you leaving?" *Good riddance.*

"No. I thought you would appreciate a second person to better explain the adoption process."

"I don't need another explanation. I got it the first time. I don't agree with you. I know what I'm doing. I'm keeping my baby."

When the clown opened her mouth all thoughts of a summer fair vanished. Sarah decided to let the woman talk until her battery ran down.

"Young woman, I'm here to make sure you thoroughly understand why adoption is the way out of your problem. Let me be frank with you. You've brought shame on yourself. Your parents have made their decision very clear. It is time for you to accept what needs to happen. It's unthinkable for you to keep this baby. You have no job nor the prospect of one. You cannot look after yourself let alone this child. I'm sure you have no idea how much it would cost. Adoption is the only answer for you. The baby gets a good home and you can forget all this." She waved her hands around the room as the grand finale and fixed a stare on Sarah's face.

Sarah stood and casually walked toward the door. Without turning, she placed her hand on the knob and announced, "I have a better plan."

Chapter Ten

January 17, 1961
Rose Hill Home

Aside from the occasional toilet flush, all was silent inside Rose Hill at three o'clock Tuesday morning. Annie was caught up in a riveting murder mystery with her feet up on a kitchen chair. A single, sharp knock on the front door sent her rushing to respond. She came face to face with a young woman wearing an elegant, long, double breasted black coat and pearl-gray cloche.

With a smile and hushed 'hello', she squeezed past Annie into the hallway. After a brief look around, she placed a large dark blue leather suitcase and matching train case on the floor. Focused on Annie, she smiled again with an engaging mix of disarming and charming. Annie was overwhelmed.

"Oh, my." Annie's eyes were like saucers. She almost curtsied.

"Hello. I'm Amelia. A little late but ready to check in."

"Are you supposed to be here, miss? This is Rose Hill Home...." Her voice trailed away.

"Oh, yes. I was expected Sunday but had things to do. Is there a problem?"

"Ah...." Annie twisted her hands together, hoping a smart answer would be forthcoming. It wasn't.

"Maybe I could sleep on a sofa until someone comes in?" Her eyes shifted to the sitting room.

"I guess so. I don't know what room is yours. Sorry." She continued to stand in the middle of the hallway.

"Do you have a pillow and blanket? I'll use the bathroom and sleep on the sofa."

"Oh, yes. I guess that's okay. Of course. I'll get them. Sorry." Annie wandered off in the direction of the linen closet.

"What's your name?" Amelia called quietly.

"Annie."

"Thank you, Annie. I'll have a rest and see you in the morning."

"Yes. Right. I'll see you in the morning."

Annie hurried into the kitchen. Her book was not nearly as interesting as the new addition. Rose Hill had its own mystery. She could hardly wait for the next chapter.

Amelia curled up on the sofa and hoped for a peaceful sleep. But her brain was not ready to grant that wish. Notes from a distant trombone grew louder. They drew closer and took control of her body. She jived and shimmied to the music of joyful memories. He was perfect. They were perfect. A delicate white veil descended as the music faded note by note. It wrapped her in soft light and carried her forward through cool mist that lifted to reveal a dark brick house looming in the distance. Continuous drumming vibrated her body to its core. The thumping grew louder as she was enclosed by a luminous orb. Faceless people in open windows writhed to trumpet and piano rhythms but they made no sound. She tossed her head from side to side begging for the bedlam to end. Her soul float away. Frightened, her heart raced to keep up but her mind was tormented with indecision. Suddenly the music stopped. Silence. From the doorway, a soothing disembodied voice summoned, "Come in, Amelia. We've been waiting for you." She floated over the threshold, sank to the floor and began to weep for her child, herself, their life.

"Good morning. I'm Matron. We've been expecting you. I hope you slept well."

Amelia rubbed her forehead, looked up and met two pair of eyes. Neither the faces nor the room looked familiar. Her thoughts were fuzzy. Her head ached. She squinted, her face reflected her bewilderment. Something about mist and music lingered for an instant, then evaporated without a trace.

"Oh, hello. I'm Amelia. This room was in darkness when I arrived last night." She needed to appear in control.

"Annie told me you arrived very early this morning. The others will soon be down for breakfast. Perhaps you should take a few minutes to prepare for the day. We will meet in my office across the hall before breakfast."

"Sure." She replied confidently not feeling one bit composed. "I'll go right now."

Amelia barely recognized the face in the mirror. Puffy eyes, messy hair, blotchy skin spelled wreck in any language. She opened her suitcase and pulled out a facecloth, change of clothes and cosmetic bag. A swift application of makeup masked some of the disaster. After running a brush through her hair, she emerged from the bathroom wearing a red turtleneck and gray wool slacks. Her blue eyes were accentuated by the pixie haircut and small diamond stud earrings.

Matron beckoned Amelia from the open doorway. "Please have a seat, Amelia." She glanced down at an open file on the desk. "I was expecting you Sunday and certainly not in the middle of the night." Her tone insinuated an apology and full explanation was due.

"Yes, well my late arrival was unavoidable. There was an unfortunate series of events in my apartment during the past few days. I had an unexpected visitor from out of town. I didn't want to be a poor hostess so offered room and board, so to speak. I am sorry that Annie was unnerved. She handled it well, though." She expected Matron to buy her rendition of the house guest story. Recounting the recriminations, pleas, threats and violence served no purpose in this room.

Matron concluded this young woman was her equal, intellectually and socially. However, she suspected Amelia's path to Rose Hill wasn't as straight as the story she told. Her pared down version of the truth would do for now. The whole truth would be unearthed in time, no matter how well buried. Sometimes it was revealed in words, sometimes in actions. She had plenty of time to wait it out. She completed Amelia's admission process then moved toward the dining room for breakfast.

Sarah was puzzled to see someone new for breakfast then totally caught off guard to hear AM introduced as her roommate. Where had she been for two days? She settled back in her chair to watch the reactions to this older, sophisticated addition to Rose Hill. She was nothing like the person she expected to share a room with for almost four months. Right now she didn't look the buddy-buddy type.

Betty appeared to have herself under control again and spoke calmly with everyone about her course and the paper she had completed. Sarah thought she sounded normal, at least this morning.

Karen and Marjorie were oddly quiet. Sarah knew they were out of their depth with the newest resident to Rose Hill. Surprisingly, they knew it too and kept their mouths shut.

Joan was calm and surprisingly agreeable but preoccupied. She eyed Matron with suspicion. Sarah felt a blow up was brewing between the two of them. Or, maybe they'd already had one. If so, another was on its way.

Ellen was absent. Nobody mentioned her but Sarah tucked toast into her pocket when she left.

Mary hurried from the breakfast table to complete her chores. She was pretty sure Marjorie delivered the yellow envelope to Ellen's room. She'd check that out right away. The new person looked old so she didn't imagine having much in common with her. At least she looked like she would mind her own business. Today, she was determined to nab Karen.

Amelia was exhausted. She ate quietly and followed Nancy to her room. After unpacking, she mercifully fell into a dreamless sleep until lunch time.

Sarah returned to her room to get a book and found Amelia asleep. Just in case, she tucked Myles' letter inside.

After lunch chores, Mary slid off the sofa and wandered into the kitchen for a hot chocolate. Carrying the mug around gave her an excuse to be a detective while feigning interest in looking out main floor windows. Unexpectedly, Karen appeared from the reading room carrying a garbage bag. She entered Matron's office and partially closed the door. Mary inched toward the door. Just as Karen dumped the waste basket contents into the garbage bag, Ellen tapped her on the shoulder. Mary spun around, put her finger to her lips and pulled Ellen with her into the dining room. "Shhhh. Follow me."

Karen exited Matron's office and sped toward the stairs. Mary counted to ten. With Ellen tagging along, she climbed to the second floor. Moments later, Mary and Ellen knocked on Karen's door and stepped in for a surprise visit.

"Nice envelopes, Karen. The blue one looks like the one I received a few days ago. Hand it over. You and I are going to see Matron today. Ellen is coming along as my witness."

Finished with Karen, Mary and Ellen went upstairs to talk inside Ellen's room on the third floor.

"Did you get a nasty note in a yellow envelope Sunday?"

"Yes. Do I really have to go to your meeting with Matron? I'm afraid they're going to do something to me if I help you."

"They're mean, Ellen. We have to stop them. Don't worry, Matron will put an end to this. You'll be okay."

Emma's mother arrived at two o'clock, dropped off by her husband. She waited in Matron's office expecting the usual warm greeting from her daughter. She stood with open arms to receive her but Emma quickly seated herself, deftly avoiding the embrace.

"What's happened? Are you ill?" Her concern was clearly evident on her face.

"No, just a little nervous, I guess. Only a few weeks to go."

"Here's an envelope with money for treats in the final weeks. New girls?"

"No."

"Anything interesting happening? New staff?" She twisted her wedding ring round and round.

Emma thought briefly about telling Alice's story but saw no good reason. This meeting was about getting information not giving it.

"No. How's the family?"

"Good. Your brother likes the new job." Round and round went the ring.

"That's good. Any news in the neighbourhood?"

"The Davidson's have a new car. Dad told me the name but I've forgotten it. You know me and cars." The ring came off her finger and back on, twice.

Emma pushed to keep the conversation going. "How are you doing with the driving lessons?"

"I've stopped 'til the snow's gone. Dad's happy with my decision. He says I hit the brakes too much." Round and round again.

"Stop playing with your ring. It's driving me nuts."

"You're high strung today. Can't we have a normal conversation?"

"A normal conversation in this place? You're joking."

"Settle down. You're getting over excited. This isn't like you. Your usually agreeable."

Emma realized she was losing her focus. She could argue another day but right now she needed facts. "Yes, you're right. I'm usually very agreeable. You don't usually come on a week day. Why are you really here?"

"Mike's dad is having some trouble with the family business." She paused.

"Why are you here about that?" She felt her curiosity rise.

"It seems the new salesman isn't working out."

"Too bad Mike didn't hang around." *Good. Mike's in the conversation. This could be easier than I thought.*

"Now dear, you know that wouldn't have been a good idea. We all felt the right decision was made."

"I was not part of the 'we' but again, why are you here?"

"Dad and I decided I should come to warn you about something."

"Warn me? What's happening? It's grandma, isn't it?"

"Grandma's fine. It's Mike."

"Mike?" Her heart skipped a beat.

"I want you to be calm and listen, just listen. We met with Mike's parents last week. Mike's dad has decided to bring him home to help with the business. There seemed to be no other way for them to solve their problem. But now, we have a problem. Dad and I have talked this over. We want you to move to Ottawa right after the baby is born and live there with Aunt Connie. You can finish high school then get a job or if you like, apply to college there. This way you can avoid seeing Mike."

"So, let me see. You've come to tell me I can't come home. Nice." Each word had a crusty edge as her body stiffened. She pushed solidly against the back of the chair, exhaled heavily and crossed her arms.

"Now, don't start being difficult again. This is not a new plan just a different way for you to be away from Mike."

"But I want to go home. Why do I have to be the one to leave? This isn't fair."

"The world is not fair. You should know that by now. Just imagine how uncomfortable it would be for both of you in the same town. People would never stop talking."

Emma softened her attitude. "When does he return?" She knew the question might reveal her plan but she needed the answer. At this moment, nothing else was more important.

"It doesn't matter. It could be tomorrow or next month. His parents aren't sure where he is. He left his last job in Yarmouth with no forwarding address. Just forget about him and live your own life now. You have a good start by being here."

Emma remained silent, assured she had collected all she could from this conversation. She was done, straightened in her chair, met her mother's eyes and thanked her for the money.

"We've talked to Aunt Connie. She's agreed to your move. It'll be fun for you in a big city with your cousins. I've always wanted to take the train to Ottawa and now you get to do it first. I'll come next Saturday afternoon so we can discuss the Ottawa details, okay?"

"Sure." *You can come but I won't be here.*

Both Emma and her mother left Matron's office convinced their personal missions had been successful. Emma however, had a new task to pursue. Her mood brightened. She waved good bye to her Mother, moved up the stairs determined to give nothing away, especially to Sarah. She was pleased with herself and fully ready to get on the train to Wolfville tomorrow. Freedom was close. She began packing in her mind. Journal, underwear, change of clothes, the money she'd been saving. The guilt money from her mother was icing on the cake. Using a suitcase was impossible. Everything must go into her coat's roomy patch pockets. She chuckled to herself about wearing her suitcase out the front door.

Sarah stared at the letter.

Dear Myles,

Congratulations on your promotion. I'm so proud of you.

Surprise, I'm well and living in Halifax too.

It would be great to see you again.

I know you are busy but we can start with a phone call. Please call Mrs. Andrews at

Darn, I don't have Rose Hill's telephone number. She hoped Nancy wouldn't ask why she needed the number and it worked. She entered the number and signed her name.

Love,

Sarah

It was simple and truthful with no mention of her earlier irritation about the unanswered August and October letters she sent via the bank. She was sure nobody bothered to send them to him. When they met he would know she had not forgotten him and they would plan a future together. But she still had a whopping big problem. She had no address to send the letter. She'd forgotten about needing the newspaper advertisement until it was in the stinky trash and didn't want to wait for another four days. She closed her eyes to focus. Who at Rose Hill would possibly help?

Matron returned to the house after a shopping trip to Fosters Grocery and found Mary waiting for her in the kitchen.

"Matron, I need to speak with you right away."

"Okay, I need a few minutes to unpack the food."

Mary was proud of her detecting work, certain Matron would appreciate her effort. When Matron asked the reason for the meeting she received an explosion of information about the nasty note and cat and mouse game with Marjorie and Karen. She ended with a request that they confront Karen and Marjorie about their behaviour.

"Karen really could have simply dumped the garbage. How do you know the envelope you received came from my office?"

"Oh, I saw her take your paper garbage and go upstairs to her room. I saw a blue envelope on her floor. It was the same kind I found under my door. For sure, she's the one planning this. Marjorie is helping."

Matron sat as casually as she could muster. Karen was no longer annoying but creating serious problems between the girls. Her file notes indicated a habit of personal boundary violations and vendettas. The blue envelope must not become a focal point in this issue.

"Okay, I will speak with Karen and the three of us will meet at eleven tomorrow morning."

"Thank you. I'm glad we're going to make them stop being mean."

During supper Emma chatted with everyone. Sarah was pleased to see Ellen eating but remained mum, lost in her challenges. The chicken with sage stuffing, carrots, creamy mashed potatoes and gravy didn't elevate her mood. She'd racked up too many problems in ten days. Perched on the top was Emma's departure. She needed a way out too. She glanced at Emma with a tinge of envy. Discouraged, she went upstairs to allow her mind to work through the developing resentment. A curious clicking sound was coming from her room. She thrust the door open, expecting to catch Bernice up to no good. Instead, her roommate was on the floor surrounded by camera equipment.

"Hey, roomie. Thought I'd play with my toys for a while."

"Hi. I haven't seen you all day."

"I took the opportunity to check out the neighbourhood. Nobody seemed to notice I was gone. I walked out and back in, no problem."

"Wow. That's very strange. They don't like us out alone."

"Guess I should remember that for the next time."

"Does Matron know you have this personal camera stuff?"

"No. And I don't plan to tell her. Hope you don't either."

"Don't worry. I won't. I have a few things myself."

"Oh, yeah? What's ya got?"

"Art supplies."

"Perfect. We're in crime together. How long you been here?"

"Ten days."

"Well, you better tell me what it's like so I'm not behind the eight ball."

"Lots of chores, feels like a prison, no information. Good food. Some girls are friendly."

"Sounds like you're not overly happy about being here. But hey, no place is perfect. Is supper ready?"

"Yes. It almost over. Nobody called you?"

"If they did, I wasn't listening. Guess I better check it out. See you in a bit."

Sarah was baffled by her new roommate's casual, accepting reaction to Rose Hill. *Nobody's here by choice so why's she so cheery?* As Sarah continued to wonder, Emma stuck her head around the door and beckoned for Sarah to follow her to her room.

"How's the roommate?"

"Mysterious is the best word. She actually sounds happy to be here. Weird. I don't know what's going on but she arrived in the middle of the night, two days late so there's gotta be a story. How was the visit with your mother? Are you leaving soon?"

Emma hesitated a moment. She had decided to keep her departure details to herself. It would be safer for Sarah. "It was the usual visit. I have extra money to help with my travel so that's good."

Sarah pressed for answers. "Are you going to speak to Matron about Bernice before you leave?"

"No. It's best not to get into a problem before I go."

"So when are you leaving?" There was a fearful edge to her voice as old feelings of being cast aside surfaced.

"A warm day during the next week. Weather will decide. I'd be leaving in a few weeks anyway."

"I know, I know." The end was fast approaching. She didn't like it one bit. The old panicky sensation began spreading across her chest.

"Your roommate sounds like she'll be good company. At least it isn't another Marjorie." A little snicker ended the sentence.

"Sarah, are you in there?" Ellen stuck her head around the door.

"Come in. Sarah and I were just talking about her roommate. What do you think?"

"She's really old. I heard she was 'way over twenty. Maybe twenty-four. How come she's here?"

Before any ideas were offered, Mary shouted up the stairwell. "Hello up there. Anyone interested in a game of Yahtzee? The more the merrier."

Emma was anxious to stay away from the topic of her departure. "You can always count on Mary to get some excitement going. Let's go."

"Not me. Got a new magazine to finish." Ellen was out the door before she finished her sentence.

Sarah declined and returned to her room to find Amelia in bed reading Ann of Green Gables. She smiled but dared not ask if she'd visited Cavendish, PEI. It seemed the perfect time to start a new sketch. At least, she could count on her roommate to see nothing and say nothing. It felt good. At nine-thirty she put the sketch book away and glanced across the room. She received a "good night" in return to which she replied, "you too".

Emma packed her pockets in the dim glow of the hall light. She glanced at the clock. Almost five thirty. Time to make it to Fosters on foot, telephone a taxi then go to the train station before she was missed. She carefully removed the Shalimar from its hiding place, then kissed it goodbye. Too heavy and breakable to carry, she wrapped it in a facecloth and placed it on her night table beside the pink envelope. She crept down the stairs from the third floor, pausing briefly at the bottom to ensure Annie was out of sight. The mixer whirred in the kitchen, so she took the opportunity to move quickly across the hall and out the door. A biting wind swirled around her face. She pulled up her collar and passed under the murky glow of a street light into the darkness of the night and her future.

Chapter Eleven

January 18, 1961
Rose Hill Home

"You're a lying bum. Get outta here. It's my decision, you jerk. Ouch. Get out, right now."

Sarah's eyes popped open. Somebody was attacking her roommate. She threw the covers off her bed ready to pounce on the intruder.

Across the room, AM was engaged in battle with an invisible foe. She punched the air and kicked at her bedding. The sheet and wool blanket fell to the floor in a heap. Finally exhausted, she rolled onto her side, opened her eyes and let out a heavy sigh. Her face was soaked in perspiration. "Good morning, roomie."

"You okay?" Sarah couldn't keep the wobble out of her voice.

"Never better. What's that commotion downstairs?"

Sarah stepped out in the hall. She'd get answers from her roommate later. Muffled words rose from the first floor. 'She's gone'. Sarah grabbed the doorknob to Emma's room as much for support as to open it and stepped into the void.

An emptiness beyond a physical absence filled the space. Emma was gone. Sarah rested her eyes on Alice's bed then Emma's. This new death sliced deep and painfully. Her legs crumbled, dropping her to the floor. She was left behind, discarded again.

Amelia patted her shoulder. "Hey, roomie. You okay? There's an envelope with your name on it." She handed Sarah a small pink envelope. "It was leaning against the Shalimar. Must be a gift for you. We better get going. I think breakfast has started without us."

Downstairs, things were not going well at all. Questions went unanswered, conversations were interrupted, food uneaten. Breakfast was the last thing on everyone's mind, except for Karen and Marjorie. Neither cared that Emma was gone.

Karen was curious about who would fill the empty room. She was bored, needed new victims to annoy.

Marjorie ate with gusto. She loved food, any food and lots of it. She chewed with her mouth open and looked at Karen. "What ya think will happen?"

"About what?"

"Emma. Perhaps she'll die too."

"Don't be stupid. She probably started to hitch hike and is miles away by now."

"Hitch hike! I'd never do that."

"You're missing out on a lot of fun. Winter isn't so good. Summer's great."

"You did that! Your parents let you? Where'd ya go?"

"Don't be dumb. They didn't know. I told them I was going to visit my sister. They never checked. I went to PEI and back. That's my longest hike so far."

"Who picked ya up?"

"Usually old people who told me how dangerous it was. Sometimes a cute guy. That was the best part." She poked Marjorie in the ribs and giggled. "You know."

Marjorie forced a giggle but said nothing. She didn't know what Karen meant.

"Where ya going after the baby is born?"

"Why do you care?"

"I'm going home. Maybe we could write to each other, okay?"

"Don't be goofy. Why would we want to remember being here? Eat your breakfast."

For months, Marjorie thought Karen was her best friend. Now she was being mean. People always did that. She tried to do everything they asked and be nice just like her mother told her. She couldn't figure it out.

In the kitchen, Eleanor asked Sarah if she knew Emma was gone. She simply nodded her head as Eleanor patted her arm. Breakfast should be easy. Her new roommate knew nothing of her relationship with Emma.

"Hi, Sarah. This is awful. How will Emma survive? I'm really worried." Ellen continued to pick at her bleeding thumbnail.

"Get some breakfast and come sit with us, Ellen. Have you met my new roommate?"

"Hello, Ellen. I'm AM."

"AM?"

"Yup. My initials. This whole anonymous business is a load of bunk." She winked at Ellen who grinned in return.

Marjorie was not finished talking. When she couldn't figure out what people meant she continued asking questions. Her mother told a neighbour she was slow, whatever that meant. She turned to Karen. "Why do you think Emma left?"

Karen scowled at her. "Who knows, who cares? Keep quiet. Here comes the new one with Eva."

Matron sat in her office with the door closed. She wanted to scream, 'time out'. Instead she closed her eyes, gathered her fragmented thoughts and picked up the phone. Emma's mother yelled and cried an incoherent rant of accusations, threats and pleas. After several minutes, she began to breath normally. At that point, Matron confidently told her the city police were searching the local area. She strongly suggested she and Mr. Evans come to Rose Hill as soon as possible. Her confidence sagged. She doubted her own words and worried the police efforts would fail. She couldn't imagine surviving another Alice episode but pushed herself to move on and think about the present. As far as she could tell, nobody knew when Emma left or where on earth she would go. Eight months pregnant, no family in the city and no money. Her only visitor was her mother. First Alice, now Emma. Then there was the blue envelope issue. With a heavy sigh, she opened the door to face a long day.

"Keep eating, Marjorie. Here comes Matron. She better forget Mary's story about me or she'll be sorry."

Marjorie didn't pick up on Karen's menacing tone and plunged on brightly. "You can keep Ellen quiet, right?"

Karen glared and Marjorie dropped her head. Their quick exchange caught Amelia's attention.

Betty leaned against the wall in the sitting room, sipping coffee deep in her own thoughts about herself, as usual. She was the next one to deliver a baby. Her self confidence was under assault, never a good thing for her bowels. Sticking to her master strategy was imperative. Have the baby and return to university. The child would have a good home with two parents. She would get on with her life, be organized. Best for everyone. Her future with Professor Richard would come when she had created a foolproof plan. She rushed to the bathroom before Matron could stop her.

Joan was in the sitting room too, totally consumed with the letter from her parents. It trumped breakfast. By the third sentence, she exploded. "Bermuda!" and charged toward the back-yard.

Matron called from the hallway. "Ladies, bring your coffee to the sitting room. Bernice, check the backyard. I believe Joan is there. She may need a little persuasion to join us."

With everyone gathered, Matron began. "Sometime through the night, Emma left the house. The police are searching for her. Perhaps she mentioned a place to go, maybe a family member or friend she planned to meet. If any of you have information, come to my office after the meeting. That's all I have to say right now. Please keep to your own routines and don't worry."

"Can we go out to look too?"

"No, Ellen. She's not hiding. She's getting far away from us. I'm pretty sure she's not in the neighbourhood now."

"But, where would she go?"

Matron wished she knew the answer. "She'll be found soon, Ellen. Let's get back to our routines."

Joan was smarting from her parent's rejection. She blasted nobody in particular. "Routines are sure to solve all our problems."

As the others rose to leave, Matron motioned to Karen and Mary. "Ladies, my office. Let's get this issue settled."

Karen smirked at Mary. She scurried to catch up with Matron, making sure she beat Mary through the door. She hurried to occupy the chair in front of Matron's desk, leaving Mary to carry one from the corner beside the filing cabinet. Karen sat casually with a confident gaze directed toward Matron. No way she was backing down from Mary's story about bullying other people. If these girls were dumb enough not to stand up for themselves, too bad for them. Besides, she had the winning ace up her sleeve. This would be over in a few minutes. She tuned in to the conversation as Matron said something about being kind and truthful.

"Mary, tell me the details about what you say Karen has been doing lately. Karen, you will have a chance to give your side of the story when Mary is finished. Go ahead, Mary."

Mary kept her eyes on Matron and explained her detective work, including Ellen as the witness. She was confident in her facts and clear explanation. It would soon be over.

Then it was Karen's turn to speak. She took a deep breath and imagined herself on stage. "Well, I'm sure Mary believes what she's saying is true." She took another deep breath, moved to the front of her chair and lowered her voice. "We all know she loves to tell stories. This is another one. Why would I do what she says I did?" A soft, haughty snort punctuated the sentence. She settled back into her chair and crossed her legs. "I enjoy her stories about other people but not this one. It's about me and it's a lie. She's making me look bad. She can't do that. Maybe her other stories are lies too. Are they, Mary?"

Matron was impressed with the theatrics. Karen had a natural talent for telling her version of the truth. She'd bet this wasn't Karen's first performance.

Mary was shaken. She absolutely knew Karen was lying and doing such a good job of it that the truth was at risk of being rejected. She blurted out, "Ellen can tell you my story is true, Matron. She was with me."

"Oh, I don't think so, Matron. I talked to Ellen last night."

Mary couldn't believe what she heard. She should have known Karen would prey on Ellen. How could she have been so gullible. Karen had just played her for the fool she was.

"Mary, did you hear me? I'll speak with Ellen later today and get this settled. That's all for now."

Stunned, Mary stood and walked out the door. Karen killed time pulling up her socks. She retreated to the door then stopped. "Matron, I happened to notice an Ottawa address on your blue envelope I threw in the garbage. I have family on the same street. Maybe they know your friend?" She smiled and stepped quickly toward the stairs.

In spite of what had happened, Mary was not afraid for herself. She'd told the truth and was boiling mad. She heard her mother telling her to cool her temper. It didn't work. No way a crafty liar was going to win this one and hurt Ellen to boot. She had to protect Ellen and get this sorted out, right now.

Mary took the steps two at a time to the third floor. Out of breath, she knocked and entered Ellen's room. Empty. Down the steps one at a time, she glanced around and exited the back door. On the bench, blocked between Karen and Marjorie, Ellen sat with her hands over her ears and feet bouncing up and down on the frozen ground. Mary moved in their direction. Time to have it out with this liar.

A rustle came from the closest spruce as Amelia emerged from it with a very wide smile on her face.

"Hello, Mary. Are you looking for Ellen? I think she's getting cold. Perhaps you could take her inside. I'm going to chat with Karen and Marjorie."

Amelia turned to Karen and Marjorie. Her lips smiled but her eyes were stone cold. "You two seem to be enjoying the cooler weather. Let's have a little chat. Don't worry, Ellen. You're safe now. Go inside for coffee with Mary."

Amelia wedged herself between Karen and Marjorie then looked at each of them in turn. "So ladies, let me be clear about what I heard while behind that tree. It stays with me only if what I heard does not happen to Ellen. Do you both understand me?" Two heads nodded in sync. "Very well, let's go inside. You two probably need coffee. Up you get, now."

Sarah escaped from the breakfast table to her room, Emma's letter in her hand.

Hi, Sarah

I hope you understand why I had to leave in the middle of the night.

I'm sorry I left without saying good bye but it was best for both of us.

I liked spending time with you.

Keep your fingers and toes crossed I'll find Mike.

Your friend,

Emma (Bonnie Evans)

P.S. Enjoy the Shalimar and think of me

The letter was still in her hand when Amelia returned from the backyard.

"Hey, what's up, roomie? You look upset. Did you know Emma well?"

"We talked quite a bit. Both of us had rooms alone after her roommate died."

"Died! What do you mean 'died'?"

"She went to the hospital and died there. It was the night of the big storm."

"That's terrible. No wonder Emma ran. She's probably terrified. How are you doing?"

Sarah ignored the question and asked her own. "How are you doing?"

"What do you mean?"

"You were yelling in your sleep this morning. Remember?"

"Oh, just a bad dream. Lots of people have them. Haven't you ever had one?"

Sarah pressed on. "I don't remember having one like that. You were kicking at someone too."

"Nothing to worry about, roomie. Wake me if it happens again. I don't want to get booted out." She chuckled.

Sarah bristled. She was getting nowhere.

"Eva, where are you?" Bernice yelled up in the stairwell.

"In my room."

"Get downstairs. Matron wants to talk to you, right now."

"Bet that's about Emma, roomie. Try to keep out of trouble down there. Emma's gone but you need to stay here, right?" She stressed the last word.

Sarah didn't answer but thought about the word each step down the stairs. Did she need to stay here? She'd tried to figure a way out from the day she arrived. This was her chance. She should take it. Get out. Maybe get thrown out. With Emma gone, there wasn't a good reason to stay. She wandered into Matron's office ready to leave if the opportunity presented itself.

"So Eva, I know you can help Emma. I'm sure you have a few thoughts about her disappearance."

"How can I help her? She left. I can't bring her back." *She's bluffing.*

"Yes, that's true but I want you to think about anything she may have mentioned that would give us a hint of where she went."

"I didn't know she was leaving last night."

"I believe what you said is true but it's not the whole truth and not what I asked."

"I didn't know when she would leave." Sarah knew she said the wrong thing the moment the words passed her lips. *Damn it.*

"Are you saying she mentioned leaving but not when?"

"People say lots of things and don't do them."

"That's true but I get the feeling you are trying not to tell me something. Am I right?" Matron locked on Sarah's eyes.

Sarah was trapped by Matron's stare. She couldn't look away or answer. This was her chance to get out of Rose Hill. She'd hijacked herself.

As Matron repeated the question, the phone shrilled. Sarah jumped.

"Hello, Matron speaking." She covered the mouthpiece and motioned for Sarah to leave.

Sarah found herself in her room not recalling any of the steps to the third floor. She was unnerved by Matron's intensity and needed to sort herself out, pronto. Dad would tell her she was discombobulated, laugh and tell her to unwind herself. *Easier said than done here, dad.*

Matron sat in her office with a fourth cup of strong, black coffee. She expected Emma's parents by two o'clock, three at the latest. Whatever Sarah might know was best saved for their visit. They couldn't be in the same room but Sarah might be convinced to share if she knew Emma's parents were in the home. In fact, she was counting heavily on it. Time would tell. She tried in vain to focus on speaking with Ellen about the envelope issue.

Eleanor tapped on the door and carried in a tray with a pot of tea, two buttered tea biscuits and jam.

"Time to change the coffee to tea and have a morning snack." She said kindly.

"Thanks. You're a real right-hand gal."

"Anything you need doing?"

"Reluctantly, yes. Can you speak with Ellen and tell her we won't meet today. I hate to cancel but I can't see how to make it happen."

"I'll spend a bit of time with her and let you know how she's doing."

At eleven, the telephone rang. Matron grabbed it and answered in anticipation of good news.

"Morning, Matron. Sergeant Cameron with the downtown station. I have news from the train station. It may pertain to your missing girl."

"Oh, thank heavens."

"Officers there have just spoken with a passenger who reported a very pregnant young woman on the platform. The passenger found it strange she was there so early in the morning without any luggage. But, he could not confirm she boarded his train for Montreal or any other one."

"The train station!"

"We don't know if it's her yet, ma'am. We'll keep you informed."

"Thank you. Bye." *Montreal?*

Tense quietness permeated the room during lunch. Everyone in the house was dealing with worries of their own making or those created by someone else.

Eleanor brought Matron a ham sandwich and mentioned Betty looked more anxious than usual but would likely be okay for a few hours.

"A new girl should be admitted around three o'clock today. Can you keep an eye out for her?"

"Sure. Anything else, Matron?"

"No, and thanks again."

So far the day was a fiasco for Betty. She couldn't eat and couldn't stay out of the bathroom. By twelve thirty, she realized all her cramps were not intestinal. She eased up the stairs and began timing them for tell tale signs of labour.

Joan was incensed by her parents abandonment. How dare they travel without her? She considered herself their equal. Therefore, they should remain at home until she returned to it. She pushed her ham sandwich around the plate with her soup spoon. A scum formed on top of the cold cream of tomato soup. She swallowed the remainder of a glass of milk and left the room. Perhaps she should call her grandparents. Maybe she should copy Emma's game plan. She certainly would not talk to any of the people here, especially those unsophisticated girls. What would they have to offer? She had a perfectly fine life without those girlfriend, best friend notions. Why start now? She told Eleanor she was walking around the block and left. Without any interruptions, she would have a solid plan within the hour.

Amelia noticed Karen and Marjorie were focused on their soup. Funny that. She smiled to herself.

Sarah decided to come clean about Emma and take her lumps. She'd never forgive herself if something happened to Emma and she'd kept quiet. She ate quietly, knowing Matron would come for her any moment. But the moment never came. She began to panic. What if something had already happened to Emma? A crushing sensation spread across her chest. It hurt to breathe. *Put the spoon down. Relax. Take a deep breathe. Out slowly. Another.*

"Don't like tomato soup, roomie?"

"A bit of indigestion. I have to relax a few more minutes."

"Take your time. I don't think we have to be anywhere this afternoon. Looks like Matron has her hands full. That door has been closed for a long time. There goes Eleanor with more coffee."

Ellen wished Mary would make eye contact across the table. She felt comforted AM was looking out for her. Anyone who stood up to Karen and Marjorie was a hero but she wanted Mary's support too. *Please, please look at me.* When Mary stood and walked from the room, Ellen raced after her.

"Mary, wait for me."

Mary turned around to see Ellen rushing toward her.

"What's the problem? Did those two do something to you again?"

"No. I want to talk to you."

"Sure." Mary's interest peaked.

"Can we go outside for a walk?"

Outside, Mary chose to remain quiet. This was new behaviour for Ellen. She did not want to spoil the moment.

"I'm not used to talking about myself with other people. That probably sounds strange to you. I have a question. Do you ever feel sad?"

"Sure, when bad things happen to myself and other people. Why?"

"I feel like that most of the time. Sad."

"You mean, before you came here, too?"

"Yes, but it's worse here. I don't have much to do here so there's lots of time to think about sad things."

Mary wanted to keep her talking. "What do you do at home?"

"School, church."

"How about brothers, sisters, friends?"

"An older brother. He lives in Toronto."

Mary was struck by the absence of friends. "So what do you do for fun?"

"I like to swim. Ride my bike."

"What do you do for summer vacation?"

"Usually church camps. I don't think I'll be going any more."

"Why's that?" She wished Ellen would ask her a question. She was beginning to feel nosy.

"It's why I'm here. I thought you had to be married to have a baby."

"Oh, my!" For the first time in a very, very long time, Mary couldn't think of anything to say. She kept walking.

"How did you get here?"

Mary didn't need a long explanation for that question. "My boyfriend."

"Are you going back to school?"

"Yes. I'm sixteen so I have to. I'm pretty sure everyone knows why I'm away right now. They'll keep quiet because they won't know what to say. But everything's going to be different when we go home because everything is changed. You know that, right?"

Ellen reached for Mary's hand. "Yes. Thank you."

They strolled hand in hand back to Rose Hill. At the door, Ellen looked up. "Can we walk and talk tomorrow?"

"It's a date."

Mary opened the front door to discover four people crowded into the front hall. A woman with a fierce face paced back and forth near Matron's door. A tall man stood like a statue near the door to the dining room. He stared at the fierce woman. A teenager wearing an over-size duffel coat slouched near the kitchen door. She clutched a small, scuffed suitcase and kept her eyes on the floor. The second woman, near the coat rack, was clearly frustrated. She leaned against the wall, arms crossed and lips pressed together. Ellen and Mary sped to the stairs.

Matron opened the door, acknowledged everyone with a nod then stepped quickly to the kitchen.

"Eleanor, the new girl and her step-mother are here already! Take them to the dining room, offer coffee and close the door. When they have coffee, go upstairs and ask all the girls to remain upstairs until we get things settled down here. Ask Bernice to help Nancy in the kitchen. Thanks. I'll take Mr. and Mrs. Evans into the office."

Emma's father sat quietly while his wife launched an all out attack on Matron before being seated.

"How do you operate this place when a young girl can walk out of it totally unseen and unheard? It is outrageous. And what have you done to get her back before something terrible happens? It's the middle of winter, for heaven's sake!" She exhaled loudly, sat, crossed her legs and removed her leather gloves. She was combat ready.

Matron opened her mouth. Her response was blocked.

"Did someone come in here and take her? This is all inexcusable." Mrs. Evans took a deep breath. Her husband took his opportunity.

"Mrs. Andrews, can you offer us some information or hope right now? What have the police said?"

"Thank you, Mr. Evans." She directed her full attention to him. "I spoke with the police while you were travelling here. We believe your daughter was seen this morning at the Halifax train station. I'm expecting a call soon. Right now, they are confirming if she went on an early train to Montreal or a later one to the Valley. I believe you have family in Wolfville or Kentville, correct?"

"Why is it taking so long? Hours have passed." Mrs. Evans resumed her sharp tirade. "Isn't there someone else to call about this?"

"Dear, the police have to telephone people at the station stops along the route who then speak directly with staff on the train. If she went to the Valley on the Dayliner, she wouldn't arrive in Wolfville until after two o'clock. In the meantime, I'm sure the police have been speaking with staff and passengers at the station here in the city. It all takes time."

"Oh please, Gerald. This is hardly the time to give me a lecture on patience. I've never had any with incompetence and I'm not about to start today. This is a case of, of, of... complete incompetence." She exhaled loudly, dropped her hands onto her lap and glared at Matron.

Matron visibly bristled, was about to respond.

A soft knock was followed by Eleanor entering the room. She closed the door but kept her hand on the knob. "Pardon me. There's a young man in the hall who wants to speak with you right away about something important, Matron. He's very calm and polite. He wouldn't tell me what it's about exactly but said there's a girl here he knows. What would you like me to do?"

"All the girls are upstairs and I will take a few moments to send him on his way. Excuse me, Mr. and Mrs. Evans."

On the third floor, Betty felt a gush of water run down her legs.

"Joan, can you hear me? I need the doctor. Joan. Joan."

"Betty, it's Eva. I'm in the hall upstairs. I'll go down for Matron or Eleanor."

On the main floor, Sarah came face to face with a guy pacing back and forth in front of the office door. He looked up.

"Hi, I'm Mike. I'm waiting for the Matron. A woman went into the office but hasn't come out. Do you know a girl called Bonnie Evans?"

Oh my gawd, it's Bonnie's Mike. "Yes, but I have to help someone. Don't leave." She darted to the kitchen.

Matron and Eleanor left the office and saw Mike watching Sarah retreat up the stairs. She ducked down on the landing to listen.

"I'm Matron. Our girls don't have surprise visitors. Why are you here?" Her tone was no nonsense.

"It's about Bonnie Evans. I'm here because I'm going to marry her."

Matron's mouth dropped. When she regained her composure, she replied, "I think you better come into the office."

Sarah's heart soared. She knew Bonnie had made the right decision. She stood in her room and cried with happiness for her.

Betty was quietly attended to by Dr. Kelly then transferred to the hospital while tense conversations continued on in the dining room and Matron's office. Bernice was kept busy serving coffee and cookies to both rooms.

Shortly after three thirty, Bonnie's cousin called. Bonnie was with her, tired but okay. Everyone in the room cried when Mike took the receiver.

"Hi, Bon. It's me. I'm here with your parents. We're going to pick you up......."

"I love you, too."

"Stop crying. We'll all have supper together. We have a wedding to plan."

Matron watched them leave together with Mike carrying Bonnie's suitcase. She intended to fill the empty bed in Joan's room with the new girl Debbie but the turmoil of the day changed her mind.

Debbie was assigned to Emma's old room. She was taken to her room by Bernice who barely said a word beyond the necessary directions. Once alone, Debbie checked all the dresser drawers. In these places nobody owned much but you never knew what goodies you might find. She picked the best looking maternity clothes for herself. The other bed looked like it had been slept in and the pillow cover was wrinkled. There were used towels in the laundry basket. *Somebody left quick. Got my own room. Hooray.*

Before supper, Sarah shared Emma's full story with Amelia. One day soon she would tell Mary and Ellen. *Good news needed to be shared with friends.*

At supper, Matron said Emma had been found safe and sound but refused to answer any questions. She introduced Debbie who smiled at everyone in turn, pausing ever so briefly at Karen. Alice's death heightened everyone's concern so she shared positive news about Betty.

"Betty is doing well. Doctor Kelly thinks she will deliver overnight or early tomorrow."

While the girls were expressing relief about Betty, Matron glanced at Sarah. She was certain Sarah knew about Mike. *Is there a Mike in her life and if so, what is she up to?*

Chapter Twelve

January 19, 1961
Rose Hill

Sleep was impossible. Every time Sarah closed her eyes, someone was leaving her. Myles, her parents, Emma. *There's nobody left to trust.*

As the hour hand inched toward four Sarah gave up, untangled herself from the wool blanket and crept downstairs. Her destination was the sitting room but Annie was baking. The aroma of cinnamon lingered in the hall. She followed her nose.

"Hi. You're a little early for breakfast. Want a muffin?"

"Sure. I know I'm not supposed to be here in the middle of the night."

"You live here, right?"

"Yes, but..."

"No buts. If you're awake, there's a reason. Food helps me when I'm figuring things out. Glass of milk?"

"Yes. Thanks."

Annie gave Sarah a hug then turned back to her work. It wasn't her job to counsel the girls but she decided to mention her concern to Eleanor later in the morning.

"Thanks, Annie. I'll try to sleep again."

"Okay, dear. Put your head on the pillow and think of something happy."

Amelia was in overdrive nightmare mode. Sarah heard her from the hall. She carefully pushed the door open and was startled by the person pacing in front of the window. Amelia's words were jumbled but 'liar' and 'wife' were loud and clear.

Sarah began speaking softly. "It's your roomie. Wake up. I'm coming closer. Wake up. It's okay. You're safe here. You're in your room."

Amelia wilted to the floor. Sarah eased herself down to sit with her.

"Okay, that was a whole lot worse than the last time. You're scaring me. What the heck is going on? If you don't talk to me, I'm going to ask to move." The last sentence slipped out but there it was. She had enough trouble of her own.

"This was your room first. I'll talk to Matron and move."

Sarah bit her tongue. *For a smart person, you're sure acting dumb. A different room wouldn't stop nightmares.* She changed her mind and responded. "If you say so but perhaps you should think it over first. In the meantime, I'm going to sleep."

"Me too."

Debbie woke early. She never had her own bedroom, no matter where she lived. She planned to enjoy every minute of it. Supper last night delivered a surprise when she recognized one of the girls called Karen. Karen was definitely not her name and Debbie couldn't remember how she knew her. She decided to play it safe and ignore this so-called Karen as long as possible.

At breakfast, Karen sipped coffee lost in thought about the latest arrival. She remembered Debbie from some place but couldn't put two and two together. The loud laugh and busty figure was familiar but her face looked different. Marjorie continued to interrupt her train of thought with a series of questions. Fed up, she turned her head and hissed, "Shut up."

Marjorie wanted to cry but figured Karen would laugh at her. She needed Karen as her friend.

"Good morning, girls. Just a few things. Betty delivered her baby last night. Miss Preston will arrive shortly. Those of you with appointments are excused from chores. Reverend Miller is scheduled to visit us on Sunday afternoon. Please be on time for his discussion group. She heard a few groans but let it go. Ellen, I'll see you in your room shortly as Miss Preston will be in my office."

A chill rippled through Ellen. She hoped Matron had forgotten about the meeting. She was afraid of Karen, despite AM's assurance. Being alone in your room wasn't safe these days. Maybe she should ask Matron for a move to Joan's room. She picked the fresh scab off her thumb.

Sarah, Amelia and Joan sat at the table but were miles apart in thought. All three had an unshakable purpose for their quietness. Sarah was day dreaming about Myles, Amelia needed freedom from the man she'd trusted and Joan wanted her power in the family restored.

As Matron returned to her office, someone was banging repeatedly on the front door. She opened it a crack and faced a man wearing a long black topcoat. He moved to push her out of the way. She countered by stepping toward him, placing both feet on the front step and slamming the door shut behind her.

"Can I help you?" She took a quick measure of him. Six feet, well-dressed, very angry.

"You have someone in there I need to speak with, now." His dark eyes never left hers.

"That is not possible, sir." She shivered as a gust of wind blew across the landing.

"Anything is possible. In this case, I'll get the police and force you to allow me in." He leaned forward. "Don't think I won't."

"This is not a public building, sir. It is a private dwelling and you sir, are not welcome inside."

"You're keeping women in there, some of them against their will." He straightened his grey silk tie. "I intend to get in there." He inched forward.

"Sir, that may be your intent but in the meantime, I'm not standing outside to discuss it with you. Leave immediately or I will step inside and call the police myself."

"This is not over."

"Good day, sir."

He clenched his fists, put on leather gloves and stomped toward a gleaming black and chrome-trimmed Buick shimmering in the morning sun.

Eleanor was waiting in the office for Matron. "I peeked out the window while you were on the step. It's not my business who he is but he looks like trouble. I was ready to call the police."

"I threatened to. That's why he left, this time."

"I wanted to tell you Annie mentioned Eva was in the kitchen early this morning. She's very unsettled."

"Thanks, Eleanor and thank Annie for me. I'll speak with Eva later today. I need a few minutes before Miss Preston arrives. Please bring a pot of coffee and another cup." *That man will be back. Who was he talking about? He's too young to be anyone's father except Ellen but she's been here for months. That leaves Amelia or Debbie.* She rose from her chair to answer a knock.

"Good morning, Miss Preston. Come in. Help yourself to coffee. Who are you seeing today?"

"Joan at nine-thirty then Marjorie followed by Karen. After lunch, Betty."

"Betty's baby was born yesterday. I expect her to return on Monday to finalize the adoption forms and pick up her personal belongings. Does that work for you?"

"Certainly. I'll be here about three o'clock."

"More news. Emma left the house early yesterday morning. Well, actually during the night. She's with her family now. I don't expect her back. Since you don't have an afternoon appointment, I'd like time to discuss a few issues. Shall we meet in here and cover the topics over lunch? I think it's grilled cheese sandwiches and vegetable soup today."

"Certainly. How is Joan doing?"

"Unusually quiet on the surface the past two days but simmering underneath. You might want to talk about the family. Something has her very agitated. When are you seeing Sarah?"

"Next week. Is there a problem other than settling in and adoption?"

"She's quite unsettled right now. Too many events have happened around her in two weeks but she'll work through it. She appears quite self-reliant."

Matron knocked quietly and entered Ellen's room to find her sitting on the edge of her bed staring at the floor. "You're looking uneasy. There's nothing to worry about. Just tell me what you heard and saw between Mary and Karen on Tuesday."

"Well, I saw Mary peeking in your office and I was curious. Then I saw Karen inside your office putting your trash into a bag. Mary and I followed her to her room and saw a blue envelope on the floor. Mary said it was like the one she got under her door."

"What was in the blue envelope?"

"I don't know. Mary said it was a nasty note."

"So why were you following Karen with Mary? You could have said 'no'."

"I got a nasty note too but Mary didn't know. I saw a yellow envelope like mine on Karen and Marjorie's floor."

"Thank you. By the way, it's good see you at more meals. A lot of things have happened here recently. How are you feeling?"

"Okay. Mary and I had a nice walk yesterday."

"That sounds very positive. Good for you and thanks for helping me."

Amelia stopped Matron on the stairs. "Is there somewhere we can talk?"

"If it's urgent, we can go outside. Otherwise, in my office at two. Is that okay?"

"That's fine."

Matron suspected the topic was more urgent than the words implied. Amelia's frown told her something had changed in the last twenty four hours.

Matron frequently went grocery shopping at Fosters when Miss Preston used her office. Today, an uneasy feeling told her to stay put. As Joan left the meeting with Miss Preston, she nipped into her office to pick up one specific file. While there, she jotted the closest police station phone number inside her notebook and sat at the small round table in the kitchen.

With lunch over, Sarah returned to her bedroom. It wasn't really her room any longer, more a source of frustration than hideaway. She'd decided to visit Ellen if AM was working with her camera. Luck was on her side. The room was empty. She reviewed the letter to Myles and sealed it inside an envelope, confident the bank address would be in the weekend newspaper. By next weekend, her problems would be over. She walked across the hall to Ellen's room.

After lunch, Amelia put on her coat and sat outside. Taking a walk around the block was out of the question. She couldn't cancel her meeting with Matron without raising suspicion about herself. If she asked for a move to another room, she would risk exposing her situation. In the end, she decided to ask general questions, citing her tiredness during admission as the excuse.

"It's not often that I have a request for a meeting so soon after admission. Is there a problem?"

"Oh, no. I have some basic questions about my time here. You probably gave me the information during admission but I was very tired."

"Yes, it was an unusual time of the day, I should say night, when you arrived." Matron paused for an explanation. None came. She continued. "Your admission information indicates you are unmarried and the father is not interested in the baby. Correct?

"Yes." *That isn't exactly correct but close enough for now.*

"So I'm presuming your questions are related to adoption, correct?"

"Yes. What is the procedure?"

"It starts at your first meeting with Miss Preston, our caseworker." Matron expected a request for a meeting as soon as possible. The answer surprised her.

"I understand. I'm not in a rush for the details."

Confused, Matron decided to switch topics. "On your form, there is no next of kin mentioned. Do you have family in the area?"

"No. My brother lives in England. I saw no reason to include his information."

"Can I presume you will not be expecting visitors?" Matron was fishing for something, anything.

"Absolutely no visitors. None at all, under any circumstances."

Matron continued. "Do you have a family doctor? If not, Doctor Kelly is our usual contact."

"I'm sure he'll be fine. I'd prefer to keep this uncomplicated."

The conversation sputtered along as Matron responded patiently to several mundane inquiries concerning mail and house routines. She hoped for a small crack in Amelia's shell but the opening didn't materialize. In the end, she cut the conversation off. "So, if there is nothing else, I'll see you at supper."

"Yes, absolutely and thank you for your time."

Amelia left the office still fearful for her immediate future. She got through the meeting but her personal safety was perilously close to being exposed. Eva already recognized something was terribly amiss. She climbed the stairs reluctantly, knowing she must act now to survive. She did not trust easily but she was cornered with no way out except to trust a pregnant teenager she'd known for two days. To her temporary relief, Eva was not in their room.

Karen and Marjorie sat in Matron's office awaiting their fate. Karen was smug with the confidence she had nowhere else to go. Matron needed the money from social services so she'd not be kicked out. Debbie had captured her attention and it would be great fun to pretend she knew her until she really did. She could whisper all sorts of threats. She crossed her fingers inside her pockets. *It would be even better if Marjorie got punted out. She was such an annoying dolt.*

Marjorie sat quietly, certain she would be sent to a wage home until the baby came in about two weeks. She felt sorry for herself. Karen was her only friend. It was so hard to figure it all out, especially with people her own age. They laughed at her and after a while, paid no attention or took advantage of her. Older people seemed to be kinder but eventually they lost patience with her. If she could just figure out what people meant, life would be easy. Why couldn't she be happy like she was in grade three?

Matron was not prepared to entertain any discussion with Karen and Marjorie. They would see her together and hear her decision. There would be no chance for Karen to spin a story to Marjorie.

"I have made my decisions about your futures in Rose Hill. Marjorie, you will remain in the room you both occupy now. Your new roommate should arrive Saturday. Karen, you need to think about your behaviour toward people around you. So, you will meet with either myself or Miss Preston once a week for the next four weeks. By that time your baby will be due. In the meantime, I expect you to stop your unkind ways right now and respect others. Meetings will begin on Monday morning with me. You will move next door with Joan immediately. I have already spoken with her."

After seeing Karen and Marjorie out of the office, Matron started up the stairs. She wanted to reassure Ellen about her safety. As she approached the third floor, she heard laughter from Ellen's room. She was tempted to turn around but moved forward and knocked gently.

"Come in." Ellen's tone was cheery.

"It's wonderful to hear laughter in the house since we've had so much to deal with lately. Eva, can you stop in to see me before supper? It shouldn't take too long."

"Sure."

Sarah entered Matron's office in high spirits. Contact with Myles would be soon and with happy results. Things were clearly looking up.

"Please sit. Ellen seems happier these days. You have been a good influence on her. Thank you. How are you doing?"

"Really good." Sarah flashed a broad smile.

"Your roommate spoke with me earlier today." Matron let the statement dangle in mid air, waiting for a response that never came.

Sarah remained silent. She wasn't about to reveal anything about the nightmares, yet.

Matron cleared her throat and continued. "It seems she wasn't listening carefully during admission and missed some information. I'd like you to help her get settled over the next few days. Could you do that?"

"Sure. Is that all?" She had to get out of the office before Matron began asking any other questions.

After hesitating briefly, Matron replied. "Yes. Thank you."

When Sarah left the office, Matron remained standing at the side of her desk. Eva was a most interesting young woman.

Things happened around her. In two weeks she's been involved with Ellen's improved eating habits, Emma's disappearance and likely her roommate's sketchy story. Tomorrow she would come to work early and stay late again. Something was about to happen at Rose Hill. She could feel it in her bones.

Sarah rushed into her room. "I just spoke with Matron. First you're moving, next I hear you're not. You better start talking or I will."

Amelia searched Sarah's face then looked around the room. She rose from the bed, closed the door and leaned against it. Her right hand covered her eyes while the left hung limply at her side. She slid down the door onto the floor.

Sarah waited for an answer. It was not her turn to speak. A whimper was followed by loud weeping. Amelia was coiled on the floor.

"He's mad, absolutely mad. He mustn't get near me."

Sarah knelt and looked into terror-stricken eyes. Tears and mucus mingled, forming a slow stream of slimy liquid on Amelia's chin. She rubbed the back of her right hand over it.

"Who is this mad man?"

"He's the father of my baby."

"And that makes him mad? That makes no sense at all to me. I'm going to get a wet facecloth then we're going to talk."

Amelia was sitting on her bed when Sarah returned. She glanced up to acknowledge Sarah then continued to stare at the floor. Tears continued to roll down her cheeks. Sarah was not going to let the moment pass. She handed over the facecloth and plunged ahead with a question.

"Back to this mad man. If he's the father, what happened to make him a nutter?"

"He expected me to have an abortion. I said 'no'."

"Abortion is illegal. How could he demand that?"

"He found someone ready to do it."

Sarah gasped in disbelief. "A doctor?"

"No, but if there's money available, you can find someone to do anything. And he has lots of money."

"Okay, I'm a little thick here. Back up. Why did he expect you to have an abortion? You could come here, which you did anyway. What's the problem?"

Amelia hesitated. This was a test for her as a roommate. Speak truthfully and establish trust or waffle around it and taint the relationship forever.

"I didn't figure that out myself until a few months into the pregnancy. We dated for almost a year and had vague conver-

sations about a future together. They were always started by
me but I didn't see that then. When I became pregnant, I expected we'd start planning that future. I hinted but he balked
every time, saying I should have the baby, that the baby and I
would have anything we wanted. When he figured out I wasn't
buying that arrangement and wanted to get married, he began
yelling and threatening me. During one of his rants it slipped
out that he was married. He told me he was paying for an abortion and if I refused I would regret it. He gave me a name, cash
and said he would be back from a business trip in two weeks. I
found out about Rose Hill and made an appointment to come on
Sunday. I don't believe he left the city at all because he showed
up Saturday to check up on me. I was still pregnant and he went
nuts, flew into a violent rage."

"And you're here now. So why are you so frightened?"

"Remember that terrible banging on the front door at breakfast? I just know it was him. Who else would do something like
that?" The question was as much for herself as Sarah.

"We don't know for sure it was him." Sarah tried to be positive but Amelia needed to get it all off her chest and continued.

"He was physically abusive. That's why I was late arriving.
I left my apartment after dark on Saturday and went to a hotel.
He's smart, didn't hit my face but my arms were a mess. I'll be
wearing long sleeves for a while. He wants to get rid of me."

"He lives in the city?"

"Yes, and I bet he's made the rounds of other homes in the
province trying to bully himself inside."

"Well, you're safe inside here."

"Probably but I'm a prisoner. Thanks for listening. I know
we aren't suppose to get personal and have friendships but a
roommate deserves to know about this danger. How else can we
support each other?"

"Does Matron know any of this?"

"Not yet. I have to talk to her soon. Everyone could be in
danger. I've really messed things up here."

"I can't argue with that but what happens next?"

"I think it depends on what Matron decides. What's your
story?"

"Mine's ordinary. My parents brought me here almost two
weeks ago. The case worker has a one track mind and it's adoption. That's not for me."

"Are you two going for supper?" Ellen stepped into the room.

"Want to go with us?"

"Yes."

After supper, Sarah and Amelia continued their conversation. Sarah began where she left off earlier.

"I have a father problem too but mine doesn't know where I am."

"What do you mean?"

"He left town without me when he found out I was pregnant. Actually, the bank moved him. I didn't have his home address but I asked the bank to forward two letters."

"You sound very sure about him." Amelia feared Sarah's outcome would be a repeat of others she'd heard about. The guys ran and didn't look back.

"I am. My parents got him all wrong. A few days ago, I found out where he works. He's here in Halifax so he'll get my letter this time. By the way, his name is Myles and mine is Sarah Gardner."

"I'm Amelia Mitchell."

"So tell me why you have all that photography stuff with you."

Chapter Thirteen

January 20, 1961
Rose Hill

Debbie began her second day alone on the third floor. She planned to rummage around and steal while the others were at breakfast. Cosmetics were her most loved finds. What she craved today was red lipstick. She itched to get started. Her maternity top was the perfect place to hide almost anything. The one called AM had a stylish haircut, expensive looking shoes and wore red nail polish, her second favourite thing. She would start in AM's room. Sure enough, the rich one had a pricey looking leather case pushed against the wall under her bed. It had trays and drawers filled with lipsticks, polishes, brushes, powders, eyeliner and shadow. She even had an eyelash curler. One drawer held a collection of Avon tiny lipstick samples. Debbie was in heaven. She wanted it all. For now, she slipped a tube of cherry red lipstick into her pocket and floated downstairs in a state of bliss.

By breakfast time, Joan had suffered more than enough of Karen's petulant silence. It had started before supper, lasted until bedtime and reappeared when the alarm clock went off. Her mind was made up. She would straighten Karen out before they went downstairs. And she did.

"Karen, you and I are going to have an arrangement while we share this room. First off, you're not my new friend simply because you're in here. However, you are going to be civil to me. No more spoiled child attitude, pouting and not talking. If you want to act like that everywhere else fine, but not here. Got it?"

Karen nodded.

"Next, if you don't smarten up and stop the bad ass attitude in here starting now, I'll speak with Matron about moving you out. And I mean really out. I don't care where you go but I'm sure there are other places for you. Understand?"

Karen nodded again. *Whatever. Debbie was more important right now than this bossy cow.*

Joan was pleased with herself. She finally had influence over someone again, even if it was only Karen. They walked to breakfast together. No words were exchanged along the way.

At the table, Karen couldn't keep her eyes off Debbie. Now that Matron and Joan were on her case, life was hell. She couldn't even send dumb Marjorie on errands. Her scowl was front and centre for all to see, not that anyone cared. She could hardly wait for this baby to pop so she could leave and go back to the youth home. Turned out, it wasn't the worst place on earth after all. In the meantime, she would concentrate all her efforts on figuring out this Debbie person.

After lunch, Mary rinsed her dust cloth and dropped it into the laundry basket. The sun was shining so she went to the sitting room and asked Ellen if she wanted to go for a walk around the block. They stepped out the front door and crossed the street toward the church. At the corner, they walked toward the school. Weekends were usually the only time the girls took this route. With school out, there would be nobody to stare or make snide comments as they passed by the parking lot. It was a painful reminder of the life many left behind. Friends and activities would never be the same. Today, the school grounds were empty, except for a big black car parked near the front door.

Mary turned to Ellen. "Must be a teacher preparing or marking an exam. Sometimes my mother goes into school on the weekend. She says she gets more done in an hour on Saturday than two during the week."

"What's your favourite subject in school?" Ellen asked.

"Math. I like solving the problems."

"I really like English." She paused. "It's good to get away from all the noise and people at Rose Hill. At my home, it's pretty quiet."

"Not my house. My older brother plays sports. His hockey and basketball friends hang around a lot. My mom keeps threatening to send their parents a bill for food. But, she likes to cook so I think she enjoys making pots of stew, hot dogs and pies."

"Your home sounds like fun."

"It is but I know it won't be the same after this. You know. When I go back, I mean." Mary stopped talking and walked with her head down. "How are you feeling these days?"

"I've got trouble sleeping."

"Betty had that too. She roamed around a lot in the last few weeks."

"I'm grumpy and sad sometimes. Is that normal?"

"I guess so. I wish someone would tell us about these things. It's like a big secret. Maybe we should ask Betty, when she comes back to get her things."

They passed the barber shop and entered Carter's Corner Store to be met by a middle aged customer who pursed her lips and stared as they went to the counter. Mary asked for ten Ganong Chicken Bones. She couldn't resist the pink cinnamon coating and soft chocolate centre. At the door, she smiled at Ellen and spoke in a loud voice, "My husband loves these."

Out on the sidewalk, they burst into laughter. Mary passed the candy bag to Ellen.

They passed an apartment building and several bunga-lows before turning the final corner. Near the alley beside the church, they approached a man walking a highland terrier. The dog barked and tugged toward the alley. In the alley they saw a man in a black overcoat slink along the side of the shed. He glanced up, darted inside and closed the door.

The man pulled on the dog's leash and stopped. "Robbie, quiet. Must be a clergyman."

Mary stared at the door but it remained shut. "Maybe so but he closed the door. That's strange. I'd leave the door open if I was getting something outta there."

"Each to his own. Robbie, come."

Mary and Ellen crossed the street. Inside Rose Hill, the girls quickly forgot about the man and the shed. The smell of peanut butter drifted into the hall.

"A cookie and milk break is in my future. Let's go, Ellen."

By mid afternoon, Sarah grew restless waiting to see the newspaper. Matron usually brought it with her from Fosters but today she came in early and hadn't left the house. Odd. Not odd but troubling were her repeated trips to the front and back win-dows. Sarah gave up, had a cookie and went upstairs before she lost all the daylight. She picked up her work on the stained glass church window and looked out across the street. As she com-pared her picture and the window, a tall man in a black coat emerged from the alley. She couldn't see a priest's collar but expected him to walk up the church steps and enter the front door. Instead, he moved to the side of the church, crept forward and tucked himself beside one of the ornate, two-storey pillars. Slowly, he put a gloved hand into his coat pocket and removed a dark item. She moved her face close to the pane as he placed the item over his eyes. Binoculars! She dropped to the floor, crawled to the door and yelled at the top of her lungs.

"Matron. He's here. He's here."

Matron couldn't hear Sarah. She was in the office, door closed with Eleanor who should have been home by now. Instead, she was back at Rose Hill. On her way home, she'd spotted a familiar looking black car parked at the school. She spun around and raced back to Rose Hill on a dead run. Out of breath, she'd pushed open Matron's door and blurted, "He's back."

Sarah screamed all the way down the stairs. As she barged through Matron's door, a cluster of girls followed in her wake. Matron and Eleanor turned to her, mouths open.

"He's here." was all Sarah needed to say.

Matron picked up the telephone and dialed the police number. With her hand over the mouthpiece, she spoke to Eleanor, "Windows and doors."

Eleanor moved quickly through the first floor and closed drapes. As she shut the kitchen curtains, she directed Bernice to quietly escort the girls into the dining room and lock the back door. Upstairs, she pulled all the bathroom and bedroom curtains shut. At each window, she briefly scanned for the angry man. Nothing, not even a rabbit.

The sun dropped in the western sky as the police officers entered Rose Hill. Soon it would set, leaving them to search in the dark, always an advantage to the bad guy, especially if he knew his way around or worse, lived in the neighbourhood.

Matron was brief in her comments to the police. "I have good reason to believe this man was here a few days ago trying to force his way into the home. He's approximately six feet tall and was wearing a long black topcoat. I'm guessing his age to be between thirty and thirty-five. He drives a black car with lots of chrome. It was parked on the school grounds at four-thirty."

Eleanor knocked and entered. "Sorry to interrupt. One of the girls is missing."

Matron's eyes met Eleanor's. "If it's who I think it is, we have a big problem."

Constable Biggar's face grew solemn. He hoped the call to Rose Hill was about a runaway. He looked at Matron and reached for her telephone.

"Sergeant McPhee, Constable Biggar here. We need a second car dispatched immediately to the area around the high school on Birch Street. We're looking for a black car, possibly a Buick. Lots of chrome. Suspect maybe on foot. Black overcoat, thirty to thirty-five, six feet. A young woman is missing from Rose Hill Home. Five five with short dark hair, wearing a long grey coat. I'll update you from the call box near the school in about thirty minutes."

Amelia hunkered down as the darkness closed around her. She stuffed her white wool hat in her pocket. *Better to be unseen than warm.* The black Buick crept past Rose Hill just as she'd rounded the corner. Now she was trapped behind the apartment building, paying dearly for a quick walk at dusk. She struggled to keep still but the cold was becoming unbearable. Crouched deep inside a dense hedge of dogwood and junipers, she was hidden by the same branches that bloodied her face. Blood trickled down her cheek, her ears were freezing but she kept her hands in her pockets, frightened the slightest sound would give her away. She was terrified to make a run for it down the street and furious with herself for being so foolish.

Sarah paced round and round the dining room table. Amelia was out there being stalked by a total nutcase and she was doing absolutely nothing. She made a dash for the front door. Eleanor grabbed her from behind just as the deadbolt clicked open.

"What are you doing?"

"I'm a decoy. He'll chase me."

"Do you really think he's looking at our front door? And what if he grabs you, too?"

"I'll scream and AM'll run into the house."

"And you know she's near the front of the house?" Eleanor exhaled and shook her head in disbelief.

"No, but..."

"Let's not add to the problem. Stay inside and let the police do their work."

Reluctantly, Sarah joined the others who looked scared stiff.

Constables Biggar and Adams crossed the street toward the shed. Neither man spoke. Hand and arm signals from here on. The nearest street light was burned out, leaving them with two flashlight beams. As they approached the shed, raspy creaks followed by bangs cut through the night air. The door was swinging open. It could be a decoy or ambush.

Adams backed by Biggar, stood to the side of the open door and commanded, "This is the city police. I'm not alone. Come out, hands up." Neither the first nor second call produced results.

Inside, they found an assortment of rusting gardening tools, push mowers with dried grass on the blades and two damaged school desks hiding nothing but layers of dust and cobwebs. A narrow window ledge displayed an accumulation of flying insects, all in their final resting place.

Quickly abandoning the shed, Adams continued down the narrow alley around the back of the church while Biggar crossed in front of the church to check out the west side parking lot and meet Adams at the church's side door.

Finding the church grounds deserted, they opened the side door and ducked behind the closest row of pews. An overpowering fragrance of lilies permeated the church interior, telling both men there had been a funeral earlier in the week.

Lilies and death mingled in Biggar's mind. *Hope it's not an omen.* He looked up to see Adams behind a row of pews across the centre aisle. They took turns moving up the rows toward the wooden communion rail with its red velvet padded step for kneeling parishioners. The baskets of lilies were inside the rail. The cloying scent made Biggar nauseous. He fought to focus on the job at hand. They appeared to be the only ones inside the sanctuary. Biggar, familiar with the church floor plan, edged to the right wall where there was a short hallway to the church office and private door to the outside. Adams trailed behind, scanning three sixty degrees as he moved forward.

Once outside, they checked the treed parking lot again, shining lights up the trees then vacated the church lot and walked toward the school. Perhaps the other constables had better luck. Voices drifted toward Biggar and Adams as they approached the other constables in the schoolyard. Neither felt reassured by what they heard.

Biggar used the call box to speak with Sergeant McPhee. "Nobody in or around the church. The car wasn't in the parking lot or on the street. We found a couple of cars near the school but they were empty and didn't match the description. Looks like he got away soon after he arrived. The young woman isn't here either."

McPhee replied a wider search for the car would be underway immediately.

All four men spread out and began a second sweep of the school grounds, speaking with each other as they moved across frozen ground and around mounds of snow. They hadn't rooted out the man, but intended to find the young woman if she had

avoided capture and could hear them. After that, they had to
believe she was already in the black car.

Biggar and his companions returned to stand in front of the
church. All were reluctant to call it quits but could see no ratio-
nale for going over the territory a third time.

Biggar put a cap on the search. "If she didn't hear us in the
last fifteen minutes, she's not close enough. I'm afraid we have
to call it off, fellas. I'm going to shut that shed door and speak
with Matron. I'll meet you in there, Adams."

Biggar was a whistler. Fellow officers frequently ribbed him
about how loud he whistled when he was deep in thought. By
the time he reached the shed, it was ear-splitting. It was a mir-
acle he actually heard Amelia's cry for help.

At supper three apple pies glowed with an odd assortment
of birthday candles resurrected from the back of a kitchen
drawer. Amelia was safe. It was a party, except for Amelia and
Sarah who knew better. It wasn't over yet.

Matron skipped the pie and sat in her office. She needed
to figure out how to deal with a man who would hunt another
human being. She must get Amelia's help but that too was a
problem. Maybe Sarah was the key.

As 'lights out' was called, Sarah and Amelia were huddled
on Sarah's bed wondering what to do next.

"What if you give the police his name?"

"I'd have to testify. Would they really lock him up for what
happened today? If so, how long?" She hesitated a moment. "I
should leave here."

"And go where?"

It was an unsolvable problem that put everyone in Rose Hill
at risk.

Chapter Fourteen

January 20, 1961
Halifax, Nova Scotia

Andy and Wendell had a Friday night 'boys night in' with Alexander Keith's beer and fish and chips from Fishy's Take Out. The evening began with a spirited exchange comparing the Toronto Maple Leafs and Montreal Canadiens hockey teams. Then it moved on to work and Andy's encounter at Rose Hill.

"I thought I had the perfect chance to speak with the matron but she told me to take a hike."

"Why would she do otherwise? You were in a home for unwed mothers during a medical crisis. You're lucky she didn't toss you out right after you arrived!"

"But I wanted to talk about helping the women in there."

"Can you hear yourself? You know about the place and have some vague ideas in your head. It makes perfect sense to you. But my friend, it made no sense at all to her. You did the good Samaritan thing and showed up at her door. You're a young guy she's never seen before. End of story. Don't you get it yet?"

"Well, a least she could have heard me out."

"Why? It's still about you. Turn it around. You have friends over for supper and a salesman comes to the door. Do you spend time with him or politely send him on his way so you can be with your friends?"

Wendell heard a reluctant grunt.

"It sounds to me like Rose Hill's taking over a big part of your life."

"No. I talked to Mrs. P and I see Aunt Helen and Liz tomorrow. That's all."

"Come on. What do you really think's going to happen?"

"Yeah well, those girls shouldn't miss out on education or something meaningful to do."

"So who says none of them are doing anything meaningful? Take that girl on the ferry. She might be doing something arty."

The longer they talked, the more concerned Wendell became. Andy continued to circle back to Rose Hill. At midnight they called it quits and pulled down the Murphy bed for Wendell.

Wendell was worried about his longtime friend. Lately, his family problem increasingly dominated social outings. Wendell was sure Liz had a great deal to do with his obsession about Rose Hill. He, Jane and Norma agreed the fixation had escalated after meeting the teenager on the ferry. They agreed to tackle the problem after Andy returned from Wolfville.

Andy laid in bed, his thoughts turning to Liz. Three years apart, they grew up together in an easy, natural relationship. Now, time together was almost non-existent and always awkward. Mother and dad were taboo topics.

Seeing Sarah's mother had reminded him of his own mother and his recent visit. He winced simply remembering their time together. She always managed to deliver sharp jabs and intentional barbs. He wanted to be calm but dreaded another lecture. When the topic of Liz entered the discussion, Andy bit his tongue and tried to remain positive.

"So, how is your sister, Elizabeth? I'm sure she's the main reason you're here."

"She's still working for the insurance company in the Valley. Aunt Helen told me she's painting again."

"Don't the insurance people know what she did? Her reputation will ruin them!"

He retaliated. "What she did Mother, was have a baby almost four years ago. That's not a crime." He took a deep breath and charged on. "At times she's angry with me. Most of the time she's distant, doesn't want me to visit." He paused and lowered his voice. "She's certainly not the sister I knew growing up. I think she's very unhappy. I want to change that."

"She should be happy? How nice for her! She's a disgrace to this family. I'm sure people talk behind my back. Having a baby and no husband is not what society expects of young ladies. Coffee?"

"So I take it that you're still not willing to talk with her on the phone?" He couldn't keep the sarcasm out of his voice.

"You are getting dangerously close to being disrespectful Andrew. Your Aunt Helen's occasional cards keep me informed so I see no urgent need to speak with her. Elizabeth made her bed so now she can lie in it. Fortunately, her father is no longer alive to be humiliated."

She rose to stand at the window, her back to Andy. "I'm the only one who has to suffer the indignity of her behavior." She turned around to serve the coffee. "By the way, why do you continue to talk to her if she's so nasty with you?"

"She's still my little sister who was sent to a home for unwed mothers then banished from returning. I want her in my life again."

"Coming home would be a constant reminder to everyone, including her. Now, she is able to live her life without any reminders of her mistake. It's easy for you to be so forgiving. You're not her mother." She returned to her chair.

"But, she deserves to have fun and friends. I don't think that's happening."

"I hope you haven't told your friends about her past. They'll judge you by her. And by the way, Andrew, do try to keep your personal life above reproach. I won't have a second family disgrace. You too can be 'banished' as you call it. Of course, it would be much easier to deal with a young man's misstep."

Andy woke worried. So far, Liz had not called to cancel his visit. He wanted to get out of the house before the phone rang.

Wendell was already in the kitchen, singing along with 'Bye Bye Love' cranked up on the radio. Coffee bubbled in the glass knob of the aluminum percolator. Toast, strawberry jam, corn flakes and milk were on the table.

"What's up today?" He asked as Wendell jived across the room, holding a slice of toast.

"I promised to help Norma and Jane shop for a television." He reached for the radio and turned down the volume.

"Lucky you! Those ruddy wood cabinets weigh a ton."

"I agreed only if the store delivers. Weather sounds good for your drive."

"Yeah. After breakfast I'll drop you off home on the way out of town."

"Sounds good."

Andy dreaded going to Wolfville. In early December Liz refused to see him saying she had no intention of dredging up feelings and memories best forgotten. In a parting shot, she told him she'd had more than enough of his lectures about doing the right thing with their mother.

Dad continued to be a 'no talk' zone with her during the past two years. Andy expected time would smooth over their cold war. But, like all cold wars, smoothing over was not a last-ing solution. He berated himself for being a coward during the few times they spoke.

His stomach began to feel queasy. A shiver raced through his body leaving him cold and dizzy. He pulled off the high-way, struggled out of the car and threw up. Then gagged at the stench of bread, milk and corn flakes steaming in the ditch. He returned to the car and turned the heater on full blast. His first thought was to run. Perhaps to Amherst and see Della? Maybe back to Halifax? He dropped his head on the steering wheel hoping for relief from the fear of facing what waited in Wolfville.

"Sir, you okay in there?"

Andy lifted his head to see a Mountie peering into the car. The cruiser was parked behind him, lights flashing.

Damn. He wound down the window and replied, "Yes, of-ficer."

"Driver's Licence and insurance, sir. Pretty cold to be sit-ting on the side of the road. You lost, sir?"

"No, just taking a rest." Andy handed over the documents.

The officer checked the paperwork and handed it back. "Where are you heading, sir?"

"Wolfville," he blurted, surprising himself.

"Drive safely, sir."

Committed to his accidental reply, Andy pulled onto the highway and began a pep talk. *Be sure to listen. Find common ground.*

As the miles rolled up on the odometer, his broken rela-tionship with Liz slipped into the shadows. His father used the word 'gumption' many times. Today, he would practice it. This visit, this day he would act with courage and understanding.

Wolfville came into view. After passing the movie the-ater, he turned left and arrived at Aunt Helen's in minutes. He knocked then stepped inside the sun porch. The resident tab-bies, Angus and Aggie each claimed one of the armchairs. His greeting 'Hi, tabs', warranted cursory squints then a return to the task at hand. Nothing but an open can of salmon could halt a nap. Miniature watercolours and framed black and white photographs decorated the walls and small tables.

"I'm here." Andy moved through the hall toward the aroma from the kitchen. Scones were a weekend staple at Aunt Helen's.

Helen wrapped her arms around him. "Hi. I've missed you. Phone calls are not good enough. How are you?"

"Pretty good and sure glad to be here." He returned her embrace adding a peck on her cheek.

"How about a cheddar and apple scone with a cup of tea. I was going to take a break anyway. Liz will be back from her art group in a few more minutes."

"How's that going?"

"Really well but she's modest. It's good to see her active in the community. Let me wash my hands. Go have a look at my latest effort in the studio. Tell me what you think. Be prepared, it's rather large."

Helen's creative talent had an impact on everyone who set foot in her studio. Her tour de force was local landscapes. Each piece had an melancholy character, evoking memories and feelings for those lost in the scenery. Andy sauntered into the studio... he was twelve again, on the shore at Minas Basin.

Helen called from the kitchen, "So, what do you think?"

"Wow, I'm a kid again. Warm mud squishing between my toes, a summer sun on my back, a blue plastic bucket in my hand."

Helen moved into the studio. "So it speaks to you. That's what I was striving for with this piece."

He nodded. "And it sure is big. Guess it had to be, eh? Low tide at Minas Basin doesn't fit on an eight by ten canvas. Very impressive, Miss Johnson."

They settled at the small round wood table to eat. "So how are things in Halifax?"

A shout came from the front porch. "I'm back."

The front door clicked shut then footsteps echoed down the hall. Liz was home and Andy's stomach churned. His big test was about to begin. He took a deep breath, stood up and smiled as Liz entered the room.

"Andy." Her demeanour was calm and collected, green eyes unsmiling. She pushed her sleeves up and shoved her hands deep into the corduroy pants pockets. The signal was clear. No hug for you today.

"Hi. It's great to see you. Aunt Helen says you're taking an art class."

Helen stood and took a step toward the kitchen. "I'll bring you a scone and tea. How was the class today?"

"The class was good but I'm not sure I am. Need help?" She twisted her blonde ponytail into a bun and plopped cross-legged in an armchair showing her red slipper socks.

"No, no. That's okay. I'll be back in a minute. You and Andy start planning our evening. How about the university basketball game?"

"Interested?" Andy prayed she'd agree so they could start the weekend in a neutral setting. He sat on the edge of his chair, leaned toward her.

"Not really. I thought you were here to talk. It's what you do best."

"I'm here to talk but the game would break the ice."

"Break the ice? This isn't a date, for heaven's sake. I'm prepared to suffer through your latest lecture right here, right now." Her face pinched, eyes narrowed.

"Come on, Liz. Be reasonable, please."

"I am reasonable. I let you come this time because of Aunt Helen, didn't I? She hasn't seen you since July. I'm not totally self absorbed." She pulled down her sweater sleeves and crossed her arms. Her face lost none of its resolute stare.

"Lower your voice, please. I've never thought of you as self absorbed, ever."

"A platitude? That's encouraging." The clipped tone continued.

"I'm troubled you would even think that."

"Right. Proves to me yet again, the past four years have been solely about you."

"Me? I'm not the enemy here. It's never been about me except my struggle to get you reconciled with the family."

"Ah, yes. The family. That would be the family that sent me to Rose Hill followed by an exile. You can't possibly think...." She stopped as Helen entered the room.

"Well you two are still talking. That's a good sign." Helen placed more scones and Liz's cup on the table. "Back in a second with tea." She returned and couldn't miss the phony smiles exchanged across the room. "So what's the plan for the remainder of the afternoon and evening?"

Andy jumped in with a response. "None so far." He suddenly realized he'd given Liz an opening to suggest he return to Halifax. "Any ideas?"

Helen recognized a blow-up on its way. "I have a photo showing with a light reception at the university library from three to five. We could go together, have dinner later. My treat. Too boring?"

"Sounds good to me. Liz?"

"Sure. Why not." Her expression relayed reluctant participation.

"Done. I'll make a reservation for six o'clock."

"I'm still working on my photography skills. Maybe you can give me pointers one weekend in the summer?"

Liz glared but remained quiet. It wasn't her place to deny Andy's access to Aunt Helen.

"Sounds good. We need more milk. Back in a jiff." Helen returned to the kitchen muttering, "This is going to be tougher than I thought."

Helen 'Ginger' Johnson, age forty-six was a nurse by profession and artist by passion. She had very little in common with her older sister Jean, mother of Andy and Liz. She'd always loved them as though they were her own and worried about their futures, set adrift from parents and apart from each other.

While getting ready for the photo event, Liz's mind went off task. It hurled her into the past, to the time she was in the hospital, her baby girl was being carried away. The suffocating loss overshadowed her life and the present moment.

Helen breezed into her room and exclaimed, "Hey miss, get your act together. We've got to be at the university in twenty minutes. Grab your long brown plaid skirt and tan sweater. My dangly wooden earrings and necklace will work perfectly."

"You're wearing a red dress! That's gutsy." Liz couldn't resist smiling.

"It's the artist in me. I know the rules about gingers wearing red but fashion rules are made to be broken and I'm just the gal to do it. See you downstairs in ten minutes. Hustle your bustle, girlie."

After the final guest left the reception, Helen, Andy and Liz packed the photos into the Bug and returned them to the house. A dusting of snow convinced them a walk down town was the best way to enjoy the wintry evening in the glow of street and porch lights.

The old home turned restaurant was alive with chatter. They hung their coats in the front entrance and were greeted by the server.

"Good evening, Helen. Great to see you again. Brought the kids with you, I see."

"Hi, Tony. You know Liz, of course and this is my nephew Andy, up from Halifax. I don't think you've met."

"Nice to meet you, Andy. The usual table in the alcove is set up. Tonight's special is baked ham with scalloped potatoes and glazed carrots. Lemon meringue pie for dessert. I'll be right over with the menus."

"You two want an appetizer? How about oysters, Andy?"

"Sure. Haven't had raw oysters since the last time I was here."

"How can you two eat those things? They look like you-know-what on a half shell."

"What?"

"You know, somebody blew their nose there."

"That's gross."

"They are gross."

"You don't chew it. Let it slide down your throat."

"Even worse. I'll have shrimp and dip, thanks."

Helen was grateful for the light conversation, mostly be-tween herself and Andy, about the Halifax storm, work, pho-tography and art. She'd experienced enough family laundry aired in public to last a lifetime. Living away from her sister was a blessing she enjoyed every day. When she mentioned Big Minas was almost complete, Andy asked about the name.

"Well, I reasoned anything that big should have a name so I nicknamed it Big Minas. We've spent so much time together, it's like a member of the family. I can't imagine anyone buying it with that name so I have to come up with a sensible one. If either of you have any ideas, I'd love to hear them.

Andy volunteered. "Muddy Toes wouldn't work, right?"

"Probably not so keep thinking."

As they walked home, Andy carried a sense of forebod-ing. A difficult but necessary discussion must begin once they reached the house. The outcome was uncertain.

Just inside the door, Liz made her move. "That was a good evening. I've had a full week so I'm off to bed. See you both in the morning."

Helen intervened. "I'd prefer you not do that, dear. I would like to speak to you and Andy together. I have thoughts I'd like you to hear. Let's go into the living room. Maybe it's time to open that bottle of brandy. Andy, can you do the honours? I'll light the fireplace."

Within minutes, Angus and Aggie appeared at the door and took over prime spots on the mat directly in front of the fire-place.

Helen shook her head and laughed, "Little opportunists." She stared at the amber liquid, savoured a sip and began the conversation.

"Both of you know I'm not into avoiding problems. I have to get things off my chest. Tonight is a perfect opportunity for us to talk about our relationships with each other. They have changed during the past four years. I love both of you but at times feel I've lost touch. I don't like it one bit."

She moved her gaze slowly from one to the other and began again. "I want to talk about how together, we can make our relationships better. I'll start with my angle on things."

She turned toward Liz. "Liz, when you arrived four years ago you were angry and sad. I do see flashes of happiness. I cannot change what happened to you but I do truly want to help you make your life more fulfilled. Honestly, I don't know what more I need to do. I need help."

She shifted her position to face Andy. "It's been difficult to connect with you during the past two years. Consequently, I'm out of your life more than in it. I don't like that one bit either."

She rose and stood in front of the fireplace. "Each of you has disconnected with the other too. I don't see either of you re-establishing a strong connection with your mother soon or maybe ever. This is regrettable but understandable. So, in the absence of that parental guidance and support, I am willing to have a more important role in your lives. But, if and only if, this is something you are willing to consider. Thoughts?"

"I would like to talk about it for sure. What do you think, Liz?" Andy's look received a blank stare as her back stiffened against the chair.

She exploded. "How dare you two plot this little game to get me!"

"Andy and I are not conspiring on some plan about you. He's here to visit."

Andy responded, "I am here to see both of you but I want it to be more than a visit."

"I knew it. Another lecture. I'm outta here." Liz jumped to her feet scaring Angus and Aggie to parts unknown.

"Please sit and hear me out. This is going to be difficult."

Helen leaned forward and placed her elbow on the armrest. She exhaled deeply as her chin came to rest on her hand. Her eyes were riveted on Andy. She had no idea what to expect next from either of them.

Liz returned to her vacated chair, crossed her arms, glanced at her watch. "I'm giving you each two minutes, starting now. Who's first?"

Andy swallowed hard and began. "During the past few weeks I've realized I'm a tormented person. I'm preoccupied with fixing something that happened in the past. I've accepted I can't continue like this. It's taking me nowhere."

Liz jumped in. "You're talking in riddles. What are you saying?"

"Here's the thing. I've beaten myself up about not helping you." He stared at Liz.

Liz was on her feet. "Stop right there, mister. Don't make this about me. I've got my own problems but I did not, I repeat did not, create yours. You own that yourself. I should have gone to bed earlier but I sure am now." She moved toward the door.

"Please, please let me finish."

Helen was on her feet, desperate to find common ground. "Liz, sit for me, please. I planned to work up to this but plunging in now seems the solo option."

Andy had wanted to get everything off his chest but his conviction faltered. Now Helen was about to expose something. He had no idea what was coming so he better stop whatever it was. He grabbed the brandy for courage and gulped. Heat scorched through his chest evaporating his breath. His eyes watered. He opened his mouth to speak. A raspy croak sputtered past his lips followed by a feeble squeak. His moment was gone.

"I couldn't trust my parents. Now you're in cahoots with him." Liz waved her finger at Andy. "This is beyond belief."

"There is no cahoots here. All I'm asking is you allow me tell you a story. Then we can see where the conversation goes. Okay?" Helen sat, hoping Liz would too.

"Go ahead. I'm still suspicious and will leave if a sniff of trouble comes my way." She sat on the edge of her chair.

Helen leaned forward and clasped her hands together. She looked briefly at Andy, met Liz's eyes with her own for a few moments then lowered her head.

"Liz, your father and I had a standing phone call date about you every three weeks after you moved in with me. He went to his friend Jack's house and called to check up on you. He made me promise to tell nobody, especially you. In the first months, the calls were very brief. I think he was afraid to trust his resistance to come here. He understood you carried anger towards he and your mother so didn't push a visit. He was unsuccessful in convincing your mother to allow you a visit home. Your cards seemed to be sufficient for her. As the months passed, he became more curious about your daily life but always, always seeking confirmation you were okay." She kept her head down, not wanting a glance at Liz to force a response.

Liz shifted back into her chair but said nothing.

Helen continued, "I believe you know your parents paid for your room, board and education. Your dad always added what he called fun money for you to participate in activities with your high school friends."

Helen lifted her head, massaged her forehead then looked at Liz. "It must have been heartbreaking for him. He never stopped loving you, never stopped worrying about you, never stopped wanting you to have a happy life. I want you to know he was very proud of your success in school and work. In June of last year, we decided he would meet you on the Island in July. We picked a small town where neither of you would be recognized. I was to make sure no one on the ferry got close enough to recognize you. We settled on July fifteenth. A friend from out of town was visiting your mother. She would not question your father taking the afternoon away from their conversation which he jokingly called gab, gossip and grub. Your dad was buried the afternoon he would have spent with you." She waited for the explosion.

Liz launched a swift, defensive response. "What do you expect me to say? I'm in a small hole with no light from any direction. That's how you feel after four years of rejection. I'm grateful dad supported me but my life for the future is what you see today. Did you really expect me to say my life is now miraculously changed with a revelation that dad continued to care for me? Nothing will change. I'm going to bed. I can't handle any more of this."

Andy opened his mouth to tell his stories but felt his resolve dissolve. He took a small, slow sip of brandy and declared, "Liz, I want to be your light."

"What a goofy thing to say. You're drunk, aren't you?"

"No, just tiddly but I want things to get better."

Helen spoke quickly. "Let's agree we've made a start and promise to talk over breakfast. Promise?" She received two brief nods and went to bed worried.

Chapter Fifteen

January 22, 1961
Wolfville, Nova Scotia

Helen reached for the coffee and spoke to Liz who leaned against the kitchen counter, arms crossed.

"You surprised me with your comment last night. Talk to me about today being your future. I want you to see the world, meet people, have adventures."

"I know I sounded ungrateful but some days life is too much for me. The future? I think it is more of the same."

Helen's response was halted by a shout from the top of the stairs. "Overslept. Give me five."

She raised her voice to Andy, "No problem," then softened it to Liz. "Today's a new day. I want to help you live for the future. This morning we all need to try a little harder. Are you willing to try?"

"Andy's anxious to go back in time but I can't go back. My life changed forever four years ago. Why can't he accept that?" Liz sighed heavily. "But for you, I'll listen to him and try to be calm. No promises though."

"That's all I can ask for."

They busied themselves setting the table and getting bacon, milk, blueberries and pancake mix on the counter.

Andy bounced into the kitchen. "Sorry, I'm late. The Valley air must have knocked me out."

Helen laughed. "Oh, I'm pretty sure the brandy did that. Liz, you're the bacon gal. Make sure you save some for the furries or you'll never be forgiven. Andy and I are on blueberry pancake duty. Maple syrup and butter are on the table. Let's get started."

Within minutes, the aroma of bacon and pancakes wafted through the house. Liz felt fur rub against her ankles. Angus and Aggie voiced their presence and sat expectantly beside their bowls.

At the table, the silence was filled with contented sighs and the occasional 'yummy'. Helen felt the pressure of time to get last night's topic started. She eased into it. "So Andy, you slept like a log?"

"Sure did. That stuff has a knock out punch."

"Liz?"

"I tossed around for quite a while."

"Maybe tonight will be better. Let's put the dishes in the sink to soak and move into the living room with coffee."

Liz felt she was walking toward the witness box. An inquisition was about to begin. Her restless sleep did nothing for her confidence to hold it together. She wrapped the crocheted throw around her shoulders and curled into an armchair, suited up to defend herself.

Andy shuffled down the hall in his thick wool socks, organizing his thoughts enroute. He faced the final chance to convince Liz of his sincerity. He was worried by her chippy attitude and fierce desire to be left alone.

Helen was followed into the room by Angus and Aggie who went to the fireplace. They sat staring into it as if by sheer willpower they could bring forth its sleep inducing warmth. She lit kindling and watched the flames curl around the logs. "Andy, I think you wanted to tell us a couple of stories last night. Why don't you start with them."

"Okay. Dad never spoke ill of you, Liz. He was a quiet, private person but I have absolutely no doubt he thought of you every day after you left home."

"Come on. Gimme a break. How do you really know that?"

"Because we often talked in person and on the phone. Our mother though, is a difficult person."

"That's an understatement. On top of every awful thing she's done to me, she wouldn't let me go to dad's funeral."

Ignoring her caustic tone, he continued. "I believe dad had a difficult life with her but he really cared about us. I have no expectation you'll reconcile with mother."

"At least we agree on that. By the way, what about the stories?"

"I do want you to think kindly about dad and I've two stories about him that will help you do that. The first one is about our Christmas tree hunt. It was the first Christmas you weren't with us. The second is about his death." He sipped coffee and glanced at Liz who displayed no emotion.

"Dad and I continued our annual Christmas tree hunt tradition after you left home."

"Let's get this straight. I did not leave home. I was sent away and not allowed to return, ever."

"You're right. Poor choice of words. As usual, we went to Jack's farm, hitched Hansen to the sleigh and headed into the wooded area at the back of the farm. Once in the woods, dad began to talk. When he began I sensed he'd given lots of thought about what he was to tell me. He started by saying we should walk into the woods on a warm summer day, tie a ribbon on a good lookin' tree and be done with it. Then he chuckled and said that would kill our family Christmas tradition and he liked tradition." He looked at Helen and received a smile and nod.

"We created a fresh path toward the large stand of trees in the south-west corner of the property line. The stream ambled its way toward the river and on to the village two miles away. Inside the little wood, the world was still and all the spruce trees looked perfect in their white winter coats. With a solid shake, the snow dropped from the boughs and all was revealed. Dad gazed at a eight foot tree and proclaimed, 'There isn't a perfect one, you know. It's like life. It isn't perfect either. Son, I need to tell you something before it's too late. But first, we'll cut this eight-footer about two feet off the ground. The wood creatures will put the stump to good use. Several young spruce are already growing nearby.'

"We bundled the spruce for carrying and dad continued his story." 'My younger sister, Margaret had a baby a long time ago. She was a few years older than our Liz when it happened to her. The guy ran off after he found out she was pregnant. Your grandfather had a cousin without children up in the western part of the Island so Margaret went there. The story they told was that she was going to help her cousin Isabel with a new baby. A few months later, Margaret returned home. She was so changed I could hardly believe she was my sister. From then on, she had a sadness about her that never went away. Her spirit was broken. She rarely went out, never married and died at age thirty-four. I think she died of a broken heart. People laugh at a notion like that but not me. So, I hope you see why I'm worried about Liz. Your mother doesn't know about my sister. She's a hard woman and believes her way is right. I don't always agree but there's no arguing with her. I send money to Helen for Liz. The two of us are in a conspiracy of sorts. Someday I hope Liz will see me. I fear she will never agree to see her mother but I can't change that. I'm asking you to keep this to yourself, including not telling your mother. When I'm gone, I want you to watch over Liz. Don't worry, Andy, I'm not leaving any time soon.'

Andy directed his gaze toward Liz. "I want you to see why I must do everything possible to reestablish our relationship. Dad asked me to do something. I don't want to let him down." Liz said nothing.

"The next story is more difficult so give me a moment." Andy held his coffee mug in both hands and concentrated on the fire. Wood crackled as a log snapped in two and another settled in the open space. Sparks flew up the chimney. After a few moments he lifted his head, removed his glasses and wiped both eyes with the back of his hand.

"Dad died on Sunday, July 12 just before two o'clock. He collapsed into the captain's chair in the kitchen just after lunch. The ambulance took him to the hospital in city. I drove like a mad man to the ferry but I was too late to say 'good-bye'. The next three days were filled with preparation, people and a funeral. I shuffled through all of it. People arrived and people departed morning, noon and night. Home was a railway station with a heavy scent of lilies. Mother's advice to 'keep a stiff upper lip' was her way of coping but it didn't change a darn thing for me. Dad was gone. I was alone. The funeral is a blur. The best way I can describe it is a mix of bagpipes, words, lots of heartfelt handshakes and embraces. The following day, I went to the cemetery alone and began a lonely walk toward the Memory Garden section in the far corner of the property. Along the way, fresh flowers in vases swayed gently in the breeze and wafted fragrances into the warm summer air. All the while, Mother Nature was quietly working her unstoppable life cycle. In a few days, the summer sun would reduce the vibrant red, yellow and purple petals to muted pastels. They would curl, drop silently to earth and drift away with the breeze. I sat on the concrete bench under the sugar maple near dad's grave and cried my eyes out. The grave was identified by a paper marker, James Andrew MacNeil 1915-1957. New sod appeared out of place with the established grass. I too felt out of place and truthfully, unhinged. Honey bees whirred among the snapdragons and asters. They were completely focused on their sole purpose in life. I smiled for the first time in days. I don't know how long I sat there but eventually calmness settled over me. I thought about dad and my future without him. At some point I got the message. I'd never really thought about what I wanted in life. I was busy with work and friends. I'd convinced myself all the activity counted for something. I left the cemetery with many questions about myself." Andy sat still, eyes on the carpet.

Helen broke the silence. "So what's happened since? Any answers?"

"The beginnings are there. I'm pretty sure my friends think I've been a little nutty recently but, so far, they haven't been blunt about it. Knowing them, that won't last much longer." He chuckled.

"What are you a 'little nutty' about or is that too personal?"

"It's pretty much about relationships."

Liz was quick to get into the discussion. "Wait. Is this about me again?"

"No, not entirely."

"That's a refreshing change. Who else is on the radar here?"

"One is Della and the other, Sarah."

This time it was Helen's turn to have an opinion. "Don't tell me I'm being asked to offer relationship advice. I'm definitely not the best person to ask. You both know that. My track record isn't stellar."

"No, not really. Della is a friend in Amherst. Sarah is in Rose Hill."

Liz shot him a stinging look. A deep crease formed between her eyebrows. "Rose Hill! What's going on here? You're totally, absolutely unbelievable."

"Wait. Wait. Wait. Hold on a minute, please. Hear me out. Here's the short version on Sarah. I met her on the ferry earlier this month. I spoke to her then realized she was very angry with her parents. I overheard her mother mention Rose Hill. I know Rose Hill changed you. Since then I've been trying to find some way to make things better in there. Any thoughts?"

The room fell silent. Liz's reply would be the turning point in this conversation. The fire paused its crackling for a moment before a log dropped into the inferno, sending a wave of heat into the room. Andy massaged his forehead and brushed the perspiration aside. Helen held her breath.

"First off, why is this Sarah so important? You met her on the ferry. What does that have to do with me? Oh, and by the way, I didn't ask for your help. You better explain this urge to be a hero."

Both Liz and Helen were riveted on Andy's face. He softly recounted the events during the snowstorm and his time inside Rose Hill. When he finished, neither spoke. Eventually Helen asked quietly, "What happened to Alice and her baby?"

Andy shook his head. "I don't know but it didn't look good. The whole thing rattled me to the core. I must do something. Was there anything you would have liked while at Rose Hill? Maybe I can work on that. Anything."

Liz leaned forward and spoke matter-of-factly. "It wasn't summer camp, Andy."

The clipped tone jarred his thoughts. He opened his mouth to respond but he was cut off as she continued. "There's nothing you can do for a place like that. Society has judged unmarried mothers for decades. Girls are hidden for months until the baby is taken away. Homes like Rose Hill are seen as the answer to a problem." Her words had lost their anger but were firm, tinged with reluctant acceptance. "I was told to take on a new name and not make any friends. They totally striped me of my self-worth, my identity. When it was over, I was told to go home and forget everything, return to a normal life." She stared into the distance. "Except I'm suffering a lifetime of exile and unpredictable feelings. I don't trust people so how can I have a relationship with anyone? I lost my baby girl. I'll never hold her again. Never know her." Tears rolled down her face.

Helen and Andy knelt in front of her.

"You both remember me as a seventeen year old. Maybe you believe that's who I still am, just an older version. But, I'm not. I lost that person long ago. I'm a lifetime away from who you think I am. I don't feel part of what's going on around me. I can't relate to it but I'm pretty good at mimicking normal, whatever that is." She gulped her coffee. "I was destroyed by being locked away from society, not allowed to make choices. At first, I had hope but then anger. In the end, hopelessness won out." She stared at the fire, cheeks flushed. "Now, there are the sudden flashbacks that jump into my mind from nowhere. To cope, I've become numb, given up. It's safer that way." She closed her eyes. "I can't help you, Andy. I can't even help myself."

Andy and Helen returned to their chairs. Andy was the first to speak.

"I think you just did. Getting art or music classes into Rose Hill seems trivial now. Can I help you in some way?"

"Not today." Her voice weak, all energy spent.

"You are brave. I don't know what else to say except I'm still your brother and I care about you. I love you."

The uncomfortable silence was broken by Helen who took a deep breath and asked, "What's the story on Della?"

"She's a gal who owns a restaurant in Amherst. Smart and funny. I really enjoy her company. I would like her to meet you both. I could bring her here. What do you say?"

"Fine by me. Liz?"

"Why not. She'd probably enjoy a weekend in Wolfville. Always something going on here."

"Thanks. I don't want to leave but I better get going. I'm going to the Island, taking the highway through the Rawden Hills."

Liz and Helen stood on the front steps and waved good bye to Andy shortly after eleven-thirty. Helen put her arm around Liz's waist.

"You've had a tough morning. It's hard to open yourself to others, especially family."

"It's strange. I'm drained but sort of at ease with it. Maybe I'll wake up tomorrow right back where I was."

"Maybe. I'd like to think it's the beginning of release from hurt and fear. They lose their grip when you lean on others you can trust. The load gets lighter. The old expression, 'many hands make light work' is true. It will take time." She hugged Liz. "Let's get at those dishes. I wonder if Andy is going to Amherst for the evening? The sky looks ominous."

"I love you, Auntie Helen."

Andy turned the radio up full blast and drove out of Wolfville relieved that Liz hadn't run him out of town. There was hope. Overnight he'd decided to take Highway 14 toward the Rawden Hills and make a stop in Amherst before heading to PEI.

The wind picked up as he turned onto the highway. Within minutes, snow was peppering the windshield. Not long after, falling and blowing snow reduced his vision. His speed was painstakingly slow with no place to turn around safely and no homes visible through the whiteout conditions. He was breaking trail on a sparsely populated country road. Buffeting winds battered the little car but it clung to the road and moved forward at a snail's pace in first or second gear. Mesmerizing snow played tricks with his eyes but the occasional glimpse of a fence post or tree was a godsend. He drove in the middle of the road and prayed nobody came from the opposite direction.

As the odometer numbers climbed, Andy counted off the miles to reach the intersection with Highway 202. The plows might be clearing snow there. He talked to the Bug, encouraging her to make each incline and hold onto the road without careening out of control into the ditch on the downhill run. The gas tank dipped below the half-way mark. The radio reception became annoying static. He shut it off. Soon he was talking to himself. Another half hour passed.

Just as he thought the daytime nightmare couldn't get worse, brake lights flashed in front of his eyes, then disappeared off the road. He took his foot off the gas, geared down and gingerly steered right. Stopped, he opened the door and was smacked in the face. Icy snow collected on his glasses, blinding him on the spot. He rubbed a gloved hand over the lenses, inched forward then dropped into snow up to his knees. Now in the ditch with the stranded car, he could see it was lying on its' side. Blowing snow collected on the driver's side window and drifted over the roof. The driver's side headlight cast a pale beam of yellow into a wall of white. If anyone survived this crash, how would he possible help them?

He peered into the car. Two terrified eyes stared back. Blood trickled from her scalp to left eyebrow. He cupped his face against the window and shouted, "Can you hear me?" A head nodded once, then the eyes closed. "Can you move your legs?" A nod. "I'm going to open the door." After three robust tugs, it gave way. He smelled gas. Without thinking he bent down and scooped the woman out of the seat. Pure adrenaline propelled him up the bank. Moments later, he had a groggy female as a passenger.

As he eased onto the road, a light flashed in the rear-view mirror. The engine in the ditch was ablaze, sending smoke and flames into the sky. With a passenger slumped against the door, he crept toward Highway 202. He had a human to talk to but he received no coherent answers, only the occasional moan.

Sandy Nicholson worked for the Government of Nova Scotia. His job was to keep the roads and highways safe for travel. Winter could be a challenge and as he said, 'Some days were a bugger.' This was one of those days. He and the other snow plow drivers were losing the battle with snow on Highway 202 between Halifax and Highway 14. He figured north to Amherst was probably the same story. That section would likely remain passable for a couple of hours. Then he expected the RCMP to close the road and he would work overnight. As he approached the intersection with Highway 14, Sandy steered toward the side road to carve out an area for traffic to pull off the highway or make the turn. He looked twice and still couldn't believe his eyes. Coming through the blowing snow off Highway 14 was a red Beetle. He flashed his lights and received one in return.

Later that night, Sandy recounted his experience and how the 2-way radio saved the day. The RCMP cruiser picked up his call and took the young woman to Doc Williams' home office. When asked about the driver, he replied, "It was a young guy called Andy. Said he was heading toward Amherst for an important meeting." Everyone in the coffee room laughed. "Yeah, I asked him the name of the meeting."

In Halifax, Wendell was walking to the Lighthouse for a late Sunday lunch with Norma and Jane. The weather was deteriorating by the hour. He expected Andy had stayed in Wolfville another day. He planned to discuss him in detail with the girls. If Andy showed up, well then he would have to be part of the discussion, like it or not. Inside the restaurant, Norma and Jane were on their second cup of coffee.

"You guys walk?"

"No. We spoiled ourselves and took a cab knowing we'd probably have to walk home. The streets will be a disaster in a couple of hours. What is it with this winter?" Norma didn't expect an answer and didn't get one.

"Heard from Andy this weekend?" Jane inquired.

"No. Sometimes he calls from Helen's house to ask if there's anything happening here with us on Sunday night. I imagine he listened to the weatherman and decided to stay put. Just as well. I plan to tell you my concerns about him. Ready to order?"

After a few mouthfuls of chowder, Wendell began. "We spent Friday evening together and he side stepped my questions about Liz. I think he's convinced he's a total failure with her. Now he's trying to save Sarah, a person he doesn't even know. Just so you know, I'm not doing anything about Rose Hill."

Norma wanted to start with a discussion not a conclusion. "Aren't you jumping ahead of yourself on that?"

"No. You know what he's been like for a few months. It's a lot worse now. We can't act on his crazy idea." Wendell threw his hands in the air. "It's guilt talking, plain and simple."

Norma opened her hands and frowned. "This isn't like you. I agree Andy has been troubled but I sure don't want to be confrontational with him right off the bat."

"I agree with Norma. Doing something helpful for Rose Hill right now is not smart. We need to help him first."

Norma nodded. "You're right, Jane. Telling him we won't help with Rose Hill should not be the first step."

In Amherst, Della looked out the diner window as the blowing snow continued to fall. She could still see down main street. The last few lunch customers told her the highway from Halifax was open, thanks to the plows. They didn't expect the ferry to PEI to be running so they were staying overnight in town and would see her later for supper. She guessed the storm would stop Andy from travelling to the Island for sales calls. She admitted to herself, the more she saw Andy, the more she liked him. She told herself to be sensible. He was a nice guy from Halifax who probably had lots of educated, sophisticated girls to choose from. What would he see in a country bumpkin like her? She glanced at her watch. She'd better get the supper food started. Liver and onions with mashed potatoes and gravy sounded good for a winter night. And for those who held their noses at liver, smothered steak done in the oven.

Shortly after three-thirty, Della was pounding steak in the kitchen and didn't hear the bell over the front door nor foot steps behind her.

"Hi. Need some help?"

She shrieked and dropped the meat pounder on the floor. "Andy, what are you doing here? You scared me half to death." Her hand rapidly patted over her heart.

"Sorry. I was hungry and drove from Wolfville for supper. What's on the menu?"

"Wolfville. Are you nuts? There's a blizzard out there."

"I noticed it a few hours ago. It slowed me down a bit."

"Are you okay, aside from being exhausted?"

"I am now. I need strong coffee. Got a sandwich in the fridge?"

"I'll get you both. Then you are going to tell me what happened on the road while I finish my supper work. Deal?" She grinned.

"Best offer I've had all day." His smile lit up the room.

At eight the customers were gone and Della shut off the lights in the restaurant. The 'closed' neon sign over the front door glowed through the swirling snow. She moved through the dark diner toward Andy who stood at the foot of the stairs leading to the upstairs apartment. Della was happy and terrified at the same time. Throughout the evening she did not speak of the overnight arrangements. She really wanted to know more about him and his family but she didn't know what to do. Mention it and he might assume her unease and tell her he was planning to stay at the hotel. That would pretty much eliminate a good conversation. Not mention it and he might assume the worst about her. She slowed her pace and feigned interest in straightening the already straight chairs. She walked to the front door, re-checked the lock and neon light switch. It was time to say something. She had no idea how to start. A quick tug on the closed drapes and her time was up. Period. No more killing time. She turned toward the stairs.

"I plan to sleep on the couch not the floor, you know. After you, Mademoiselle." He stepped aside and waved his arm in a sweeping motion.

"I have a bottle of red wine. Would you like a glass?"

"Sure but first I have to make two phone calls."

"I'll go into the bedroom."

"No need. One's to Aunt Helen in Wolfville and the other to my buddy Wendell, in Halifax. He'll call my other friends and check on my neighbour, Mrs. P. She's the granny I never had. I'll call the office in the morning."

Della popped the cork on the wine and poured. *So, no special girl to call in Halifax.*

"I'm all yours. Want the record player on? I see you have a photo album on the coffee table. May I?"

"Yes to both. The album's a collection of my family and friends photos. I'll introduce you to everyone."

"I'll have to bring my albums the next time. Whose the little cutie with blonde pigtails and red plaid bows standing between the guy in the wheelchair and the German shepherd?"

"Me when I was five. On one side is Bill, my friend and neighbour. He had polio before I was born. The one in the fur coat is Roger, my dog."

"Tell me about your family and the diner, of course. How did it get started?

"My life story! You sure? It's not exciting."

"What better way to get to know each other? When you're finished, I'll tell you my story. Deal?"

"Deal. Gosh, where do I start. I was born in 1933."

"An older woman. I love it."

"Okay, smarty. If you're going to interrupt at every opportunity, we will be here for hours. And by the way, I'm not that much older, just wiser. My parents were Clifford and Evelyn. We lived on a farm a few miles from Amherst. Dad's club foot and the Great Depression made life a struggle. When I was nine, he sold the farm and we moved to town. He used to say he gave away the farm. Dad became a car salesman."

"Big change for everybody."

"Mom loved town. She joined the weekly quilting group. It was a world of women who shocked and invigorated her, thanks in part to the war. She thought some of the women were downright rebels. But she liked it. Enid Murphy's daughter was serving overseas. Gert Barlow moved to Toronto to work in a manufacturing plant. Joyce Chisholm was preparing to run for a seat in the provincial election."

"How about you?"

"I liked town. I made friends, had places to go and parents who encouraged independence. I have a vivid imagination and rarely kept my opinions to myself. That last part was not always appreciated."

"Your parents are not living?"

"They died in a car accident almost fourteen years ago. I lived with my aunt, uncle and cousin for six years."

"So how did the diner happen?"

"After high school, I went to work as a cashier in the grocery store. I loved the smell of spices, fruit, anything baking and family memories that went along with food preparation and eating. I decided to find mom's recipe books in the attic and started to bake. People began asking me to make goodies for special events. That's when the bug bit. I wanted to work for myself and cooking was the way to do it. I did bridal showers, baby showers, weddings and every other possible event for miles around. Eight years ago, I rented this tiny store front with living quarters upstairs. Wedged between the record store and bank, it seemed an ideal eating spot to do business. The end."

"Worst day since opening?"

"The first day. Boy, it was a shaky one. I was so nervous on opening day, I thought I'd throw up. To boot, I was horrified people would think I was sick on my own food! Your turn."

"Your story is wonderful. Mine is not nearly as exciting. Better fill the wine glasses."

Chapter Sixteen

January 22, 1961
Rose Hill Home

Sarah woke on Sunday filled with excitement for what the day would bring. She gathered her clothes and rushed to the bathroom. In the tub, her worries popped with the bubbles. Her world was finally right side up. Tears of relief spilled down her cheeks. She was light-headed with joy. After breakfast, she would get her hands on the weekend paper. This time, she wouldn't let it out of her sight. She needed that bank address. Tomorrow her letter to Myles would begin its journey. By Thursday, he would call her at Rose Hill.

Sarah closed her eyes and lovingly massaged her stomach as the cocoon of water rolled over her body. She heard Myles' voice utter her name and call her his beautiful girl. She felt his passionate embrace as they nestled together in a quiet restaurant. She saw them wander arm in arm through the streets shopping for rings and a wedding dress with long sleeves and flowing lace.

The water cooled and Sarah stepped out of the tub in a panic, a delightful panic. There was so much to do in a short time. She was dizzy thinking of all the scurrying about they must do in preparation for the wedding...tell her parents, meet Myles' family, find a church, plan a reception? Who would be maid of honour?

Wrapping her arms around the baby, she whispered, "You're going to a wedding, little one!"

Then she spoke softly to Myles. "I should have understood what was happening to you sooner. You were worried about the bank training and new job. Now those problems are gone. It's the ideal time for my letter. A wife and child will be the crowning touch to your achievements. Your family will love me as you do. They will be over the moon about a grandchild on the way. The bad times are finally over."

After dressing, Sarah looked in the mirror and frowned. She had to add pretty maternity clothes to the shopping list. She could hardly wait to give her parents the biggest shock of their lives. She was getting married.

A second celebratory atmosphere enveloped Rose Hill during breakfast. Eleanor and Annie splurged with buttermilk pancakes, crispy bacon and Canadian maple syrup. Amelia was feted with a chocolate cupcake, complete with chocolate icing and yet another candle.

Matron stood quietly in the kitchen. She worried about Amelia. Constable Biggar mentioned nothing beyond an overnight detainment for the angry man. He'd violently resisted arrest following the car chase for a traffic violation. Could charges be laid related to his threatening visit to Rose Hill or the spying episode? Would Amelia have to lay the charges? The whole matter was hard to even imagine being possible, let alone safe, private or successful.

Laughter rippled up the stairs into Debbie's room. It sounded like a party. She stood in front of the mirror, lipstick in hand. Lipstick for the party. Why not? What harm could it cause? As far as she was concerned, she was locked up anyway. She pranced down the stairs and beamed a shockingly bright red smile to everyone in the kitchen.

Karen laid eyes on Debbie's smile and it all fell into place. She was standing inside Woolworth's department store with her friends on a Saturday afternoon in August almost three years ago. It was so hot, her sleeveless blouse stuck to her back and her armpits were dripping wet. But she had a job to do. She sized up the store. Aisles were filled with mothers and excited, noisy children doing their weekend shopping. It was the ideal time to create a distraction and shop without paying. They'd pulled it off several times before. She started an argument with a friend in the group. The clerk sent them outside. During this kerfuffle, the leader of the day pocketed what she wanted and then joined the group outside. They walked to the alley and shared the take, which was usually gum, candy or a comic.

That day, Catherine jumped up and down with glee. She'd scored the mother lode...a small cosmetic case containing red lipstick and nail polish. "I love, love, love red lipstick. It's my favourite. I'll never forget this day."

Karen wondered if Catherine did forget that day. Within the week, she was gone. Town gossip was her oldest sister was fed up with her antics and sent her to live with another sister out of province. Karen couldn't wait to ask 'Debbie' if red was still her favourite lipstick. Gotcha.

After breakfast, Sarah settled into a comfy chair in the sitting room with the business section of the newspaper. Expecting to see Myles' picture and bank advertisement again, she turned the pages hastily. Nothing. Convinced she'd missed it in her hurry, she poured over every page, especially those without a picture. Still nothing.

Beside her, Mary was sipping coffee and reading the society section. She had no reason to know anyone in Halifax but was amused by pictures and stories of big events, engagements and weddings. It was her Sunday morning entertainment.

"Here's a whopper of an wedding story. People are attractive but the name dropping makes this one fun to read. My imagination is running wild with the juicy possibilities behind the words in this one. This girl probably shopped to marry up. I'm going to write a book about this stuff someday."

Sarah poked her in the ribs. "Yes, I can hear it now. Mary the best selling author of stories about society's darkest and spiciest secrets. Names changed to protect the guilty, of course."

"Wow, what a stunning wedding dress. French lace everywhere. Scoop neckline with beads and it's ankle length. That's different. Big crinoline. Swanky. Bride's smile looks real. Groom looks glum. Why would they put that picture in the paper? They must have had a better one. Okay, listen up. Here's the write up. 'Doctor and Mrs. Melvin Ellison are pleased to announce the marriage of their only child, Grace Marie to Myles Alexander, eldest son of Mr. and Mrs. William Alexander.' It goes on to say, 'the happy couple will settle in Halifax where Myles is Assistant Manager at the Regional Head Office of a large national bank'. La-di-da."

Sarah snatched the paper from Mary.

"Hey, what are you doing? I was reading." Mary was miffed and it showed.

"It's him!"

"Him who? What are you muttering about?"

"Nothing important. Here, you can have the paper back. I'm just surprised to see those two are married." Sarah's voice died away at the end of the sentence.

"Yeah? Well, I'm not surprised. Looks like a sizable bump in the front of the wedding dress, if you ask me. Betcha your friends just had a shotgun wedding."

Sarah climbed the stairs by pushing one foot in front of the other, her body along for the ride. No reasonable thoughts passed through her numbed brain. Paralyzed on her bed, she tried to count the flowers on the wallpaper. Anything to hang on to sanity. Over and over, she failed to get past five.

Mary showed Amelia the newspaper and suggested she check on her roommate. "I have no idea why she ran out of the room. Seemed serious though."

Amelia understood immediately. She found Sarah on the bed and pulled a blanket up to her chin. She knew about foul surprises.

"I saw the wedding announcement in the newspaper. Try to sleep. I'll stay for a while and we can talk later."

By lunchtime, there was no denying the obvious. A change in the weather was on its' way. The kitchen door rattled non-stop as the wind carried a violent storm into the city. The clincher was a telephone call from Reverend Miller. He'd heard the weather forecast and decided to cancel the afternoon dis-cussion group. Joan was noticeably unhappy when she heard. She'd been looking forward to getting the good reverend on the hot seat for another grilling.

Sarah slept through lunch. Amelia mentioned to Matron that Sarah was feeling tired and took a sandwich and glass of milk to their room. By mid afternoon, Sarah stirred and opened her eyes. Amelia put down her book and offered the sandwich. Sarah shook her head but eyed the glass.

"I'll have the milk."

"We're in for another storm so no neighbourhood walks today. We'll all be more than a little stir crazy by tomorrow morning. Want to get up?"

"No."

"Okay. This book will keep me occupied for another few hours. I'll pop in between now and supper. You rest."

Snow drifted across the walk and packed against the front door. Matron pushed thoughts of the last storm out of her mind but decided to clear the walk, just in case. Marjorie was due in ten days.

Just before three, Betty stepped out of a taxi carrying a small overnight case. She was back a day early due to the storm. It was a relief to leave the hospital where she was called 'miss' too many times and left unattended on the ward. It hurt to see happy families with babies even though she never intended to keep hers. She inched up the walk not wanting to be inside but knowing the inevitable was about to happen. Matron would be matter-of-fact while the girls would be dying to ask questions. They knew so little, she knew so little... until three days ago. One part of her wanted to tell them everything while the other wanted it flushed from her mind forever. What would be best for her? Either way, she would leave in the morning as planned. Rose Hill would be a dreadful episode she'd amputate from her life. She knocked and was met by Matron who motioned toward the office.

An awkward silence began Betty's meeting with Matron. She fought hard against the urge to leave the room.

Finally, Matron asked, "Feeling okay?"

"Yes, a bit uncomfortable. I have stitches. The baby was eight pounds, two ounces." *The truth? I can barely sit still on this hard chair and oh, by the way, I'd like to scream at your face.*

"Are you still bleeding?"

"Yes. But the clots are smaller."

"Good. Were you given any medication to bring back?"

"No. I'll be okay." *Get me outta here before I yell and wake the dead.*

"Go to your room and rest. I'll have Bernice bring up some food and pads."

"Thank you."

Betty was in control up the stairs until she reached the second floor. Without warning, she was encased in a wave of overwhelming sorrow followed by huge tears. She stood paralyzed outside her old room, unable to step over the threshold.

Mary heard Betty weeping outside the door. Their relationship had not been close but Betty's plight threw all the rules not simply out the window but down the street and around the block. She grabbed a blanket, wrapped Betty in it and helped her onto her bed. By the time Bernice arrived, the sobbing had slowed so Mary went to the kitchen for a coffee to settle her own worries about mid February. She thought carefully about asking Betty questions but sensed she would be soundly rebuffed.

Others in the house did not share the same inhibition about questions. Marjorie, Karen, Ellen and Joan appeared in Betty's room the precise moment Bernice left. They materialized as if from thin air, all with yearning looks.

Not one able to understand the scene before her, Marjorie blurted, "Was it a boy or girl? Was the food good?"

Karen elbowed her and snarled, "Don't be so nosy. Keep quiet for once."

Ellen had planned her questions with the hope that Betty would come back. "Did it hurt?"

"Yes, but they gave me drugs so I was knocked out when the baby was born."

"Did you have your own room?"

"No, there were others in the ward with me."

"Were the nurses nice?"

"Some were. I was left alone most of the time in labour. They didn't pay much attention to me."

"How long can you stay here now?" Marjorie was planning to stay as long as possible after the baby arrived.

"I'm leaving tomorrow morning. I'm tired and want to be alone now."

Joan heard enough answers to get the picture. She pushed everyone out of the room and closed the door behind her.

Amelia peeked in on Sarah shortly after four-thirty. It was getting dark outside and everyone was in their rooms, except Mary who was curled up in the far corner of the sitting room. Amelia joined her.

Sarah heard Amelia on the stairs and got out of bed. She listened at the door then crept downstairs, carrying her boots. Bernice was in the dining room and Eleanor in Matron's office. No voices came from the sitting room. All was perfect. She spirited out the kitchen door toward the big spruce and huddled down against the fence.

Sarah did not appear for supper so Amelia went up to wake her. Initially, everyone thought she was somewhere inside, probably the bathroom. When an indoor search turned up nothing, everyone went into full alarm mode.

Matron asked everyone to dress warmly, exit the front door and break into two groups at the sidewalk. The girls were told to hold hands and walk the front yard. Nothing but snow drifts. They regrouped at the side gate and entered the backyard to walk toward the back fence. It was there they discovered the mound of snow.

Doctor Kelly nodded to Eleanor inside the front door and handed over his medical bag. He pulled his feet out of brown leather snow boots, grabbed the bag and ran up the stairs, two steps at a time.

"Another attack?" He looked at Sarah and scowled.

"No, doctor." Her voice was weak and raspy.

"No more talking. Let me check your feet and hands, temperature, blood pressure and the baby. Matron, a few more hot water bottles wrapped in towels, right away. We'll get them packed around her. You're very lucky, young lady. Whatever in gawd's name possessed you to wander outside in this weather? You sure you didn't have a second attack outside? Another thirty minutes and you'd be in the hospital or morgue. No more outdoor walks until I say so. I'll be back tomorrow."

Sarah didn't care about any of Doctor Kelly's words except the part about going out thirty minutes earlier.

Matron took her turn. "I called your parents. They'll be on a morning ferry and hope to be here by mid afternoon. Eleanor will be up with more warm soup. She's going to stay with you while you eat. No funny business."

Inside Matron's office, Doctor Kelly was more explicit. "That young lady needs to be watched closely for the next few days. I don't want to prescribe medication because of the baby but she appears to be in considerable emotional trouble. Did something out of the ordinary happen to her in the last day or two? Death of a family member or other damaging news? Emotions are out of whack during pregnancy but this is over the top."

"Nothing to her personally that I know about but since she arrived two weeks ago, we've had three big issues in the home. She's been spunky since arriving. Was she trying to take her own life?"

"I'm not a psychiatrist so can't say one way or the other. However, she displayed very troublesome behaviour by isolating herself in the backyard during the storm. It may have been one extreme response to bad news that won't be repeated. In any case, I am worried enough for you to ensure she is not alone overnight tonight. I'll re-assess tomorrow. In the meantime, it would be helpful if you pinpoint someone or something that caused today's behaviour. What's her roommate like?"

"A few years older, mature, has her own issues but I believe she's a stabilizing influence."

"Thank heavens. I'm off to fight the snow back to the hospital. Call me if you need. I'll figure some way to get here."

Chapter Seventeen

January 23, 1961
Amherst, Nova Scotia

Andy stood at the window of Della's apartment captivated by the view across the street. Light bounced from snow held in recesses of bricks, turrets, window ledges and arched oak doors. The early 19th century sandstone church was aglow with reflected light. The white wonder sent him rummaging for his Brownie.

"Good morning. Lose something?"

"Look out the window. I've got to take my camera out on the street."

"Wow. Go while it's still there. I'll make coffee and start breakfast."

Freshly-brewed coffee welcomed Andy back into the diner. Della was already at work slicing brown bread in the diner kitchen. Bacon and eggs sat on the kitchen counter, ready for customer orders.

"I'll have a busy morning. The hotel guests will be here soon. Can you unlock the door and turn on the open sign? Thanks. How'd the picture taking go?"

"Great, I think. But you never know until the film's developed. I've had nasty surprises. Do you have a camera?"

"What would I shoot? Hey, cut that out!"

"Don't you want new pictures for your albums? You look good in an apron."

"Is that really a compliment?"

"Oh, oh. Here come the starving hordes. Can I help or do you want me to pretend I've just arrived?"

"Don't try to hide anything. Small town people know everything anyway, even if they stretch it a bit sometimes."

"Got it."

"You might as well make yourself useful. Here's your apron."

"How do I look?"

"Very fetching. The red roses look lovely with cord pants. Now hustle out there, greet those folks and take their orders. You can keep the tips, if you get any!"

"Just watch me."

Andy left Amherst after the lunch rush. Work at the diner and of course, the time with Della was fun. He hit the road in a positive frame of mind.

Most streets in Halifax were single lane until late afternoon. Snowplow drivers widened streets where it was possible but drivers were lucky to find a passing lane every few blocks. Sometimes, they got out with shovels and did the work themselves. Many homeowners shovelled the street end of their driveway first, allowing cars to pull out of the way for oncoming traffic, especially ambulances and police. It took a community effort to get the city moving again.

Wendell and Norma walked to their respective schools in less than an hour. Jane wasn't as lucky. She was scheduled for a clinic day with out-patient appointments between ten and four under the supervision of psychologist, Nathan Stewart. She left the apartment at seven-thirty with lots of time to think while plodding through the snow. At least the sun was shining and the wind was light. Most of her thoughts revolved around Andy. She was concerned about his focus on Rose Hill. She didn't want the role of psychologist with a good friend. However, she believed his focus was directly related to his sister, Liz. Her challenge was to help him recognize it without damage to their friendship. She planned to ask for Nathan's perspective and advice today.

The phone was ringing when Andy opened his front door. He dropped his grocery bags on the floor. It was Mrs. P. in a worried tone of voice.

"Thank heavens, you're home. How long have you been on the road?"

"I left Amherst a few hours ago. It was slow but no problems."

"I'm sure you have things to do. I wanted to know you were okay."

"I'm good. Do you need anything? Food, snow shovelling?"

"No, all taken care of. But can you pop in a bit later? I have something for you to read."

"Sure. I've a few telephone calls to make. In an hour work?"

"Sure. Bye, bye for now."

Andy was eager to talk with Wendell then Jane and Norma. Within minutes he organized supper at his apartment for the next evening. He promised them homemade spaghetti. They agreed to bring bread and dessert. Carefully following Della's recipe, he assembled the sauce ingredients in the slow cooker and set it on 'low' to simmer. Next time, he'd try beef in a blanket. This cooking thing was cool.

Wendell had barely hung up the phone when it rang again.

"Norma here. Did Andy call you a few minutes ago?"

"Yes. What's up?"

"Did he tell you what's going on?"

"No. What's going on?"

"Jane and I don't know but something is. We're supposed to bring dessert. Maybe it's something big."

"You two are overthinking this. Remember we agreed to talk with him. This is the perfect chance. Make the dessert and let tomorrow happen. Have a good evening."

"You sure he didn't give you a hint?"

"Yes, I'm sure. We'll wait together. Good night."

Norma hung up and shrugged her shoulders in Jane's direction.

"Well, you heard me. Wendell is as clueless as we are. Let get those brownies started for the mystery soiree." She shook her head and grabbed the Robin Hood Flour cookbook from the shelf.

On Tuesday, the city was back to normal except for the heaps of snow left to melt in yards, beside driveways and in parking lots. Andy saw his last customer of the day on the Halifax side of the bridge, then played taxi, picking up Wendell, then Norma and Jane before five-thirty. They were full of questions when they entered the hallway.

Jane breathed deeply. "It smells great in here. Who made the sauce?"

"Me."

Wendell wasn't convinced. "Sure. You became a chef in a weekend?"

"Kinda."

Norma wasn't convinced either. "Yeah, yeah. Someone else made it. Bet it was Mrs. P."

Andy grinned. "Nope, you're wrong too. Being a chef is one part of our supper conversation. Hang up your coats. There are extra slippers in the closet. Let's go into the kitchen. Can someone open the wine? Norma, can you set the table? Things are on the counter. I'll start the pasta."

Andy's home was a second floor apartment in an older residential area of the city. He splurged and bought a new bed and mattress set then trolled garage sales. In the finish, he owned a Formica and chrome kitchen table with four chairs, a couch, two comfy living room chairs plus a big coffee table.

Refilled glasses in hand, everyone sat around the table for salad, spaghetti and bread.

Andy raised his glass. "To the future."

"The future," chorused Wendell, Jane and Norma.

Norma was too curious to endure any more pleasantries. "How was Wolfville?"

"Tense at the beginning but hopeful at the end. Bear with me and I'll give you the short version. I'm sure you'll all have something to say at the end."

Wendell was the first to speak after the update. He hoped to keep the discussion as light as possible for as long as possible. There would be more than enough drama to come.

"Well, you're certainly a different guy after Wolfville. I put all the success on the brandy." He chuckled.

"Explain the 'different' part." There was no mistaking Andy's touchy tone.

Wendell rubbed his hand over his eyes and leaned forward. *Now or never.* "All three of us have been concerned for you since early December. As your friends, we agreed to speak about it with you as soon as you returned from Wolfville. And now, here we are. Tonight though, you are different. So far, I've not heard much about Rose Hill. You've spoken about Liz in a positive way. Surely you must feel different. Do you?"

"Yes, but this isn't only about me. Let me get back to this conspiracy the three of you cooked up. You were going to gang up on me. Explain how that works."

"We weren't going to gang up on you. I volunteered to tell you how concerned we all were then ask how we could help."

"What were you all worried about?" Andy kept his eyes on the wine bottle. He refused to make eye contact and lose his resolve. "I'd make a fool of myself or worse?"

Jane was unnerved. They were losing Andy, not bringing him closer. She seized control of the conversation.

"Andy, we think more highly of you than that. We've held each other in safekeeping through all sorts of uncertainty. This is no different. Trust has always been a watchword for all of us.

This rough patch calls for us to embrace that trust once again." She held her breath.

Andy exhaled loudly but kept his head down. Norma needed a tissue and bolted to the bathroom. Wendell thought it best to keep his mouth shut, despite his hankering to add his two cents worth.

An ear piercing ring broke the dead air.

Andy raced to the bedroom. "Damn, I forgot to turn the ringer down earlier. Sorry."

"What the heck was that?" Norma rushed from the bathroom. "It sounded like a fire truck."

"The phone and thank goodness for whoever it is. It broke the tension."

"No kidding. Here he comes."

"So I better move off my soapbox, eh? Jane was right. You were only trying to help. Mea culpa."

"Listen you goofball, that phone nearly scared me to death. And I was down the hall in the bathroom. Don't ever turn that ringer up again. Geez."

"Have more wine. It'll fix what ails ya." Andy handed Norma the bottle.

"I thought that was brandy, smartie."

Wendell was feeling his old self again. "Okay, back to the weekend. Did you drive from Wolfville yesterday?"

"No, I left Wolfville Sunday morning and drove smack dab into the storm about an hour later, on the road to Amherst."

"Amherst?" Jane's brow crinkled.

"Makes sense to me." Norma glanced at Jane. "Visit the client in Amherst then come home."

"Not exactly. I have a friend there. That brings me to the other part of my story. It was a last minute decision to visit Amherst on Sunday. A friend owns a diner where I've stopped several times. The storm was the curve ball so I had to stay overnight. So I spent Sunday evening and part of yesterday being a waiter and dishwasher. It was busy. Stranded people, plow drivers, Mounties."

"I get the spaghetti sauce now." Jane grinned.

"Yeah, in three months, I used that slow cooker once, for stew. I'm smarter now."

"Bet your buddy was happy he had help." Wendell shook his head. He couldn't imagine himself a waiter. A classroom full of children seemed a breeze compared with a room full of starving grown ups.

"I'll get the coffee. Jane, can you bring dessert. I'll finish my story when we are settled again."

Wendell and Norma stared at each other across the table. Norma leaned forward. "I think we're all in for a big announcement."

"So, back to part two of my weekend adventure. My buddy with the diner is a girl. Guess you guys are surprised by a girl owning a diner."

Wendell was the first to speak. "I'm not."

Norma smacked Wendell's arm. "Come on. Give me a break."

"You never give me enough credit for my forward thinking."

"You're quiet, Jane."

Jane met Andy's eyes with hers. "I'm happy for you as I'm sure these two sparing partners are as well." She paused. "Is it thoughtless of me to ask about Rose Hill at this moment? Just say 'yes' if you think so but we do have some unfinished business." She helped herself to another brownie.

"Top up your coffee. We'll get off these uncomfortable chairs and go to the living room. I've news on that front too."

Andy stepped into the living room and scooped up a few sheets of paper off the coffee table. He waved them in the air.

"Mrs. P did homework for us. Since 1916 Nova Scotia has offered correspondence education to people unable to attend school in person. She thinks it might work for Rose Hill and has contacts for us. Ladies and gentleman, we have an opportunity. What say we give it a shot?"

Chapter Eighteen

January 23, 1961
Rose Hill Home

The storm left Rose Hill neighbourhood smothered in drifts. A few locals strapped on cross-country skis or snow shoes to claim ownership of the street and break trail to Fosters Grocery.

Sarah's empty eyes stared vacantly at the wall, her back to the room. The bud of hope with Myles had bloomed then perished in moments.

Amelia woke from a watchful sleep even though Annie was in the room for Sarah. She nodded and received a smile in return. Amelia took this as a sign that none of her own nightmarish words or behaviour had betrayed her during the night. Following a quick glance at Sarah, she left the room to shower and dress for the day.

When Amelia returned to the room, Annie stood and beckoned toward the hall. They stood silently until Debbie went down stairs.

"I'm going to check in with Matron. Are you okay to stay until I return?"

"Sure. I'll suggest she have a shower and see how that goes."

Amelia returned to the bedroom, closed the door and pulled a chair to sit behind Sarah's rigid back.

"Sarah, I'm not asking you to say anything. You're crushed and know all is lost with Myles. I have felt the same way. Both of us have been betrayed and rejected. You will feel better, just not today. I will do my best to help with your privacy today. None of the girls will come in unless you say so. Today is a survival day. I have two requests. One, you have a bath. Two, you have breakfast. After that, let's see what the day brings us. Unless you ask me to leave, I plan to stay with you."

Sarah stirred, moaned then rolled over. An ashen, puffy face with two lifeless spheres rimmed in red stared at Amelia. She audibly gasped but Sarah didn't seem to notice.

"Bathroom."

"Put your feet on the floor. Now take my arm and I'll help you up."

In the bathroom, Amelia placed Sarah on the toilet. "You're weak so don't lock the door. I'll return with a clean nightgown, get the bath ready and sit outside the door."

Annie arrived with breakfast shortly after Amelia heard Sarah get in the tub. She took a tray into Sarah's room then walked toward Amelia with a cup of coffee in her hand. "This one's for you. I guessed you weren't moving off the third floor for a while. Milk, sugar?"

"No. Always black coffee for me. I'm a bit of a purist about it. If it's good I know it. If it's bad, I know that too. Thanks."

"There's breakfast for two on the tray. If you eat, she might too." She patted Amelia's arm.

"You're a gem, Annie."

"Thanks. I'm off home right away. Nancy will come up a bit later to give you a break." She managed a brave face with Amelia but choked back quiet sobs down the stairs then darted into the bathroom to wash her face before appearing in the kitchen.

Karen purposely sat between Debbie and Marjorie for breakfast. She intended to take a poke at Debbie before meeting Matron after chores. Intent on her prey, she did not notice Matron standing in the doorway when she leaned over and said, "Nice to see you again, Catherine."

Matron smiled and turned away from the dining room.

Betty was visibly uneasy and agitated during breakfast. She planned to leave immediately after eating but the snowfall meant she would likely be in the house for lunch too.

Marjorie didn't help matters by asking her two personal questions back to back. "Who gave you that pretty ring? Where are you going to live now?"

"Marjorie, I'm not answering any questions from anybody today." The emphasis on 'not' and 'anybody' made it clear all conversation was over.

Marjorie looked confused and received an elbow jab from Karen.

Mary had counted on getting advice and guidance about labour and birth from Betty before she left. It was now obvious that would not happen. She felt terribly alone and wondered if this was what Ellen meant about sadness. After chores, she would have a talk without a walk with Ellen.

Joan rushed through her chores and waited for Karen to begin her meeting with Matron. Having a roommate was a pain in the butt. Upstairs she pulled her scribbler out of hiding and added a few more notes. Her plan was working. Since last Wednesday she had written detailed notes about the incidents at Rose Hill. She wrote stories about the girl who escaped at night, a nutcase who tried to get inside the house, the police who visited three times, her new roommate who lied and bullied others and the topper, a girl who nearly froze to death in the backyard. She got out her best writing paper and began...

Dear Grandma and Grandpa,

It is not safe here. I think you better come and take me home. I would be much safer in your guest room until mom and dad come home. I'm lucky to be alive to write this letter. Here is what happened since Wednesday.

It ended...

Your loving and terribly frightened only granddaughter, XOXO

In high spirits, she addressed the envelope ready to be mailed. *I'm outta here.*

Nancy popped in to see Sarah at nine thirty. She found her asleep and Amelia reading. She quietly removed the breakfast tray and noted that only one breakfast was finished. The other was missing one piece of toast and the milk. *Better something than nothing.*

Karen was eager to attend her first weekly meeting with Matron. She was certain Matron's blue envelope held the key to her protection. There would be no reason to cut short her fun before the baby arrived three weeks from now. Bring on your best shot, lady. She knocked sharply and opened the door.

"Come in, Karen. No need to sit. This will be quick. How are things going with Joan?"

"Great. We've hit it off. Talking lots together. Nothing personal, of course."

"Good. Any trouble following my request to be kind with others?"

"Oh, no. Not at all. It's easy when you put your mind to it."

"Hmm. Then you'll have no trouble explaining why Debbie looked so frightened when you spoke to her at the table this morning."

"No. I told her I hoped the crazy guy wouldn't come back. She didn't know he was a madman. That must have been it."

"Well, Debbie came to see me after breakfast. Apparently, the two of you lived in the same town a few years ago. She was afraid you might tell nasty stories about her. There will be no stories. Do you understand"?

Karen ignored the question. "You have a friend in Ottawa, right?"

"What does that have to do with Rose Hill?"

"Well, your name is Andrews and you wear a wedding ring. Mark Rousseau sends you letters in pretty blue envelopes with red hearts on the envelope flap. Sounds like a secret story to me. Maybe even a secret love story. My family in Ottawa might want to drop by Mark's home for a visit." Her body language was laced with swagger.

"Mark Rousseau's my brother. He's a detective with the Ottawa Police. Perhaps you would like him to check up on your family... just to make sure they're okay?" *Two can play the fib game.*

"No. I'm sure they are fine."

"Now, back to my question about Debbie. No stories, correct?"

"Correct."

"See you next Monday, same time."

"Yes, Matron." *Maybe.*

Mary found Ellen sitting on her bed using a chair as a footstool. As Mary entered, Ellen placed an open book face down on the bed.

"Hey, feel like a chat?"

"Sure. We can share the footstool."

"What's the book?"

"A murder mystery. Do you know about Agatha Christie?"

"I know the name but haven't read any of her books. I could use something new to think about. Where'd you get it?"

"AM. She has several books in her big suitcase. What did you want to talk about?"

"Do you find Betty odd?"

"What do you mean?"

"I know she kept to herself before but I was hoping she would be willing to talk more about what happened in the hospital."

"I try not to think about that part. Maybe you need to ask her anyway. She was your roommate."

"Yeah, maybe. I'm not as sure about myself these days. I've lost my sense of humour, feel gloomy most of the time. Sometimes I cry and don't know why. If my mother could see me, she'd say I'm down in the dumps. Our brains and bodies are all mixed up so I guess it's the hormone stuff. You're doing better, right?"

"Yes. Guess my brain and body are less mixed up. You, Eva and AM have been kind. That's been important to me."

"You see AM this morning?"

"No. She's probably staying with Eva. Do you remember when I called AM old?"

"That was dumb. Old is good."

They started to laugh and fell sideways toward each other into the middle of the bed.

Betty returned to her room after breakfast. She dreaded Mary's return after chores knowing she would have questions. Determined not to spend another night at Rose Hill, she stripped her bed, including the plastic mattress cover. It gave her something to do. Still at loose ends, she re-packed her few clothes and notes from the university course, leaving the art textbook on the night table. Feeling weary, she reached for the book intending to sit and pass the time. The room began to spin around her. Perspiration gathered on her forehead, above her upper lip and around her neck. She cooked from the inside out. Unappealing as the bare mattress looked, she fell onto it and closed her eyes. She stayed still a few minutes then squinted with one open eye. The door had stopped chasing the window around the room. She stood and shuffled toward the door where she used the wall to take halting steps to the bathroom.

Joan heard the 'thunk' from her room and raced toward the bathroom. Betty was put to bed with strict orders to remain there until Doctor Kelly completed a check-up later in the day. Nancy delivered a dinner bell if she needed to go to the bathroom. Betty reluctantly resigned herself to another night in Rose Hill and promptly fell asleep.

Sarah opened her eyes before lunch and asked Amelia to help her to the bathroom. When they returned, she sat on the edge of the bed, not speaking or looking at Amelia. Instead, she began to rock back and forth, slowly wrapped her arms around her abdomen. Mournful whimpers were followed by tears. They ran down her cheeks and dropped onto her nightgown. She curled into a ball on the bed. Whimpering gave way to the agonized moans of the gravely wounded. A quick series of shallow breaths satisfied her body's need for air. Her body could no longer sustain the assault. The rocking ceased. The well of tears went dry. The gasps for air became peaceful and measured. Grief itself was dying… for now. Amelia witnessed its' passing, covered Sarah with a blanket and waited for her to wake.

Hushed voices in concerned tones floated into the room. Amelia recognized them and stepped into the hall. She tapped her index finger over her lips. A whispered conversation began.

"How's she doing?" Ellen's look was solemn.

"Can we bring lunch for both of you?" Mary tried to sound positive.

"Thanks but I think Nancy will bring a tray for us. It's been a difficult morning but I'm hoping the afternoon will be a bit better."

"When are her parents expected to arrive?" Mary spoke as if this was something Amelia would know.

"Oh, dear. I never even thought about that!"

"Okay, Ellen and I will fish for information over lunch and let you know. Let's hope the snow really, really delays them. In case you heard a kerfuffle on the second floor, it was Betty. She had a fall in the bathroom. She's back in bed."

"Will this day ever end?" Amelia returned to the bedroom as Sarah was getting out of bed.

"Hang on. I'll help."

"Bathroom again. Please."

Amelia needed to remind Sarah of her parent's visit. There would be an explosion or a repeat of the earlier collapse. She decided to speak of it after lunch then opened the curtains allowing sunlight to flood the room. Whether it was the sun or hunger, Sarah smiled weakly and picked up a cheese biscuit and dipped her spoon into the chowder.

"Feeling better?"

"A little. Still shaky."

"Food and rest. That's the recipe today."

"What happens to me now?"

"What do you mean?"

"Doctor Kelly and Matron will send me somewhere to be locked up."

"Locked up! You had a big shock yesterday. I'm guessing they don't know about that. You reacted to the shock."

"I guess so. It's all a blur to me, like fog. How long will this feeling last?"

"Better ask Doctor Kelly that one. When I was threatened, the world became a scary place. I needed to hide. Thinking back now, I had shock too. I didn't realize it at the time. As I told you, I muddled through on my own for a few days, made up a story at work and here I am."

"But you're not safe yet, are you?" The question was more a statement and Amelia knew it.

"No, but I'm not on my own any more." She felt a sense of belonging, struck by the irony of this as she was in a house full of strangers with phony names and no future together. "We'll take each day as it comes. Let's eat then you can rest."

Despite their best sleuthing efforts during lunch, Mary and Ellen came up empty handed. Undaunted, they decamped to the sitting room and waited to eavesdrop on Matron's telephone conversations. Ellen was reluctant to listen in on Matron's private calls and told Mary so.

"It's not right, Mary. We're being nosy."

"It's for a good reason. We'll only tell AM what she needs to know. The rest we forget. Tell yourself you're solving a mystery."

The telephone finally rang. Good fortune smiled on them... sort of.

"Hello. Rose Hill Home."

"And good afternoon to you, Constable Biggar...."

"Oh, my. That is very startling news..."

"Yes, I will share your information. Thank you for calling. Good bye."

Mary's wide eyes met Ellen's. "Who the heck is Constable Biggar?"

"I have no idea but this is not a pretend mystery. Should we stay here longer? Nancy has already looked in twice."

"Yes, we need to. Get a couple of magazines from your room. I'll stay here just in case."

At three-thirty, they threw in the towel and went to the kitchen for hot chocolate. Dejected, they walked toward the stairs but made an abrupt left turn when Matron's telephone shrilled. They strolled across the hallway to the dining room.

"Rose Hill Home. Matron speaking..."

"She's eating and resting..."

"We'll look forward to seeing you about six then. Good bye."

Mary and Ellen scurried up the stairs. Without knock-ing, they tip-toed into the room to find Sarah in a deep sleep. Amelia rose and all three went into the hall.

"So, what do we know?"

"They'll be here about six."

"Thanks, you two. I hope Doctor Kelly leaves before they arrive."

"He'll be here a while. Remember, Betty is in bed, too. What a day. By the way, do you know a Constable Biggar?"

She frowned and shook her head. "Don't think so. Why?"

"Probably doesn't matter then. He called Matron when we were downstairs. Sounded like some bad news."

Amelia returned to her room and took a deep breath, exhal-ing slowly. She racked her brain trying to remember the name of the policeman who found her in the hedge. She tried her old trick using the alphabet. Abbott, Albertson, Anderson, Bain, Bernard, Brown, Clement, Clow, Crane, Dillon, Drake.... It was no use. No name rang a bell. It was more likely about the girl who ran away.

Sarah opened her eyes and Amelia edged into the topic of her parents. "I have to talk to you about your parents. Do you know they are coming to see you today?"

"I figured they would."

"They'll be here about six o'clock. You should think about their visit before they arrive."

"What do you mean?"

"Well, they'll have ideas. They'll talk to Matron before see-ing you. They might know about the newspaper. What do you want to happen and don't want to happen. For example, do you want to stay here? Would they want you go to a relative's home?"

"Can you stay with me when they arrive?"

"Oh, no. I won't be allowed to do that."

The engine's roar was music to Matron's ears. She watched as snow flew into the air and landed on sidewalks, driveways and front yards. A couple of the neighbours had shovelled their driveways. Now, they had the dubious pleasure of doing it again. A lone car crept along behind the snowplow and forced its' way into Rose Hill driveway. Doctor Kelly had literally blasted in and was now firmly stuck until he was shovelled free. He waved in the direction of the snowplow's cab and received a salute in return. He stepped out of the car and sank up to his knees. Matron saw his mouth move and a singular expletive es-caped into the frosty air. Fortunately, drifting snow had packed against the fences so after three giant steps, Doctor Kelly found himself on a clear path to the front door. Matron greeted him with relief and big smile. He returned the favour.

"Is this snow ever going to end? How are things here?"

"Could be worse, I suppose. You now have two patients to see."

"Who else?"

"Betty. She's weak. Probably bleeding too much but you're the doctor."

"Okay but before I start, a scalding hot cup of tea with milk and sugar would be appreciated."

"Earl Grey's your favourite, I believe."

"Absolutely. Mind if I use your office while I wait?"

"No. I'll be in shortly with tea, biscuits and jam."

Amelia also heard the snowplow but it did not signal relief. The snow had kept her safe inside Rose Hill, out of harm's way. Now, it could no longer be depended upon. She sighed heavily, knowing she was exposed to danger again.

"Sarah, Doctor Kelly's here. I'm going downstairs now."

Sarah was frightened. Doctor Kelly would step into her room, deliver a lecture about her unstable behaviour then write a prescription for some kind of mind numbing drug. Next, the words about the move to a safer place. It would have more people to look after her and maybe locked rooms. The best she could hope for was to stay at Rose Hill until the baby was born. Her plan was always to get out. Now she wanted to stay. Perhaps she really was wacko. Tears started again.

"My, my. What's going on here? Why are you crying? Are you in pain?"

"Where are you sending me? I don't want to go to the asylum. Please, I can't go there."

"Asylum? Either you have a vivid imagination, young lady or somebody put that idea into your head. Sit up. Let me see those hands and feet. Have you been eating?"

Sarah nodded and sat still for the usual round of heart, blood pressure and baby checks.

"You both are doing fine. Now back to that silly notion. Did someone talk to you about an asylum?" His tone changed from concern to annoyance. She wouldn't want to be on his bad side, an expression her father occasionally used about people.

"No, I just thought...."

"Stop thinking about that."

"Yes, doctor."

"Can you tell me what you were thinking about yesterday before you went outside?"

Answering the question didn't feel like a choice. "I had bad news that upset me."

"And how do you feel about that news today?"

"I'm sad and angry but can't make what happened go away."

"Sounds sensible to me. Are your parents coming to see you?"

"Yes, today."

"Hmmm. No doubt they will be very upset. You're doing well so I want you to join everyone for supper. I'll call Matron tomorrow to ask how you are doing. Bye, bye."

Amelia was fearful about Sarah's fragile state of mind. She waited impatiently for Doctor Kelly to appear. When he entered Matron's office she sped to the third floor to find Sarah getting dressed for supper.

"How'd it go?"

"He said I was sensible."

"Well then, let's eat."

At the bottom of the stairs, Matron approached Sarah and Amelia.

"I need to have a quick word with each of you separately. Eva you first, please."

"I had a call earlier today from Miss Preston. Because of the storm, she will see you a week from today at ten o'clock. Any questions?"

"No. Not today."

"Please send AM in."

Amelia entered Matron's office not knowing what she was about to face. Did she find out something about me? Did she receive a threat and needs me to leave? Whatever it was, Amelia was frightened.

Matron spoke softly. "I have unexpected news for you. Earlier today I received a message from the police. Late last night a head-on collision occurred on the highway outside the city. There were no survivors. One of the bodies identified was the person arrested the night you were hiding in the hedge down the street. I don't know your relationship with this person and of course, it's none of my business. Nevertheless, it is a shock for you. Is there something you need to do?"

"No, there's nothing I need to do."

"Would you like the office to yourself for a few minutes?"

"No, thank you."

"Supper in your room?"

"No, I'm fine."

Amelia left the office but Matron was riveted to her chair. Secrecy cloaked Amelia's story and journey to Rose Hill. Amazingly, chapters continued to be written, including today. It was the stuff of fiction in real life at Rose Hill. Sylvie Goudreau-Andrews was captivated.

Supper conversation revolved around the storm and the expectation that life would return to normal tomorrow. Betty and Sarah were welcomed back from 'not feeling well'. Karen spent the time hatching new ideas for her personal enjoyment. She would let Debbie off the hook but had no intention of exiting Rose Hill in three weeks without leaving her mark on as many others as possible. Amelia leaned toward Sarah and told her the angry man was dead and she'd explain later. Plenty of questions went unasked and several went unanswered but that was life at a Rose Hill supper.

Sarah's parents arrived at six-thirty. Mrs. Gardner was in a tizzy, demanding answers from Matron who calmed the waters, deftly avoided any mention of the possible reasons for Sarah's behaviour. She led them upstairs and left them with their daughter.

A big surprise awaited Matron in the front hall. Bernice was standing beside a very pregnant older woman wearing an unbuttoned, thread bare coat which revealed a faded yellow cotton house dress. On her feet a pair of oversize rubber boots dripped melting snow. Her badly battered suitcase sat on the floor. A fresh bruise marked her left cheek. She removed her mitts and revealed work worn hands and a thin, gold wedding band.

"Please, Mrs. He threw me out. I've no place to go. I'm beggin' ya."

Upstairs, Sarah's mother fluttered around the room spewing a series of endless questions and flapping her arms. Sarah sat on the bed with her back ramrod straight. She focused on breathing and counting until the rhetorical questions and drama came to an end. She'd seen this display many times. So had her father. He rested his elbows on his knees and twirled his hat forward and backward. He learned long ago to let his wife run out of steam. Eventually, she did and asked the only question that mattered to her.

"Why did you stay outside in a snowstorm?"

"I saw a picture of Myles..."

She cut Sarah off. "That boy is no reason for anything let alone for you to act in such a childish, dangerous way." She followed it up with a sharp reprimand, "Don't you ever, ever do that again."

Sarah glanced at her father. He had a worried look but remained quiet.

The verdict on Sarah's future was next on her mother's to do list. It came without delay.

"Now about Rose Hill. We have decided you will remain here. None of your relatives know you are 'in trouble' so we can't possibly ask them to look after you. Do you have anything you'd like to say?"

Sarah had lots to say but absolutely nothing to them and certainly not today. She couldn't trust herself to utter one word without her resentment turning into fireworks. Counting on her parents for support was long gone. Awkward moments of silence preceded their hugs and departure.

Sarah was sitting on the bed, rocking back and forth when Amelia came into the room. She suggested board games downstairs would pass the time. Sarah was too exhausted to object.

Chapter Nineteen

January 23, 1961
Rose Hill

Jenny caused a big stir with her late evening arrival. Matron rushed her into the office and through admission. Bernice accompanied her upstairs to Debbie's room where she was given clean clothing and told to have a bath before returning downstairs for something to eat.

Sarah was grateful for Jenny's unusual arrival. The hushed exchanges about the new woman during board games allowed her mind to wander away from her own troubles. She listened to all the idle talk without comment. At nine-thirty, she walked toward the stairs, eager to have a heart to heart conversation with Amelia. As she waited for Amelia to return, her mind drifted into treacherous territory. Sketching didn't help either. It was impossible not to think about what might have been. Her future ripped from her, she was a raw wound ready to bleed with no way to stem the flow.

Amelia wandered into the room carrying a cup of coffee. "Well, that was quite the evening. Jenny just raised the average age in the house." She paused mid thought and sat on the bed beside Sarah. "What's the matter?"

Sarah responded with a trace of irritation. "How can you be so cheerful? Jenny's a mess. We're all a mess."

"Everybody has messes in their lives from time to time. I refuse to dwell on mine all the time." She took a deep breath and continued in a low voice. "Do you remember the survival day comments I made to you?"

"Not really. What did you say?" The tinge of annoyance lingered.

Amelia's soft tone continued. "Mostly things about surviving day to day. We all cope in our own way here....reading, eating, annoying others. You sketch. What's happening?"

"I don't know what to do. I need help." She covered her face with both hands.

"Something in particular tonight?"

"No, it's everything. I can't even think straight. My head's everywhere." She twirled her index finger in midair.

"I'm like that sometimes. I feel out of control by all that's going on in my head and around me. Sound familiar?"

"Yeah, the more I think about everything, the worse it gets. When does it end?"

"Honestly? I haven't a clue. As I said, I still have awful days. For me, I still have to take each day as it comes."

"That's really easy for you to say. You've got everything.... a job, somewhere to go, a future waiting." Sarah let out a deep sigh followed by a long pause. Her voice softened to a whisper. "Sorry, sorry. That was a mean thing to say." She looked around the room. "There's no future for me or my baby anymore." She looked around the ceiling, eyes searching for the answer she wanted.

Amelia began gently. "You do have a future but it's not the one you dreamed about with Myles. It'll be the one you bring to life, not the one society dictates. Your art will give you strength to manage difficult times just as it has here. When your survival skills kick in, planning will begin. I know, it sounds easy but it's very hard work, every day."

"How do I even begin?"

"Did you have ideas and dreams about your future before Myles?"

"Yes. Some were probably dumb."

"Maybe, but that doesn't matter at the moment. Can you start thinking about one idea tonight?"

"Right this minute, no." Sarah wrapped her arms around her stomach. "How can you stay so calm?"

"You don't remember the basket case that arrived last week? I have to work at it every day. I tell myself there will be bad days, then move on."

"This one sure is bad for me." She paused. "Can you tell me what happened with the angry man?"

"He died in a car accident. I'm relieved my fear is over but he left me with scars that can't be seen. Some will never fade away. And, I still have fears to face in the future."

"Fears? The nutter's gone. You can leave here and go back to your life."

"A work life, yes. My fears are people fears....their questions, looks, assumptions."

"About what?"

"My coworkers think I'm visiting family in England."

"Why's that a problem?"

Amelia thought about revealing more but chose to remain silent. "I'll have to make up lots of stories about people and places I didn't see." She immediately felt guilty but it was the best answer for the moment.

"Can I ask what you will do when you leave?"

"I'm a photographer, as you probably figured out days ago. I understand my return to the outside world will be different than yours. But, it will not be easy for either of us."

Sarah managed a fleeting smile but held back the question she'd agonized over for so, so long. An unthinkable question she'd tried to hide from herself and dared not speak out loud. Once uttered, it would become real. The dreadful words would demand an answer. She glanced at Amelia who was clearly waiting for her to say something. "I know."

Amelia took Sarah's hand. "You're upset and afraid. Talk to me."

Sarah suddenly felt aching heaviness as pain spread across her chest. She closed her eyes.

"Breathe slowly, Sarah.....and again. Good. Breathe. Again. Once more. Okay?"

"Better." Then a whisper. "What about my baby?" She moved her hands in slow circles over her stomach. "I love my baby. What's wrong with me loving and keeping my baby?" A pause and a slow, deep breath. "Why can't my parents love my baby?" She lifted her head. "Am I a bad person?"

Amelia shook her head 'no' but remained silent. The dam had burst. She knew there was more coming. She also knew this would be the first of many times.

"How can I go home? So many people know what I did. They're not fooled by my parents. They'll pretend they don't know but laugh behind my back. I trusted Myles and abandoned my friends for a good-looking liar. I'm such a fool. I believed every word he said. I won't ever, ever do that again. My life is destroyed."

Amelia stroked Sarah's hand. "Don't you dare believe a word of that last sentence."

"But right now, it feels that way." She sobbed and wrapped her arms around her stomach, caressing her baby. "I can't leave my baby behind. I can't." Emotionally drained, her head dropped, words silenced.

Amelia sat quietly for a few moments. "Remember a while ago I asked about ideas and dreams? Can you tell me one or two?"

"I love to sketch, paint......maybe do what my summer art teacher does?"

"That's a great start. Think about your art in bed. Maybe we should get some sleep?"

"Thanks for listening."

Amelia soon heard the deep breathing sounds of sleep.

Sarah's big challenge for the next day would to remain patient until she could talk with Amelia in the evening. She desperately needed someone to help keep the anxiety attacks at bay.

During supper, Sarah looked around the table. With no job and no money, almost everyone would have no choice but adoption. Fighting back tears, she wrestled with her own situation. She had no education, no job and no money either. Her dreamworld was gone forever. "Ow!" A jab took her breath away and tears flowed down her cheeks.

After supper and a brief walk in the backyard, Sarah found Amelia and Mary chatting about cameras. She sat on her bed and listened. Lenses and filters sounded way more complicated and boring than creating something beautiful with pencils, brushes and colours.

"Lights out."

Mary said good night and left the room.

Sarah plunged in immediately. "Have you felt your baby yet?"

"Yes, a few weeks ago. Fluttering movements then a kick. You?"

"For sure at supper tonight but maybe last week too. I thought it was gas bubbles."

Amelia knew the excitement and joy of a baby's first kick. She couldn't imagine how wondrous then disheartening it would be for Sarah. She waited.

"I don't want them to take my baby away. At first, I thought my parents would think of my baby as their grandchild and I would come home with my little boy or girl. I'm such an idiot, they locked me up. At supper, I thought about adoption."

"And what did you think?"

"I don't have a job or money or a boyfriend to come for me but I do not want to do it. There has to be a way." The words were strong but Sarah's usual confident voice was not in them. Suddenly, anger took over. "Some families keep the baby. My parents didn't even give me a chance." The volume shot up. "I'll never forgive them. Everybody thinks they're right and I'm wrong.....parents, caseworkers, all those people out there walking around who think they are so good. You're lucky, you don't have family here."

Amelia let the fury subside. "Any dreams last night?"

"I don't remember any. I've wanted to paint for a long time so that's a start, right?"

"It sure is."

"But I have to finish high school. All those people talking behind my back, shunning me. This is so hard." She looked at her stomach and began to cry.

"That's true. If you want art school bad enough, you'll get through high school. The paths you and I are on right now are difficult. The choices and sacrifices we make to create our own paths aren't easy either."

"Are you getting off or staying on?"

"What do you mean?"

"Your path. Are you getting off, maybe going somewhere else to live?"

"No, I am staying on."

"So you're keeping your job, staying here?"

"Yes..... and I've decided to keep my baby."

Sarah was stunned by Amelia's revelation. "You are? How?" She wanted her baby too. Crying was pointless but she burst into tears again.

"I couldn't keep you in the dark." She paused briefly then continued. "I don't want to get married, ever. I trusted someone too. Never again."

"The case worker's going to fight you."

"I know." She nodded. "It's going to be a big battle but I'm ready for it. I have a job and place to live. People have nasty opinions of unmarried mothers so it's going to be a rocky path for me and my baby."

Sarah sat still for a few minutes. "I sing to my baby in the bathtub. It's my baby...inside my body. How is it fair that someone can steal your own baby from you? That's what they're doing to me."

Chapter Twenty

April 1961
Rose Hill Home

Sarah and Amelia walked countless miles around their neighbourhood during the weeks following the fateful events in late January. Their daily routine moved from quiet strolls to brisk walks. It looked like exercise but was so much more.

With each step, Sarah struggled to widen the distance between her past and her future. She did her best but sometimes crippling grief washed over her without warning. In the late night darkness, she moved her hands back and forth over her swollen stomach, whispering softly to her child. "You are loved."

Amelia fought to close the distance between herself and the unknown future as an unwed mother. Questions tested her determination. What would she face living in a community as a single mother? How would her child be treated?

Surrounding Sarah and Amelia's individual journeys, life inside Rose Hill moved along with predictability during late January, February and March.

Marjorie went into labour early. She left for the hospital in tears and returned the same way. When her sour-faced mother arrived to pick her up, she cried.

"Poor little soul. She doesn't belong anywhere." Mary whispered to Ellen at the top of the stairs.

During Sunday lunch on January twenty-ninth, Matron reminded everyone of Reverend Miller's afternoon meeting. As soon as her last word was spoken, Joan marched out leaving her lunch unfinished. She was still smarting from the Friday meeting with Matron. On the preceding Thursday, Matron had been invited to the home of Joan's grandparents. There, the three of them had a candid conversation. Joan would remain in Rose

Hill until the baby was born. She would go home alone. Matron was charged with delivering the family message. No negotiations would be considered.

Reverend Miller was gun-shy. He'd been fired on too many times by Rose Hill girls, especially by the one called Joan. He entered the sitting room cautiously, greeted everyone and started the meeting with a prayer. Keeping his head down, he announced 'hope' as the topic of discussion. He lifted his head. All eyes were on him but not a word was uttered. For a moment he thought Joan must be ill. But no, she was there but with a surly face. An hour later, the meeting was over.

After supper, Sarah rushed upstairs. Tomorrow she would meet with Miss Preston. Her mind raced through the past. It always ended with a gaping hole in her heart. When Amelia entered the room she broke down, sobbing loudly.

"Tomorrow?"

Sarah nodded. "It's a death. I'm losing my baby."

"Let's get through tonight. Bring out your art supplies and I'll read out loud."

Mercifully, the meeting with Miss Preston went quickly. Upon entering the office, Sarah was asked if she'd reconsidered adoption. When she replied 'yes', the consent forms immediately appeared on the desk. After signing, her legs turned to jelly but somehow managed to carry her to the front hall. There, Amelia was waiting with her coat and boots. "We're going to Foster's to buy the biggest ice cream cones we've ever eaten. Then we walk."

The friendship between Mary and Ellen continued to strengthen. Matron openly displayed her concern and assigned a new roommate to each of them, hoping it would weaken their bond.

Mary fretted about leaving Ellen behind to sink into sorrow. She vowed to find a fix before she left and settled on asking Ellen if she wanted to exchange real names and addresses. Ellen agreed.

Karen was lost without Marjorie. Not because of a missing friendship but she was now without influence. Desperate for recognition, she faked interest in Debbie. At least, she could reminisce about the good old days and keep on Matron's good side before she had to leave in a few weeks. She was looking forward to seeing the old gang at the youth home again.

***

Sarah's mother telephoned once a week in April. Like previous conversations, they were brief and one-sided. Sarah answered all the questions but never asked any. When each call was over, she treated herself to a strong coffee adding plenty of sugar.

On Saturday, April twenty-second, Sarah woke in a soggy bed.

"Amelia. The bed's soaked."

"Cramps close together?"

"Yes."

"I'll see Nancy."

From their bedroom window, Amelia watched Sarah get into the taxi. She and Debbie were the only ones of the original group remaining. She didn't know much about the newbies and didn't care to find out. In a month, she'd be gone too. She'd already made private arrangements to go directly home from the hospital.

Sarah's taxi ride to the hospital was an unsleeping nightmare. Between fleeting glimpses of buildings, she grimaced and breathed through grinding pain. The plastic sheet on the back seat crackled. She squirmed to find a comfortable spot but did not succeed.

Wordlessly, hospital staff whisked her into a wheelchair then onto a bed in a ward with three other beds. A nurse timed her contractions and announced, "You'll likely deliver later today, miss."

Sarah looked around at the other women. All had visitors who held their hands and smiled in anticipation of a new family member. Alone, she stared at the ceiling and choked back tears.

As the contractions increased, Sarah conjured up images of a calmer place: a warm bath, homemade soup, picking raspberries in the summer sun, sketching blossoms in the apple orchard. They worked until a woman released a blood-curdling scream.

"Miss, I'm here to check on your progress. Do you need a pain killer?"

Remembering Betty's words, she nodded.

Later when she woke in pain, the privacy curtains were around her bed, it was dark outside and the overhead room lights were on. She thought she was alone in the room until she overheard voices.

"She's the perfect granddaughter."

"Shhh, mom. Nobody's been to visit the one across the room. Probably not married. Poor thing."

Sarah took a sip of water and reminded herself that she was not a 'poor thing' and had a plan. Not long after, she felt nauseated so pressed the buzzer. A nurse arrived, put a stethoscope on her abdomen, timed her contractions, completed an internal examination then announced it was time to go to the delivery room.

"Hello, Miss Gardner. I'm Doctor Brown. We'll give you a needle to help with the pain but you'll be awake. Let's get started."

Sarah closed her eyes against the glaring lights and pushed on command. She'd expected the delivery room to be filled with dialogue, including guidance and encouragement. Instead, it was eerily quiet. She got the message. This was a medical procedure, not a celebration of new life. Her numbness cancelled any sensation. She was reduced to a passive participant in her own life and her baby's birth. At ten thirty-two, she gave birth to a seven pound, three ounce baby boy.

Back in the empty room, Sarah held her son, told him she loved him forever and always then watched as a nurse carried him away. There were no tears left to shed. She curled into a ball and rocked herself into a dazed world of half sleep.

Sarah woke to find a nurse gently rubbing her arm. On her night table, a tray held toast, jam, a pot of tea and a banana. She was awash in emotion and cried. "Thank you."

"Can I help you to the bathroom before you eat?"

"Yes, please."

As the nurse left, she smiled kindly. "Breakfast's in a few hours. Sleep well."

On Sunday morning and afternoon then twice on Monday, Sarah shuffled to the nursery to look through the window. She tried to identify her little boy. Early Tuesday morning, there were no boys in the nursery. He was gone.....forever.

After breakfast on Tuesday, a doctor examined Sarah and discharged her. The return taxi ride was painful too, but in a different way. She truly was alone, on her own with an unknown path to travel. She filled the time preparing for a longer ride after her parents arrived.

Amelia was waiting for Sarah's return. She helped her up the stairs then brought lunch. They talked about the hospital visit and the future until Matron entered the room.

"Eva. Your parents will be here in a few minutes." She left quickly.

Sarah embraced Amelia. "I don't know how to thank you, except to say it. Thank you."

"Our new lives are about to begin, roomie. Keep in touch."

Sarah picked up her suitcase and started down the three flights of stairs, each step blurred by a flood of tears.

Wordless, she led her mother out of the home and to the car. She got into the backseat then greeted her father who responded, "Feeling okay?"

"Yes, today is the beginning of my future."

"Oh, I'm so glad you feel that way, dear." Mrs. Gardner turned toward the backseat. She sighed with relief.

"What way is that?"

"You're happy to be going home, of course."

"I don't belong there now but I'll stay for a while. I have plans, special plans."

Chapter Twenty-One

June 1961

When Eva walked out of Rose Hill Home on April 25, 1961, Sarah Gardner vowed never to set foot in the city again. She returned home but the baby boy she left behind was never far from her thoughts. She cried herself to sleep most nights for the first few months.

In late June, Sarah wrote a short letter to Amelia.

Hi, AM

Sorry, I haven't written sooner. Just a note to let you know I'm still alive. I have trouble sleeping though.

I haven't had to return to school. Somehow my parents convinced the principal I was completing art projects in May and June for the course I took in Halifax during the winter. Can you believe it? At least that's what they told me but I don't trust them. The best part is I don't have to face people every day until September.

So far, my mother is mostly okay with my 'aloofness', as she calls it. She makes little hints about my lack of social life but so far she's not actually done anything about it.

People avoid me probably because I ignore them. Whatever!

Miss Mayne will be back for the summer art program. Great news.

How are you and the baby? What name did you choose?

Please, please write soon,

Sarah XO

In a week, she received a reply.

Hi, Sarah

Julie and I are well. I went back to work a week ago.

I found a young woman down the street to care for her. She has a little girl too so it works out. He husband is in the navy and away a lot.

People at work are quite curious. Guess they notice I have less free time. At some point pretty soon, they will have to know I'm a mom. That should be interesting, to say the least.

Keep healing and keep in touch,

Love, love, love, AM and Julie

Sarah used the summer as her personal training ground for the future. She maintained zero interest in being personally close to anyone and offered an excuse for every social invitation. She'd learned all too well where trust got her and vowed never to forgot the lesson.

In mid December, Sarah's vow had its first test. Her mother shouted up the stairs, "Sarah, are you helping at the library Saturday evening?"

"No, I am off. I'm working on Sunday afternoon instead. It's the children's Christmas card-making event."

"Wonderful. Bert and Doris Shaw have invited us for dinner Saturday."

"Okay." *Easy. Nice people. Good food.*

Bert Shaw was delighted that Sarah could make the dinner and it showed. As she stepped over the threshold he whispered, "My dear, I was afraid you had to volunteer at the library this evening. Now our nephew will have someone nearer his own age to talk with. Wonderful."

The Shaws were childless. Sarah had never heard of this nephew but managed to mutter, "No problem." However, she thought it was definitely a big problem.

Entering the living room, the Gardners greeted Doris and were introduced to William Stevens.

"Everybody calls me Bill. Nice to meet all of you."

It took Sarah no time to recognize her mother knew about Bill. She was hopping mad but she would deal with her mother later.

During dessert Bill mentioned he was going to an art gallery in the city the next day. "Sarah can I take you along? It should be right up your alley."

"Sorry, I work at the library tomorrow."

"Too bad. I leave Monday morning."

At home, Sarah decided to say nothing to her mother. For now, she'd keep the uneasy peace and be more suspicious in the future.

During the summer art program Miss Mayne and Sarah became more like colleagues than instructor and student. She watched Sarah's talent and passionate drive to chart a life path in art grow. And she had an idea.

"Sarah, what are you doing after grade twelve?"

"I don't know. I really want to go away for college and take art but I can't find anything about where to go. Any ideas?" *Please don't suggest Halifax.*

"I'm in Halifax and I have connections in Ontario? Either one sound okay?"

Sarah tried to sound casual. "Ontario would be fine."

"Won't your parents object to you moving far away?"

"No. I'm sure it won't be a problem." *I'll make sure of that.* "What would I have to do? How much will it cost"?

"Well, lots of paperwork when the time comes. Your art awards and summer art program training will be important. In January, I think you should apply for admission and a scholarship. Would you like my help and a recommendation?"

"Is there any other answer but 'yes'? Thank you, so much."

Entering grade twelve in September was a big personal test for Sarah. Could she maintain what Amelia had stressed? Take strength and joy from your art to build your future.

Her old classmates had moved on from school. Many had moved away. She easily isolated herself from the younger students. Days and nights were filled with sketching, painting, reading and helping in the village library.

In January, Sarah mailed the art college application, complete with references and samples of her work. The answer was
due by the end of April. By the end of March, she was bordering
on panic. What would she do if the answer was the wrong one?
Anxiety and its' associated chest pain returned. In a letter from
AM, she was reminded of the miles the two of them walked. She
laced up her sneakers.

April 22 was her son's birthday. Sarah spent the whole day
reading and in quiet reflection. On that day, she committed to
do the same every year for the rest of her life.

On April 27, Miss Mayne called. Sarah could barely walk to
the phone. *She's calling to warn me about the rejection letter!*

"Hello...."

"No, the letter hasn't arrived yet...."

"Really. I am." Then the tears came. "How can I thank
you....?"

"Okay. I think I can do that." Sarah replaced the handset.

Sarah's mother called from upstairs. "Everything okay,
dear?"

"Everything is absolutely fine now. I've been approved for a
two-year scholarship. I have to be there by September 1."

Art college was an eye-opener for Sarah. For the first time
in her life, she experienced a world where others shared her
passion. Art wasn't the only thing her fellow students were
passionate about. An exhausting social life rivalled art for su-
premacy.

By the end of September, Sarah was forced to tell lies. Her
fragile grip on a new future had to be protected at all costs.
Nobody would fool her again.

'I've got a paper due, I promised my roommate to spend the
weekend with her family, the girls are going out or I'm helping a
friend with an essay' became standard answers to fend off real
connections, especially male.

By mid December Sarah invented a boyfriend at home. After
the Christmas break at home, she returned wearing a ring. 'Art'
had proposed and she'd accepted.

Epilogue

Victoria, British Columbia
Twenty-Six Years Later

Sarah eased into her favourite chair and considered the watercolour on its pewter easel. 'Rock Candy' was her first piece of art finished at Rose Hill in 1961. It held painful memories but also a reminder of her personal strength. Most days she scarcely noticed it but today was different, very different. The envelope in her hand felt as heavy as a brick.

For three days, Sarah had been incapable of dealing with the contents of the envelope. Each time she'd glanced at it, panic rose in her chest. She took a deep breath and placed the envelope back on the coffee table.

Since late 1964 Sarah's life in Victoria had been anchored in routine, a lifestyle she cherished. Then the letter upended everything. The return address unearthed deeply buried memories.

As a celebrated artist and art teacher, she was accustomed to requests for workshops within a day's drive of her home. This one asked for her presence on the other side of the country. The opportunity was tempting but she was terrified by the horrors such a visit might spew forth. For her own well-being, she'd decided to decline the invitation. One niggle remained. How could she refuse a two-week workshop in Halifax without insulting the college's reputation and tainting her own?

Sarah's front door opened. "Hey neighbour. I brought chilled white and dessert."

"Come through, Barb. I'm in the sun-room with the glasses."

Barb poured, slipped off her sandals and curled into a padded wicker chair. She glanced at the coffee table. "Very fancy embossed letterhead. Going somewhere?"

"Nowhere."

"May I?" She nodded toward the letter.

"Sure."

Barb looked at the envelope with a Halifax return address then read the invitation. "Oh, I get it. But, it's more than twenty years. What are the odds someone will recognize you?"

"It's possible. You know what small cities are like." Her lips pursed as she exhaled deeply.

"Anything's possible but please give it more thought. It really is such an honour and opportunity."

"The teaching part isn't my worry. It's the reception at a gallery called The Knot. Anyone could show up." She sighed heavily. "I have to reply on Monday. Facing fears is a good thing but I'm truly frightened of this one."

Barb continued. "Let's think about this. You weren't Sarah Gardner in Rose Hill and you were a teenager. How could people in Halifax possibly recognize you now?"

"A few national art magazine interviews?"

"Maybe...ish."

"How about people who've purchased my art?"

"In my humble opinion, iffy at best. Your business cards don't have your picture, just an image of 'Rock Candy', correct?"

"That's right."

"Okay. I've made my point and besides, do you think they would say anything?" Her eyebrows lifted and left hand shot into the air. "Really?"

"But it's not only them I'm worried about, it's me. What if I recognize someone?"

"Ahhh. Now the real reason is on the table. That's what planning ahead is about. Don't let 'what if' stop you now. It hasn't since 1961."

***

The cozy two story Halifax gallery had been a family home for almost forty years when it was purchased by a couple with a teenage daughter in 1975. They converted part of the main floor into a studio for local artists where photographers, painters and potters could sell their work.

Normally, The Knot was filled with all forms of nautical art. Tonight a different theme. A Canadian watercolour artist on a teaching visit to the city had accepted an invitation to a social evening. A few of her pieces from private collections were on loan and prominently displayed.

Guests wandered through the rooms while catering staff offered guests Maritime fare, local beer, wine and coffee.

Sarah arrived by taxi. "Here we are, Miss Gardner. The Knot. Enjoy your evening. I'll be back in an hour, as you requested."

"Thank you."

"Good evening, Miss Gardner. I'm Rudy Abbott, chair of the college foundation. Welcome to Halifax. It's a great delight to have you with us. Is this your first visit to our fair city?"

"No, but it has been a very long time. Thank you for your invitation to the college and this evening."

"Our pleasure. May I introduce the owners of The Knot, Mr. and Mrs. Porter and their daughter, Sarah Alice." The Porters stepped forward.

Mike recognized Sarah's face and Bonnie detected the faint scent of Shalimar. They shook Sarah's hand as she stared at three pair of eyes, unable to speak.

Bonnie didn't miss a beat. "Welcome, Miss Gardner. I understand you've had a long travel day. Would you care for a quick coffee in our family kitchen before beginning the round of shaking hands and conversation?" She looked away. "I presume this will work for you, Rudy?"

"Absolutely. See you shortly then."

"Mike, maybe you and Sarah can circulate while Miss Gardner has a moment of peace and quiet."

Bonnie led Sarah to the kitchen, placed her in a chair and closed the door. She took Sarah's hands.

"It's okay. Mike and I will personally escort you through the evening."

Sarah began to cry and wrapped her arms around Bonnie. "This is impossible!"

"No, it's very real. We knew you were coming so all's okay."

"I invited a photographer friend Amelia to be here tonight.......just in case. I'm sure you'll like her. I've worked so hard to forget. I couldn't face trying to find you."

"You don't need to explain anything to me. We didn't know what to do the first time we saw you in a magazine. I'm ashamed to say we did nothing. Guess I was afraid you wouldn't reply. But you're here now. This is so wonderful."

"Thank you." She paused. "Sarah Alice?" Her eyes overflowed.

"Yes. You and Alice made Rose Hill bearable for me. Our Sarah has no idea who you are and we'll keep it that way if you like. Mike and I know about her name and that's all that matters." She paused. "Now, let's get you that coffee and a tissue. But first, we both need another monster hug."

"I can't believe this. I just arrived and I've met people I know. What's going to happen during two weeks?"

"Nothing Mike and I can't handle. You have family in this home. When we saw your picture in the college announcement, we appointed ourselves your personal tour guides."

"I can't believe it's you. My Emma."

Inspirational
Resources

Gone to An Aunts - Remembering Canada's
Homes for Unwed Mothers
> Ann Petrie, McClelland & Stewart, 1998

Mother & Baby Homes 1960s
> Rose Bell, www.motherandbabyhomes.com, 2013

Not by Choice
> Karen Wilson-Buterbaugh, www.eclectica.org, 2001

Nowhere Else to Go – Homes for Unwed Mothers
in Canada during the 20th Century
> Nancy Schnarr Curatorial Research Assistant
> Canadian Clay & Glass Gallery, 2011

Public Attitudes in Canada Toward
Unmarried Mothers, 1950-1996
> Susan Crawford, https://journals.library.ualberta.
> ca/pi/index.php/pi/article/view/1425, 2008

The Children They Gave Away
> Sarah Karnasiewicz, www.salon.com/writ-
> er/sarah_karnasiewicz, 2006

The Girls Who Went Away - The Hidden History
of Women Who Surrendered Children for
Adoption in the Decades Before Roe v Wade
> Ann Fessler, The Penguin Press, New York, 2006

The Shame is Ours: Forced Adoptions of the Babies
of Unmarried Mothers in Post-war Canada
> Standing Senate Committee on Social Affairs,
> Science and Technology, July 2018

Book Club
Discussion Questions for
In Trouble

1. Were you quickly engaged in Sarah's story? Why?

2. What emotions did you experience while reading? Surprise, sadness, confusion, fear, anger, frustration?

3. Was the story's pace appropriate for you?

4. What was the central idea of this story?

5. Did the book's title reflect the theme of the story? Why?

6. Did the book's cover convey what the book is about?

7. Describe the main characters' personality traits and motivations. Were they believable?

8. Would you like to meet any of the characters in this story and if so, why?

9. Were you satisfied with the ending? If not, how would you change it?

10. What do you think the author's purpose was in writing this book?

11. If you could ask the author one question, what would it be?

12. Has this book broadened your point of view, provided a new perspective or provided new information?

Thank You

To my husband Rudy: Thank you for your continuing support and assistance with biography and cover.

To John Ashton: A meticulous reader who provided positive, helpful editing.

To author Kathie Sutherland: A supportive reader with sage words of advice from her years of writing.

To Kristin Woychuk: For her enthusiastic belief in my ability to finish.

To authors Richard Van Camp and Michael Hingston (Edmonton Metro Writers in Residence): Your expertise made me a better writer. Take credit for truly helping me cross the finish line.

To the members of the Fort Saskatchewan Writers Group: Thanks for listening.

Finally, for the PageMaster team in Edmonton - Dale, Kim, Vanessa and Cindy. Your "know how" and patience brought In Trouble to life.

To order more copies of this book, find books by other Canadian authors, or make inquiries about publishing your own book, contact PageMaster at:

PageMaster Publication Services Inc.
11340-120 Street, Edmonton, AB T5G 0W5
books@pagemaster.ca
780-425-9303

catalogue and e-commerce store
PageMasterPublishing.ca/Shop

About the Author

As an adoptee herself who grew up in the 60's in Atlantic Canada, Dianne (Taylor) Palovcik was inspired to write In Trouble and bring this hidden part of Canadian history to life for a new generation. She has a Bachelor of Science degree from Acadia University, an education certificate from the University of Alberta Faculty of Education, an employment training specialist certificate from the University of San Francisco, and a travel writing certificate from Lakeland College. Dianne worked with People with Disabilities for more than 20 years, and co-authored a training course for Human Service workers in Alberta. Dianne and her husband live in Alberta.

facebook.com/DiannePalovcikAuthor